H^{the}ounds of Set

Troy A. Carrington

The Hounds of Set / by Troy A. Carrington – 1st edition

ISBN-13 978-0-9848889-0-0

Printed in the United States of America

To Tina, my endless source of love and positivity.
To Zach for your quiet strength and patience.
To Mason for your eternal imagination and boundless energy.
This book would not have been written without you.

"Reality is merely an illusion, albeit a very persistent one."
-Albert Einstein

"Destiny is something that happens while you're waiting for reality to stop."
-Troy A. Carrington

One

War was coming. That much, Alex could see. He was safe for now, hidden and crouched behind the massive concrete pillar. He was waiting for the perfect opportunity. A sliver of time hidden somewhere between existential freedom and utter annihilation was all he needed. The heavens above were suddenly filled with an example of his enemy's awesome firepower. Its missiles darkened the sky.

Armed and ready, Alex reeled back and opened on his target. He had waited his whole life for this moment, it seemed. He held his breath as he waited for the impact. The arrogance of his foe was ultimately his undoing. Alex's assault had landed as intended. He wasn't prepared for what happened next.

The whole lunchroom erupted in cheer. Alex smiled and stood, both arms raised high in the air in celebration. Then he saw Jackson's reddened face. Not good, he thought; not good at all. Alex's smile completely disappeared when a battalion of teachers flooded the room. That was yesterday. Today, however, was quite different.

Bounding down the stairs this particular morning felt somehow new to Alex. There seemed to be far more bounce in his step than usual. Like every other morning, he could hear his grandmother singing in the kitchen. For as long as he could remember, it had always been the two of them. Alex believed she was perfect in almost every way . . . *almost*. He found them rather annoying, her episodes. But he wasn't going to let any of that bother him. It was meaningless at this point anyway. He'd tried to talk to her about it before, but had never gotten far. He wasn't going to ask today, not on this special day, not on his thirteenth birthday!

"I'm a *man*," Alex reported upon entering the kitchen. His grandmother spun on her heels as if she were thirty years younger. A smile upon her face indicated she must have shared in his joy. Underneath her smeared apron, she was wearing a full-length dress of light blue with small yellow and white flowers speckled across it. Alex suspected the yellow flowers had once been white and had simply aged over the years. In fact, at times, he swore some of them had even *moved*.

The kitchen had always been plenty large enough for the two of them but, he surmised, was probably small by most standards. It had a bit of country styling, with heavy wooden cabinets rising from a narrow slatted oaken floor, run smooth from wear over the years. The lower cabinets were topped with sections of butcher's block and white marble. Alex thought it was exactly what a baker would want, if a baker could have. The upper cabinets were, well, not. There were shelves scattered in a complete disarrangement, all manner of towering plates, crooked glassware, and teetering jars filled full of curious objects she had collected over the years. If it weren't for the hint of faded blue brush strokes on the sides of the shelves, his grandmother's dress, and the curtains slung around the windows, the room would actually be quite drab. He was pretty sure that the curtains and his grandmother's dress were from the same cut of cloth.

Then, of course, there were the jars. They had color, too, lots and lots of color. In the past he'd tried not to focus too long on them, or more precisely their contents, for if he did, his stomach would always lurch and the room would begin to spin around him. This would always make him turn a slight shade of pale green. He was determined not to stand in a spinning room today, and most certainly *not* turn green.

Despite all of this, the kitchen was surprisingly bright with rays of light streaming in from the many windows that wrapped the room like a glass box. The largest of them looked over the seaport, and the ships docked on the other side of Sandpiper Lane.

"Then would the *man* of the house please take the garbage out?" she quizzed.

"But gra . . ." Alex started.

"Time and space have left my side, through the years I shall glide . . . te de, te dumm," she began.

Alex knew it was useless to continue. He grabbed the sack and hoisted it over his shoulder in one swoop. Leaning to the right with his knees buckling under the weight of the past few days' trash, he did his best to boldly display both his strength of the feat and his hatred of the task. And so he trudged off through the torn screened door at the back of the kitchen, slamming it as he passed.

The force of the screen door was actually more the result of a broken spring than his dramatic exit, but Alex appreciated the effort it had made on his behalf.

He worked his way down the garden path to the side of the old shed where a pile of neatly stacked wood sat. He had spent most of his summer chopping that same wood, he recalled in angst, and dropped the sack.

"Eighteen inches exactly," Alex muttered to himself, reflecting back on that particular summer's chore and his grandmother's insistence for perfection in this matter. There has never been firewood cut so perfect in the entire town, perhaps even the whole state, he thought with a forced smile. "I hate chopping wood."

The shed, he surveyed, had seen better days with its sparse and weathered grey clapboard siding, broken glass on the side window, and an ancient door that would swing open by no less than gale force winds. Alex winced a little when he recalled exactly how the window had broken. It seems his aim may have been a bit off that summer. Distracted, he thought; not my fault.

He'd spent most of his free time in this small, picket-lined back yard. The grass always seemed to run a bit longer than the neighbor's yard and a bit browner, while the fence itself was missing some boards. It, too, was weathered grey like the shed. Where the front yard looked down the hill over the small busy seaport, the back yard was tucked up behind several other small neatly kept yards, each surrounded by rigid white picket fencing.

They had always been short on storage outside and many of their garden tools were either leaning against the shed and fence or scattered and rusted across the yard, barely visible in the grass. Kicking the broken handle of a hoe, Alex's thoughts were interrupted with a thunderous noise.

"Crap," Alex spoke, his head jerking up. By the sound of that blast he knew he was running late. For as long as he could remember, Captain Shovers has risen at the crack of dawn every morning, meandered down from his seaside roost to the Mermaid, made his way aboard the vessel to its bow, and loaded Matilda. Matilda was a convincing piece of iron mounted just off the bow and was pointed out toward open sea. The Mermaid herself was a non-sailing, non-operational vessel of days long past. As the Captain would say, "She's a nod to the brave who still navigate the local waters and dream of the open sea." The Captain was a frail elderly man "of about 150 years old," as Alex would always say.

"Twelve are lost, never to return. Never to return," bellowed the Captain in a somber, almost haunting voice.

With a blast like that, Alex thought it gave new meaning to the phrase *raising the dead.*

Alex ripped the dented steel lid off the top of the garbage can and shoved the oversized bag inside, slamming the lid in response. He no sooner turned to run back up the garden path when . . .

"Alex!" shouted her voice from the screen door. "Time for breakfast. Get a move on."

"I know. I know. I heard it," Alex complained and rolled his eyes in contempt. Despite what Matilda's original intention had ever been, Alex and his grandmother had long ago begun to set their schedules by the deafening blasts.

As he took the stepping-stones two by two, he glanced over the fence into the neighbor's back yard and was surprised at how much Mugsy, the Moores' Doberman, had grown since he'd last saw him. Without thinking anymore about it, he made the back steps in one effort and was sitting at the kitchen table in another. He figured he'd try again.

"As time passes by, you too shall leave my side. But for your safe return, I shall forever yearn . . . te, te, te, te, de, te dumm," she sang with a hint of a skip in her step.

She was in a cheerful mood, even by her standards. The table had no cloth on it, but several of her mismatched plates had been placed out, brimming with breakfast foods of steaming hot sausage links; scrambled eggs mixed with crabmeat, cheese, onions, and green peppers; golden yellow homemade biscuits; fresh bacon from the Bowery Bros. Butchery; hand-squeezed orange juice; and crab cakes soaked in butter, lemon, and pepper. "Awesome!" Alex belted out. There were always crab cakes. He loved crab cakes. Of course, living by the sea, he ate them practically every day. But Alex didn't mind; he devoured them first, then moved on to the eggs.

"Gramma, anything different today?" he asked.

"No. What do you mean?" she responded with an indifferent stare while filling his plate with another round of scrambled eggs.

"I mean *today*?" he repeated desperately as if this would jog her memory back down to earth. A look of disbelief washed across his face from beneath his uncombed brown mop of hair. He wondered how on earth she could have forgotten. It's not like it's difficult to remember, Alex rationalized. He'd been leaving signs all week, and now his frustration was bubbling over.

Despite how she was some of the time, he loved her. They shared a special connection between the two of them. She had plenty moments of clarity, and they enjoyed every one together. She had been more than a grandparent to him over the years, more than his guardian. This woman had been his mother, father, friend, confidant, and . . . something more; something he couldn't quite explain.

"Never mind," Alex continued, feeling deflated. Rather than continue with the conversation, he finished the rest of his meal in silence. Clearing the table and starting to feel depressed, Alex decided he would depart on his long journey to school a little earlier this morning. When all of the plates and dishes were scraped clean into the trash bin, he set them on the counter and ran back upstairs. He knew there was no reason to dawdle anymore. What he'd been anxiously anticipating the entire summer wasn't coming.

It was fall, and although mornings were still brisk, by late afternoon it became warm. Those days made it hard for Alex to figure out what to wear. His school wasn't air-conditioned and always relied heavily on the cool harbor breezes to provide a break from the sun. With this thought, Alex took special note of the weather when he passed by the upstairs hall window that had been left open the day before. The window faced the Moores' house to the right, and he could just make out the end of the stone wall that lined the harbor entrance if he poked his head out far enough. From this location he had a partial view of the harbor and beyond to the lighthouse and, if looking in the opposite direction behind the houses, could easily see into four other back yards.

"*Hunnhh?*" said Alex as his eyes dropped down to the Moores' back yard. What was that movement? "A dog," he answered. Mugsy, he thought. No, wait, not Mugsy, but another dog. It was one he didn't recognize. Must be a stray, he realized. Alex noted its movements weren't like most others he'd seen. Not that he'd seen a lot of dogs in his time. There weren't many dogs in his town that he could recall. Just then, a delivery truck rattled up the way, and Alex turned toward the noise. When he looked back, the dog was gone.

Pulling himself out from the window, Alex rushed into his bedroom to ready himself for the rest of the day. He loved his room. It was comfortable enough for him and actually one of the largest rooms in the house. The temperature was kept fairly constant here if he could just remember to open and close the windows at certain times of the day.

"Shoo!" Alex yelled. Mittens, his grandmother's Cheshire cat, was sleeping on the foot of Alex's old four-post bed. The sun, rising and passing through the east window, was landing squarely where Mittens rested. The bed was massive, but matched the room size nicely. It was comfortable and warm, covered by hoards of his grandmother's handmade quilts and worn out woolen blankets purchased in town. But still, it was *his* bed, Alex resolved, *not* the cat's.

"I SAID SHOO! SCAT! GIT!" Mittens was curled in a large tuft of white and orange hair barely registering that Alex had even

7

entered the room. She opened her eyes, licked her front paw, and rolled onto her side. She was asleep again. Alex's frustration at the way the day was shaping up was growing and building a head of steam. He needed to vent. To the side of his door sat one of many piles of dirty clothes cast all over his room. At some point in time this particular pile had become home to a pair of his tennis shoes. Alex eyed the pair with a devilish grin and slowly slinked down to the pile. It was only four short steps to the foot of his bed where Mittens lie quiet. Alex stretched out his arms as far as he could, a shoe in each hand.

The flat soles of the shoes came slapping together about a foot above the cat's head. Mittens shrieked awake from her warm slumber. The attack couldn't have gone anymore wrong if he'd wanted it to. It all happened within a moment. So frightened was Mittens that she pounced on Alex's shoulder, scratching and hissing through the entire onslaught. Alex clamored to get her off from his shoulder, his head; she was on his back, now his stomach.

"Get off, get off, get OFF!" he cried in desperation. The force of the assault sent Alex backwards toward the pile of clothes. Alex was unusually clumsy like most teenagers with obnoxiously oversized feet. The momentum sent him tripping into the open closet door with a thud. Years of neglected board games, books, and collectibles that had been shoved into such a small space rained down from above onto his head. Alex sat there in a slump, dizzy and confused at what had just happened.

They never liked each other much, Mittens and Alex. In fact, Alex had always thought that Mittens resented him. She'd been with his grandmother far longer than he could remember. Taking what seemed like minutes to shake it off, Alex saw the cat darting across the room in a zigzag fashion, under the bed and out the door.

"Hah! Good," Alex shouted in triumph. He knew that he hadn't won anything, considering that he came out far worse than his foe. After all, he justified, *he* didn't have claws. Still, Mittens was gone, and with a glimpse toward his alarm clock out of the corner of his already swelling eye, he realized that he was now starting to run late.

Like most teenage boys, Alex never gave much thought to the clothes he wore. Old, new, clean, dirty; it didn't matter to him. On special days, weddings, funerals, and such, he would make the effort to comb his uncut shabby brown mane, but not on school days. *Never* on school days. He'd like to think it was in some sort of silent rebellion, but the truth fell more with being pressed for time, as he was this morning.

He sprang up from his current state in the closet and cleared the distance to his dresser in two steps, opened the middle drawer, and muddled around inside. In less than fifteen seconds he had spun around and was attempting to pull over a wrinkled flannel shirt, not bothering to unbutton it as he tugged. On his way out of the room he scooped up the two shoes he'd used in battle only moments earlier. Yesterday's jeans at the end of the bed made for a good compliment to his outfit, and he hopped down the hall, alternating legs as he dressed.

He'd become an expert over the years at hooking his backpack around his arm and grabbing the little brown paper bag his grandmother had set out on the entry table during his morning rush to school. He was at a flat run by the time he met the sidewalk. Heading northward up Sandpiper Lane was always a race against time for Alex. He'd never beaten the morning bell; *never*. He tried.

"Morning, Captain Shovers!" Alex shouted from the hilltop.

"Morning, lad," replied the elder townsman with not so much as a glance. Alex was in too much of a hurry to wonder why the

Captain hadn't bothered to corner him as he did so many mornings on his way to school. They had logged hours of conversation between the two of them about the sea and tales of adventure and toil on the open waters. No, in fact, Alex was glad that this particular morning the Captain paid him no mind. His friend seemed to be preoccupied with something else this sunny morning.

" . . . damn animals . . . broke, destroyed . . . *food, too?* Damn! Need a trap next time," muttered the Captain.

"I'm late. I have to run. Sorry," Alex said. And with this, his mind was back on the race toward school. He'd made it about three doors down the lane when it happened.

"*Ummnff.*" Alex was sent flying against a nearby tree, shoulder first, but somehow managed to stay upright. His shirt was torn where it had landed against the rough bark. He heard it pop.

"Owwww!" Alex shrieked. He turned to find Jackson Styers and his cohorts standing in a group next to the squared, neatly trimmed hedge that lined the Styers' property. The Styers lived well; far better than Alex and his grandmother. Far better than most, in fact. It wasn't that they were rich; they just showed it off more than most. They had the biggest house, the biggest yard, and the best view. It was a tree-lined bit that sat just a little higher than the other houses in town. Alex had always suspected that Jefferson Styers, Jackson's father, purposely chose this location so that he could look down on everyone else.

They were all laughing; one, far more than the rest. It would appear that Jackson had planned the assault and executed its timing perfectly. Not much consolation to Alex, who had been on the receiving end, though.

Jackson was a typical school bully. He towered a good foot taller than the rest and was built solidly like a slab of marble, with about the same intelligence. His square jaw and head were topped by a short straight haircut that rose sharply only inches above his Neanderthal-like head. For the past year Jackson had made it his mission to torment Alex.

Of course, Alex made for an easy target. Unlike Jackson, he had no followers, was a bit of a loner, and his stature was nowhere near that of Jackson's. In fact, as far as newly aged thirteen-year-olds go, Alex was about average height, but was roughly fifteen pounds lighter than his peers. More times than not, this made him look awkwardly thin and gangly. His arms flailed about routinely when he moved and looked uncontrollable. It appeared as though the only thing keeping Alex upright much of the time were his unusually large feet.

It wasn't that the others liked Jackson; they seemed to follow him more out of fear than favor. What they feared was sharing Alex's same fate if they didn't laud him. Heck, even the older kids avoided him.

Alex hadn't been awake more than an hour, and already it was shaping up to be an exceptionally bad day. Alex had enough. His thoughts of what happened next were only flickering shadows of the actual event. He remembered standing toe to toe with Jackson, coming only up to about his chest. A few words were exchanged, and Jackson became heated. He couldn't remember what it was he said, but he remembered lunging at Jackson and sending what he believed was a solid fist against his opponent's lower left jaw.

Then there was a dog. It was one that Alex had never seen before. It landed between him and the pack, pacing and growling. It seemed to have jumped out from nowhere, perhaps from behind the hedge, Alex guessed. It wasn't growling at him, no, but rather at the others. This strange canine was pushing them back, away from

11

Alex. The beast was frightening, yet somehow Alex sensed it was there helping him. As he stood staring in disbelief at this creature and the crowd of scattering peers beyond, he noticed this animal was exceptionally thin. He remembered seeing bone under its skin. It reminded him of a greyhound, only thinner, and one that hadn't been fed in quite some time.

Another muffled sound came up from the depths of the creature's throat. The only one brave enough, or stupid enough, Alex thought, to have not moved was Jackson. Too intent on returning the blow that Alex had landed, he was focused more on his foe than the danger that was between them.

He recalled the dog turning about and looking at him.

Run.

"Hunh?" Alex no sooner heard the words echo in his head and he was off. It was a different tone than earlier. This wasn't *his* voice. Then whose was it? Alex wondered. His mind searched for answers but only gave him questions. Whose dog was *that?* Where'd it come from? Did the dog . . . ? Humph? Yeah, right. He must have imagined it. He *had* to have imagined it, he decided. Dogs can't talk. He shook off the thought as soon as it came.

He vaguely remembered hearing some words shouted after him, but nothing more. The encounter was over.

One good thing about being thin and the object of torment for the local school bully, Alex learned to run pretty fast. It was another half-mile to the school, and he didn't bother looking back the entire distance. Alex was panting as he reached the doors behind which were the hallowed halls of Peabody-Styers Academy for Secondary Learning, or 'PSA' as his classmates liked to call it. He paused for only a moment against the stone building to catch his breath.

"Safe," he said, " . . . or not." He recoiled with the realization of having to endure the entire school day looking over his shoulder. Not just in the halls and at lunch, but during World History class, where he sat directly in front of his oppressor.

History class, in fact, was a particularly grueling hour taken from each day of his life with no chance for escape. He spent his time dodging both flying objects from Jackson, as well as searing comments from his teacher. It was always Alex who would be called out, despite the proof of numerous battle wounds and available witnesses. Those who defended Alex to his teacher soon learned it wasn't a deed that went without its own form of punishment. Eventually his classmates stopped trying to help and could do nothing but provide quiet pity.

While it was admittedly true that Ms. Flowers' looks gave credit to her namesake, inside she was no rose, Alex thought. Well, maybe the thorns. He laughed. Outside, she was a vision of beauty, with shoulder-length yellow hair done up in curls. A fine featured younger woman who looked down at him through her wire-rimmed glasses from her 5' 6" stature. She was neither overweight nor too thin and was always appropriately dressed for her position as a "purveyor of knowledge" as she put it. But it was her inside that Alex hated. To him, she wasn't just mean; she was nasty-mean. She was downright go-out-of-her-way-to-break-him mean. Sadly for Alex, he was her sole object of public humiliation, and she always did so under cover of a flat smile, with never a loss of temper. But he could see it in her steel cold eyes.

Of course, it didn't help that Ms. Flowers was dating Jefferson Styers. Much to Alex's dismay, this unholy union created many opportunities for Jackson to find unique ways to hurt, maim, and otherwise bludgeon Alex's life out of him without fear of consequences. Alex found his World History grade failing miserably as a result.

This particular morning went almost without incident. He'd made it through lunch and had successfully navigated down the back halls of the Academy the entire day, feverishly avoiding any further interaction with his foe. Alex had grown tired from the trials of the morning's events. It wasn't until Alex found himself drifting off to sleep in Ms. Flowers' class that Jackson retaliated. Poised to strike, he let it go.

The rubberband snapped the back of Alex's bare neck. At a distance of about three inches, the projectile was sure to leave a welt.

"*AAAHHHH! Sheeshus!*" Alex jumped back to life. Grabbing at his neck, he could hear Jackson and a few others snickering under the concealment of their hands. But it wasn't Jackson who stole Ms. Flowers' attention; it was Alex. She was on him like a coiled pit viper on a field mouse. His uncontrolled outburst not only earned him a forceful twist of the ear to the door and a slip to the principal's office, but detention as well. He didn't care. He was glad to be rid of those people, if only for the next hour or so. Besides, he liked Crunch, and Crunch liked him.

Alex and his classmates took to dropping the formalities of titles long ago like most preteens and referred to the man in charge as only 'Crunch.'

Crunch was a short fellow, not much taller than Alex, and reminded him of a large egg that waddled slightly when he walked. It was his taste for all things sweet that gave away Crunch's weakness. One couldn't visit his office without noticing all of the candies and chocolates about the room. The only thing that existed in more volume than the sweets themselves were the wrappers from those he had previously eaten.

Truly one of the nicest people in town; Alex smiled. That's not to overlook Mrs. Crunch. She was the exact duplicate of her husband in all forms. In fact, Alex thought, together they looked like a couple of round bookends, but still nice, at least to Alex. It seems Mr. and Mrs. Crunch were long-time friends of his grandmother and this, Alex was happy to report, was a blessing in many ways.

Entering Crunch's office wasn't as imposing as one would think. There was always music and singing, humming actually, coming through the cracks of the large wooden, hand-carved door. A few people even claimed to have seen the figure inside gliding in time with the music. The room itself was average sized with traditional woodworking and thick surrounding shelves. Open windows behind the large tattered desk seemed to frame the man, who often would crouch, hidden behind the brass nameplate perched at the edge. The dust over the years had settled on the teetering books and brimming file cabinets. Two matching chairs in need of desperate repair sat just this side of the desk to keep company.

A large white wire cage in the corner behind the desk seemed out of place, as it was kept unusually neat and tidy in comparison to the rest of the room. Two small white lovebirds sat in the cage, while their food fell to the floor. As Alex entered the room, he noticed Crunch was in his usual position, standing next to the cage cooing to the birds with his finger poking inside.

Without turning, Crunch spoke, "Interesting little cusses. Come in, Alex." He paused as if to contemplate the meaning of the universe or some complex scientific theory, then said, "I understand Ms. Flowers has sent you here to speak to me? Candy? No? Are you sure? There are all types. How 'bout chocolate? I do so love these little things. OW! They bit me."

"Uh, the *candy* sir?" Alex inquired a bit confused.

"No, no, son. The birds. One of them bit me," Crunch replied.

"Oh," was all Alex could think to say.

"Crun . . . umm, I mean, Mr. Crunch, sir. I didn't do it. *Really.* Jac . . . someone . . . *thing* hit me in the neck, sir," Alex tried desperately to explain but despite loathing Jackson, he was no tattletale.

"*Hmmmm.* I see. Perhaps you're hungry? No, not you boy. The birds. They need to be fed. Right. Here you go," Mr. Crunch said as he began scooping birdseed in through the cage door and into the cup inside, seeming completely distracted.

"Um, sir?" Alex said persistently.

"Yes. Well then. That's settled. Right? Good," responded Crunch.

Alex was bewildered at the conversation. He didn't know if Crunch was speaking to him or the birds at this point. Just then the afternoon bell rang. He'd survived another grueling day of school at PSA. Taking full advantage of the sudden charge of students into the halls just outside the door and the preoccupied man before him, Alex slinked backward through the heavy door, giving a meek, "Th-Thanks, sir."

Thankful indeed. He was thankful for the commotion in the halls. He could blend in and hide all the way to the freedom beyond. Bursting through a lesser-used side entrance, Alex cleared four steps and was off running. He moved past the parking lot, stooping between the cars, hiding every movement as best he could. He ran down past the row of neatly kept houses on Harbor Point and through the adjacent field.

Alex felt as if someone was following him, watching him. He immediately thought of Jackson. But it wasn't like Jackson to scurry about and hide behind trees and bushes. Jackson was an "out-in-the-open" kind of guy. Jackson would want to punish him where everyone could see, as public embarrassment was more his style. But still, all of his senses were telling him differently. Every hair on the back of his neck was standing up. Not knowing when Jackson would pounce was worse than knowing. His entire body stretched for confirmation, but couldn't find it.

Then he heard a noise. There was a scuffle from between two houses. Just a dog, Alex thought. Wait! *A dog?* Not again. What's up with the strange dogs? He wondered. Was it the same one that had come to his rescue earlier that morning? He recalled for a moment the voice he'd heard earlier, not knowing where it had come from. Alex shuddered as he looked over his shoulder, not quite sure if he actually heard the sound. He ran even faster now, fearing both beast and human.

"Home. Finally," Alex spoke, finding relief that there had been no second encounter with Jackson, or anything else for that matter.

"Gramma, I'm home," he announced loud enough for any pursuer to hear in the hope that company would deter them.

"In the kitchen," she replied.

"Of course you are," he said quietly to himself, still trying to push his heart back into his chest. Dropping his backpack, he relaxed and went into the living room. He'd decided the living room was his best chance to avoid any potential questioning from his grandmother. The routine mid-afternoon barrage of questions about his day would likely bring his insides back to a boil, and he was anxious to dodge the impending queries. He dropped into the worn brown leather chair that flanked the brick fireplace. As he began to melt into its soft, warm comfort, his eyes searched for something to occupy his thoughts.

He'd looked hundreds of times at the different pictures hanging on the dingy panels of the room. The panels had been whitewashed at one time, but so much time had passed that the only white now found on the walls existed beneath the pictures themselves. The thing that always struck him as odd was that the pictures were mostly of scenery. And not the type of landscapes he'd ever seen first-hand.

There was one picture, however, that always stood out above the rest. It was a black and white of a young man roughly in his early thirties. It was positioned next to a similarly framed picture of his grandmother when she was much younger and was probably taken around the same time, he assumed. He could recognize her a mile away, he thought with a smile. But the picture of the young man hung on him much the way it hung on the wall. Sort of . . . well, heavy and out of place. Yet even this odd young man with a wiry smirk of an expression and three distinct scars across his face seemed vaguely familiar. Although he'd never met the man, he knew him. Or at least he *felt* that he knew him.

"Alex," said the voice from the other room, "where'd you go?"

"In here, Gramma. The living room," Alex spoke lazily, his eyes half shut.

"You know where I got that chair, don't you? Brought it up from our ol' place down by the shore. Used to be where our people lived. But such a long time ago, I dare say," she informed him.

"Down by the shore. It's never more. Ta tum. Ta te. The sea will always be, while the shores will never more. Ta tittle le dum te te."

And she was out of the conversation as quickly as she had begun it. Alex just rolled his eyes. Of course, his grandmother had always been a bit *off.* "Tetched," the older townsfolk would say. He knew she was different from most people. He preferred it that way. He loved and cared for her so deeply that it didn't matter what other

18

people said in their low whispers behind closed doors. Yes, he'd heard them, seen the looks. But it didn't matter. He actually thought she was cool. Cool or not, he was still mad at her for forgetting how special this day truly was.

"How could she have forgotten?" he whined quietly.

"Dinner's on," came the next recognizable words from the kitchen. He must have dozed for a while, he surmised. He tried to convince himself he hadn't fully fallen asleep, but given the time, it was too probable. A familiar orange glow had entered the room through the window, indicating that the sun was setting, also giving away the onset of the new season. It felt like it was going to be a cool night, so Alex took count of the logs set neatly by the fireplace as he left the room.

It was a quick, quiet dinner. Despite the silent banquet, the odor filled enough of the room to entice all of the senses. It was a pot roast sliced thin and smothered in brown gravy, homemade, *not* from a jar. Green peas and mashed potatoes were steaming out of their side dishes.

Alex took great pride in how he arranged his plate at the dinner table. He filled his plate with a towering heap of food, until every last visible sign of stoneware was gone. Everything had to get covered with gravy, and for every forkful of mashed potatoes, he would mix his peas. This combination had to be what heaven tasted like, Alex equated. He didn't waste any time to load up on seconds either. A second helping took a little longer to put down, but Alex made a valiant effort and was as triumphant in his glory as a conquering gladiator, or in most cases, the lion that they fought.

He quickly cleared the table, much as he was accustomed to doing "every day since birth, if you please," he muttered. He then darted upstairs to do his homework, grabbing his book bag along the way.

Reaching the solitude of his sanctuary, he moved to his desk set across the back corner, dodging the toys strewn about the floor; toys, he thought, that were too young for him now that he was thirteen. He'd have to put those away tomorrow. Sliding into the hard wooden school chair, he jumped back up so quickly that he dropped his book bag onto the floor, sending its contents spilling in all directions. This same motion sent the desk upward about two inches when his legs caught the drawer causing it to come crashing down.

"Ow! Man, that's the second time this week I got a splinter from this piece of junk," he complained as he turned to pull the 2 x 4 from his hindquarters. He sat down a bit more gingerly the second time, leaned over, and began collecting his spilled tools.

Sitting upright again, he started on the long journey of mathematics and science. Learning of theory and equation, he wished he had paid closer attention today in his classes. But how could he have when he was busy just trying to stay alive? he wondered.

Hours seemed to have lagged by like the waves lapping against the gunnels of the ships he'd played in down at the docks. How he longed for the familiar warmth that only came from beneath the covers of his bed. He paused every so often to savor the thought of what waited for him at the end of his long, difficult journey. He imagined how wonderful it would feel to sink into his soft pillow at this moment. Begrudgingly, he moved forward with the task of all things academic. He was done.

"Finally," he said.

Unfortunately, like most teenagers, the opportunity of forethought left him for a moment, and he bounced out of his chair.

This sudden burst of energy again sent his books and papers flying in every manner possible. Again, the desk came crashing down.

He'd had enough. He left everything in their new-found places and decided he would collect them in the morning. Depressed at the finale of his efforts, he lurched toward the end of his bed. He ducked under the model airplanes he'd worked so hard building two summers ago. They were hung from the ceiling, smack in the middle of the room. *Smack* was right, he thought. He *smacked* his forehead every time he passed.

He barely made an effort to remove his clothes and replace them with his sleepwear. He collapsed, exhausted. As he drifted off to sleep, he saw the images of the day swirling by. He wasn't happy. It had been an awfully long day; not quite boring, but it did come with all of the usual disappointments. He thought for a split second that he ought to be used to the disappointments by now. He often thought that his parents' disappearance, Jackson and his gang of mutant thugs on constant prowl, and a grandmother who only made sense about one third of the time was almost too much for anyone to handle. This day, of all days, should have been different, he lamented.

His anger was quickly replaced by guilt. Alex suddenly felt ashamed. He was acting like a child and not the man he'd hoped he'd be today. It was with this remorse that he fell asleep, stirring only once in a while to accommodate the lumps in his ancient mattress.

It felt like mere moments had whisked by when a noise so thunderous shook his bedpost off the history book that it was perched upon, simultaneously releasing the window shade up in a flutter. He instinctively sat straight up like a board and rubbed his eyes just in time to see the table lamp wobble to a halt on his dresser and the money left over from the day roll off on to the floor. The two pictures hung next to his closet door had fallen crooked from the unearthly noise. His heart thrust through his shirt as he grabbed at it, and his ears rang so loudly he thought they were bleeding. What the heck was *that?* he thought with a start.

It was difficult to quickly shake the dizziness from his brain and sit still long enough to stop the room from spinning, but with some effort he was able to collect his thoughts. As he sat in his bed, still half covered by his sheets, his eyes reached through the darkness of the room. His ears strained for some small sign that his grandmother had also been woken by the noise. They were listening for anything actually. It was odd that there was nothing now. It was dead quiet. Not the best choice of words, Alex thought, but still, he couldn't hear a thing. Surely, he thought, his grandmother was awake after that. He strained to hear any movement down below. Had he imagined it? Was it part of a dream he couldn't remember?

Alex slowly turned, certain that any sudden movement would bring out the source of the noise, something he definitely didn't want to see. As he turned to scan the room and all things in their place, he noticed his alarm clock. His mind desperately tried to sort through the details. How could it be 11:58 already? He *just* went to bed.

A desperate thought of Captain Shovers on the bow of the Mermaid raced through Alex's head, and suddenly he was certain what the noise had been. As he settled back down, pulled his covers toward his neck, and closed his eyes, he jumped back up with a start. Captain Shovers had never fired Matilda off at this time of night, of that Alex was also certain. No, this noise was not Matilda calling out to the beyond. This had been something different.

There was something else. He had to strain for it, but it was there, under the cloak of darkness. A wisp; more like a faint shuffle or dragging noise. He listened harder. It was coming from outside. He was too scared to move, but his curiosity was killing him. Alex slid off his bed and moved toward the window without a single controlled movement. It was as if something or someone had a grip on him and was forcing him toward the window. He approached the glass from the side because he was sure that they would see him otherwise. Alex became anxious. *They;* wait--who were *they?* He peered from behind the soldiered prints of the bedroom curtains, believing the darkness of the room kept him hidden.

Then he saw him, or her; he wasn't quite sure. It was dark outside, and the figure was cloaked from head to toe. From the tiny space between the curtain and the window's edge, Alex peered down upon what looked like a shimmering mass, gliding seemingly without any movement except for the heavy dark cloak flowing in the breeze.

From this angle, perched in the safety of his familiar bedroom, Alex could see that the figure was moving hunched over and, if standing straight, would be roughly twice the height of its current stance. But then, that would make him almost ten feet tall, Alex reckoned, and that was impossible! The thoughts had no sooner left his head when, almost in response to them, the cloaked figure turned and gazed upward toward the window from beneath its hood. Alex fell backwards from fear, bumping against his dresser and once again sending his table lamp into a wobble. Catching it to quiet the noise, he whirred back to his former position peering through the window, but the figure was gone.

Alex searched his distant memories for something familiar, anything. What was that thing? Ten feet tall, not likely. Had he been seen? He must have. Think. Remember. Was there a face under that

23

hood? An eye, a nose, perhaps a mouth . . . *teeth?*

Slowly he formed a picture in his mind of what he'd seen. Too dark for any details, he remembered seeing the darker shadows of a long nose and a glint of light from where one of the eyes should have been. He couldn't be sure of much else. It was beyond him at this point. Why was it on his doorstep? What did it want? Where did it go? Too many questions were coming too fast. He remembered seeing a light; no, not a light, a glow. But assuring himself the mysterious glow had come from reflections of moonlight off the sea, he readily dismissed it. But he couldn't and wouldn't dismiss the rest of what he saw.

Alex looked out onto the street and farther past, on down the shoreline to the docks, but the only movements he could see were the waves lapping up onto the shallows and the ships rolling against the docks. His tired eyes searched, but found nothing. He knew that if he stood looking out his window long enough, he'd surely see things that just weren't there. So he decided, after much thought on the subject, to return to the comfort of his bed where, by morning, all of this would be a distant memory. He turned to climb back into his warm pile of tattered quilts and worn woolen blankets, when he saw it.

A small box was outside on the front stoop exactly where the shadowy figure had been. It couldn't be more than three-inches square. It was obvious whoever, or *whatever* it was, had left it behind. It was decided in a flash. He would go down and get the box. He wanted, no *needed*, to see what was inside.

Without much more consideration of the matter, or even his own safety, he reeled toward the foot of the bed, stubbing his big toe on his dresser. Strangely, all of the fear he'd possessed just a moment before was gone, replaced by determination, his growing curiosity, and raw agonizing pain, of course.

In one motionless effort, he had on his robe and was sliding his feet, pain and all, into his slippers. The pain from his toe made it difficult to move around the room quietly, so he paused a moment to lay out a plan for moving across the hall and down the stairs without waking his grandmother, who, he was sure by now, was indeed sleeping. With this pause came the sudden realization that what he'd seen may not have been real at all, but rather his imagination playing tricks on his tired, over-active mind. When he turned back to the window to check for the box, he couldn't tell if he wanted it to be there or not. It was still there.

So he tripped and clamored across the room as softly as he could over the piles of dirty clothes. At one point he knocked over the stack of video games, regaining his balance against the teetering three-legged side table next to his bed. Alex let out a muffled curse of his situation and took aim at the clutter with his foot without thought. This second assault on his toe proved almost too much for him as he landed on his bed in a heap of the material, grabbing at his toe. The pain was so great that the only way he could dispel some of it was to grind his teeth and force his yelps into the fluffy goose-down pillow now pressed against his face.

Two

Alex never had any real friends. His grandmother didn't count. He wanted to believe, *needed* to believe, that what lie outside on the stoop was a sort of present; a gift from someone, *anyone*, who may have remembered that today was his birthday. After all, it was still Friday, and by all accounts 11:58pm, so it *was* possible.

There were two scenarios, however. The first was that this was a dream. Or was it? he questioned with reluctant uncertainty. So far it had seemed quite real to Alex. The pain of his swollen toe was real enough, he thought, as he rocked back and forth on his bed, squeezing his toe as if that would stop the pain.

He scanned across the darkened room to assess his situation. The chair where he'd earlier received his more discreet injury was still in the place he'd left it, he reconciled, grabbing his backside instinctively. The schoolbooks on the ground were still strewn about from the earlier spill. His jeans were at the top of an ever-growing pile of clothes that somehow seemed to have taken on a life of its own. The little red light on the back of his gaming system was still on, casting an eerie red hue across the inside of the closet wall. It was the same closet where his scuffle with Mittens had landed him that morning before school.

The second, more obvious, scenario was that Alex knew that this was quite real, and that posed a problem. There was something outside, and that something had left a box behind.

The throbbing of his toe was leaving him now, and his desire to investigate began to grow again. He again paused, took a deep but quiet breath, and slid out of bed. Despite his injuries, his

26

movements were stealth-like. He was cautious, purposely taking advantage of every shadow and dodging every cast of light to avoid being seen. Hiding, Alex reflected, was all he seemed to be doing lately.

He moved down the oversized wooden staircase, complete with missing balustrade, toward the front door. Stopping just shy of his destination, he listened for any sign of stirring from his grandmother, although, if she hadn't been thrust about from the earsplitting noise outside, she wasn't about to wake up from the sounds of his footsteps tip-toeing about.

His eyes trained on every shadow looking for something out of place, he moved closer to the door. Alex leaned in, ear first, landing against the door with a muffled thud. His heart popped, and he drew back, scared that he may have given away his position to the terror on the other side.

Alex tried to convince himself that it was nothing to worry about . . . nothing, of course, except the big, hairy mass of a creature slung over his front porch waiting to attack at the mere sight of movement. There was a cloaked evil of the worst kind waiting for the unsuspecting fool who dared cross paths with this fanged behemoth, and Alex knew it. "Okay. Okay. Calm down, Chronos, ya baby," he teased himself. But still, he was certain he saw teeth.

Alex crept closer again to the front door. Sensing neither sound nor movement from the other side, he placed a shaking hand on the knob. Every creak groaned and echoed through the halls like a diesel train pulling out of the station. Alex peered through an opening so slight that paper could barely slide through it, and as he did, the grandfather clock chimed to life twice from the living room. "WHAAAAAA!" Alex screamed, jumping out of his skin.

Three more times it boomed. "*Sheesh,*" he uttered, returning back to earth in realization of what the source of the noise was. His cries trailed off down into the harbor, causing the gulls to stir and scream with sudden flight.

Twice again it struck and echoed.

Alex searched feverishly, his body still inside while his head poked through the now fully opened door. In his new position now on all fours, he wrenched his neck up and down the road to get some sort of glimpse of movement.

Twice more the clock continued to count.

"Would you please stop?" he pleaded with the clock. Twice more it responded with its count. Wait, how many was that? It was too late, of course. The damage had already been done. If anything had been slinking around outside, shrouded in darkness, they . . . *it* was sure to have heard the commotion. But there was nothing outside. No movement, as Alex had expected. Better yet, no attack. At exactly midnight the grandfather clock gave its final report.

"AUGGGHHHHNN!" Alex responded hopelessly. He looked again just to make sure. He scanned up to the left, toward the fields and down to the right, past the boatyard and the wooden skeletons of ships that had been dry-docked and forgotten over the years. He looked across the lane and down toward the harbor. Even Matilda was quiet.

Remembering his original purpose, he looked down. It was still there. The box wasn't particularly covered in any sort of special birthday wrappings, nor was it overly large in size. Reaching slowly forward with hands still trembling, he could feel warmth from the box as he drew nearer. He hesitated and looked up just one last time. Nothing. Still, as he grabbed at the box, he decided he would retreat back up to the safety of his bedroom where, behind closed doors, he could thoroughly examine the contents of the mysterious package.

Scurrying backward like a mouse, as he was still on all fours, he closed the door slowly to minimize any sound. Alex rolled to a position at the base of the stairs, sitting in total darkness, staring at the box. He held the box gingerly, moving it from one hand to the other and back again. The box mesmerized him, or rather, what may be inside. His mind raced with excitement and terror at the same time. It was with great effort that he lifted himself off the floor.

Alex made his way upstairs without any further disturbance to the silent night air. "*Now* it's quiet," he whispered to himself in disbelief as he ascended the great stairs. Carefully, he twisted and felt his way through the blackness of the night, back up to his haven. Alex continued to move cautiously and closed his bedroom door slowly behind him. He slid over to the same three-legged nightstand that had provided him with support earlier and pulled the chain to his bed lamp.

Slowly, the light flickered as if cold from fear itself, then flooded the cavernous room, casting the sense of fear away. At first Alex was shocked at the intensity of the light, concerned it may be too bright for the deed at hand, but as the moments ticked away and his eyes adjusted, he realized the light barely cast any shadows and only provided mild relief from the monsters that still lay dormant under his bed these many years.

Alex sat himself at the head of the bed, leaning against the loose headboard and facing in the direction of his front window. It was through this same window that only moments earlier he'd witnessed one of the strangest events of his entire life. He wasn't old enough to have had many strange experiences in his life but, after all, he was thirteen years old now, he beamed. However, in those thirteen years, this is the first time he'd seen a terrifying, cloaked dark figure

29

stooped over on his front steps surrounded by a mysterious blue glow, he thought. Alex cringed and drew his knees up to his chest, placing the box at his side on the bed. He stared at the window. Before he moved on to the task at hand, he believed it wise to consider the matter further.

So there he sat, deep in thought on the recent events. He dissected every sight, every sound. There was the blast. It had woken him up from a deep sleep and made him sit straight up in bed. The glow that followed, he remembered, was blue and shimmering and surrounded a large mass. He remembered the realization that the mass on the front stoop appeared to be hunched over and, if standing straight, would place him at almost ten feet in height, according to his estimate. Everything he knew was telling him that it just couldn't be. Alex strained his already overactive brain for knowledge of anybody or anything that tall.

"Impossible," he said softly. There was a sudden, not so subtle reminder of exactly how real these events were when he moved his foot and felt throbbing. *That* was real. So what does that mean? he thought. A vision of a long snout and teeth flashed into his head as a response. Alex shuddered and pulled the quilts up to his knees for safety.

Had this creature seen him staring from behind the curtain in the window? he wondered. With no clue as to what it all meant, more questions flooded his aching head. Why the box? Why now? Why *him?* The idea of the box being a birthday present quickly left him on this thought. Alex knew it was no present.

His eyes dropped to the package. It was time. He knew he had to open it. He gave a deep sigh and snapped up the box. It was still warm to the touch. Carefully pulling back the top, he peeked inside and couldn't quite make out what was nestled within. Anticipation got the best of him, and he jerked the top back fully to reveal something at the bottom.

It was a small chain. Alex squinted and looked closer. It was a rope, actually, with fine gold strands laced through it. The ring-shaped pendant fixed at the end of the necklace was no larger than a silver dollar, made of what appeared to be bone. Curious, Alex removed the contents to take a closer look.

The ring encircled a shaft that cut it equally into two parts, allowing the ring itself to spin around the shaft on an axis. The carving inside the circle was of a man and a woman situated on either side of the staff, facing each other. They were dressed in what appeared to be long ceremonial robes, and each was wearing a different type of headdress or crown. Alex guessed they were important, like royalty. The shaft was carved into a tree, tall and narrow. Wrapped around the entire length of the tree was a snake, slithering upward.

"Yikes," Alex said quietly.

Alex noted that the outer part felt slightly rough as he ran his thumb and forefinger across it. Strange little bumps, shapes rather, ran the entire length of the outer ring on both sides and were barely visible unless someone knew what to look for.

The entire pendant was a hard bone-white material not unlike the scrimshaw carvings he'd seen crafted by some of the locals down at the harbor. These seafaring men would spend hours, days, even weeks on a single carving. The difference was this pendant was far more detailed and intricate and had a blue vein of material that streaked through the entire framework.

Alex had learned all about scrimshaw this past summer from running up and down the docks, visiting with new people from strange, far off places. He enjoyed listening to the stories, each told with an air of mystery and adventure. It was these stories that sparked his growing interest in traveling someday. Listening to the sailors, Alex would drift off, daydreaming of his own adventures one day.

Scrimshaw, he'd learned, was a favorite pastime of whaling men, who would carve away the hours on the teeth and bones of whales. The beautiful pictures and artwork were made almost effortlessly once the sailors began to lure any unsuspecting listener into his tale. Alex had listened to many of Captain Shovers' tales in the past and was keen to recognize truth from fiction. But still, a boy needs adventure in his life. Alex, it seemed, needed more than most.

"Why would someone give me some ol' necklace?" he asked, still under cover of quilts and shadows. He glanced around his room again, still not sure if he was being watched.

"Maybe it's not for *me*," he answered. Alex took to speaking to himself sometimes, but would often catch himself for fear that others would liken him to his grandmother.

He could hear them now, "Apple doesn't fall too far from the tree," they'd say. "Just like Camille," he'd hear them whisper. He knew how they meant it, but chose instead to be proud of those particular statements.

"Who else then?" he continued. "From who? From what?" he quizzed. His thoughts converged back to his birthday. "It *must* be for me."

Alex continued to pass the necklace through his fingers, deep in thought. His mind was racing. Yep, that's it, he decided. Over the summer he'd witnessed entire scenes etched in just one sitting. Their artwork would be sold either at the docks or at Trudie's Treasures.

These people were gifted not only in their craft, but also in the stories they told. Alex would often sit and listen to these courageous men and wonder what it would be like to live free like they did. These were men's men. They were true and tough sorts who would talk for as long as someone was willing to listen. Captain Shovers had been one of those men, but at his ripe old age, could barely navigate his way to the bathroom, let alone home from sea anymore. No matter, Alex liked him just fine. He'd always been raised to respect his elders.

With the chain draped through his fingers and the pendant resting in the palm of his hand, he spent the next hour examining the object, only stopping once to check the bottom of the box to see if there was anything more inside. Dangling the pendant from the chain in one hand and flicking the pendant with the forefinger of the other, Alex made the ring spin with ease. He wasn't sure, but he thought for a moment that it felt warmer when it spun. This object was so intriguing that all thoughts of his birthday left him. Eventually, his eyes began to droop, and he recognized the feeling of sleep washing over him. He was too tired to dwell on this anymore. His last thoughts before his eyes closed were actually of his grandmother. He wondered what she'd think of all this.

Morning came way too early for Alex. But when the sun washed in the next day's salt air through his window, Alex wasn't about to lie around all day. He was up with a start. Kicking off his covers and sliding from the bed, Alex landed squarely on both feet. Taking note of his surroundings was a regular morning exercise for Alex, for if he hadn't, he'd surely trip over the latest pile of discarded unwanteds.

It was Saturday morning, and nothing felt better. Moving into his closet, Alex rifled through the pile at the bottom in the hope that there was something that resembled *clean*. Unfortunately, the only pants he could find, he'd already worn earlier that week, twice. He grabbed them anyway and turned back toward his bed to seize the red t-shirt tossed over the footboard. He gave each armpit a whiff and a shrug, and it was on. No time to comb his hair, it was Saturday. Smiling he went out to the hall and down the stairs.

His grandmother was up now, stirring in the kitchen. She'd spend her entire day there if she could, Alex mused. No matter, breakfast was ready and hot, as usual. Cinnamon bread, juice, and cereal were all laid out, and truthfully all he had time for was the cinnamon bread. He snapped up two large pieces and a swig of the juice and headed back toward the door. His grandmother smiled. She was used to his Saturday morning routine. She knew she couldn't keep him inside on such a beautiful day.

As he exited he heard, *"Someday you'll see; that you'll wash away with the sea . . . te, te, te, te . . ."* trailing off from behind him.

Nothing but the familiar slam of the door followed. Whether it was the noise of the door meeting the wooden jamb or the blast of fresh air that hit him square in the face, the feeling of loss or that he was forgetting something jolted him to a sudden stop. Alex stood in his rather small front yard lined with the same broken picket fence that circled the back; he tried hard to shake this feeling of forgetfulness. He scratched his head in hope of remembering.

"THE NECKLACE! Of course!" he shouted. He spun around so quickly that he lost his balance tripping over his own unusually large feet. Charging the front door, he was in his room in less than five steps.

"Where is it?" he asked, searching frantically. His bed was the last place he remembered seeing it. Alex threw his quilts first to one end, then back to the other. No luck. Mittens made the mistake of coming in at the exact wrong time and was smothered in a shower of blankets and bed linens. The sheer weight of the pile of blankets was much heavier than the cat herself and pressed her to the floor in a loud howl. Although she could barely move and seemingly only in lurches, she made her discontent known. Alex stopped only for a mere second to tug the mountain off, sending her to her freedom hissing and scurrying.

"Where the heck is it?" he asked again much louder. He began looking everywhere. Under the bed seemed to be a logical place.

"I *REEEALLYYYY* gotta clean this room!" Alex admitted, throwing a scuffed dress shoe behind him without looking up. Pushing his video games out of the way, he continued hunting. Then, while leaning into the closet atop a rickety hill of toys, he felt something light against his chest. Something was out of place, something *warm*. He grabbed at his shirt, feeling it beneath.

"Whoa? No way! No way, no how." He gasped. It was the necklace! He pulled his shirt away for a visual confirmation and saw it against his chest. Alex was shocked! He quickly pulled it out and held it in front of his face.

"I put you on top of my bed last night. I know I did," he spoke to the trinket as if it were alive.

"Naaahhh. Silly," he said. He was tired, so he must not remember placing it around his neck before dozing off. There was no other explanation. His room was now in total disarray and, if it were possible, even messier than before. So he tucked it back under his shirt and went downstairs a second time. This time his trip through the front door was much more deliberate somehow. Now he had a purpose. He had a job to do. As he passed through the front gate held on by only the upper hinge, he laid out his day's mission. It was good that it was Saturday. This may take awhile, he thought.

Because the necklace bore a striking resemblance to the

scrimshaw artwork he'd seen in the past, he decided the best place to sleuth this one out would be down on the docks. It was a quiet and warm fall morning with the wind wafting in both sound and smell from the sea. These docks were different than most.

Alex could tell this had been a busy port long ago, but over the years many failed attempts at progress had left their mark. It was a sad reminder of a dying way of life, but most of the seafaring men still frequented the docks by noon each day. That is, if they weren't busy sleeping off a hard night of drinking. These were rugged men, whose skin had been worn to leather and whose eyes would stare completely through a person, as if they were looking into their very soul; characters, each and every one, and Alex preferred it that way.

Making his way through the maze of plank board pathways, Alex poked and prodded along. He first twisted his neck into one vessel that listed slightly, similar to the Mermaid, but not as bad, then into another. He came upon a group of three sailors sitting on small wooden folding chairs like those typically stored inside the boats. Two were younger men, one smaller than the other. The third was much older and appeared as if the only thing holding him up was the wind itself. They wore different clothing than Alex had seen before. Greek perhaps; not that he would know, he quickly thought. They looked tough and mean and had positioned their chairs in a circle about halfway down the first lead dock, right in the middle, as if daring anyone to tell them to move.

Alex decided it would be best to keep on moving and skirted well around the group. As he did, he saw the thin man lean over to the larger and whisper something to him, pointing at Alex's chest. Alex quickened his pace, but strained to listen. They were foreign, that's for sure, as he had no idea what the man said. It didn't matter because he didn't particularly like the tone of what was said or the looks he was now getting from these men.

"Greeks. Humph," said Captain Shovers. Alex had guessed correctly and, at this point in time, had never been so happy to see the Captain before. As the Captain spoke, the older man snapped to and sat upright, seemingly insulted, and whipped back what appeared to be a return gesture, rambling in his native tongue. As he did, both younger men quieted him and must have shared their earlier thoughts about Alex, for he, too, trailed off and now was staring at Alex's chest with great curiosity.

Alex asked Captain Shovers for permission to board the Mermaid as was customary, and permission was granted.

"Good to see ya lad. How's your grammy?" the Captain asked as he finished pouring his morning cup of tea.

"She's fine, thank you, sir," Alex replied.

"Fine woman, Cam is," the Captain stated. "Known her for some time now. Must be . . ." He paused, deep in thought, presumably about the past.

"Twenty years, sir," Alex said, completing the old man's sentence while rolling his eyes.

A bit startled at Alex's response, all the Captain could say was, "Yep, these twenty years now."

Alex had the same conversation with the Captain for the past three or four summers now, over and over again, he thought. He knew it was impolite, but he was on a mission, so before the Captain could drone on about how pretty his grandmother had looked and how young and strong he used to be, "still am," as the Captain was always quick to clarify.

Alex interrupted, "Excuse me sir, Captain, sir. May I ask you something?"

Stuttering at being cut off, the Captain conceded, "Uh, sh-sure,

Alex my boy. What is it?"

"It's just . . . I have to ask you something. You see, I have this necklace and . . ." he explained hesitantly.

"Ahhh, a girl, is it?" the Captain said imploringly.

"No sir, not a girl. I wish, but no, not a girl. The necklace is mine. I have it here, see?" Alex said, pulling it out from its hiding place and held it out for the Captain to see.

Moving closer, the Captain adjusted his eyes for a clearer look. "Hmm, I see," said the Captain. But Alex could tell he couldn't *see* at all, and after a moment the Captain walked over to one of the cabinet drawers, pulled out a magnifying glass, and returned to face the boy. Reaching up, the elder adjusted the overhead lamp to shine between them where they stood. Alex noticed this cast the strangest shadows across the inside of the Mermaid and, with the rolling of the ship, felt his stomach pitch slightly. He grabbed the table behind him to steady himself, and the Captain made a motion for the bench seats surrounding it. They both eagerly sat down, although for completely different purposes.

"Ain't got your sea legs yet, eh?" the Captain joked with a big, toothless crack of a smile. It was still dark in the cabin of the Mermaid, so the Captain lit one of the oil lamps on the table. Focusing intently with the pendant merely inches in front of the magnifying glass, the Captain did his best to size up the object he now held in his own hands.

"Dunno. Seems I've seen it before. Or leastways, something like it. Can't recall," the old man explained. Disappointed in his scant recollection of the past, the Captain returned the object to Alex. But as he did, the light of the oil lamp bounced off the object, and something caught the Captain's eye.

"Hold up there. What do we got here?" he asked, snatching it back out of Alex's hands before the boy could close his fingers around it. Alex jumped back, on edge since he witnessed the cloaked creature on his porch the night before. Captain Shovers paid no attention to Alex's reaction and tilted the lamp in, toward the pendant.

Alex's jaw dropped. He saw it, too. He hadn't noticed it before. He'd spent what felt like an eternity looking at it, but had never seen this. Had it always done that? he marveled. He rubbed his eyes just to make sure. They were both leaning in now.

As the Captain held the object in one hand, he rolled the base of the table lamp in the other, forcing the light to bend toward the pendant. When it did, and everything was just right, it happened again. They both jumped this time.

Stray beams of white light shot through several tiny holes along the ring and spread shadows onto the wooden hull of the Mermaid, while other streaks formed shapes on the walls, catching the edges of the ridges and bumps on the ring along the way. The whole thing reminded Alex a little of a mirrored disco ball.

The two were in shock. Their eyes were fixed on the swirling shapes and lights that were moving not unlike a choreographed dance company performing their season finale. Shapes, figures, and letters, or at least what looked like letters, trickled off from the hand-hewn oaken beams of the vessel. The walls and ceiling were covered.

"Boy. BOY!" the Captain shouted, and Alex whipped back to his senses. "Go get a pen and paper, now," he said.

"Hunh?" was the only response Alex could muster.

"I said go and get me a pen and a piece of paper from the drawer, over there," the Captain spoke slowly, trying not to scare Alex anymore than he was. Cautiously, Alex stood, took two deliberate steps toward the drawer, and pulled. It was stuck. He tugged harder. It budged about an inch outward and stuck again. Salt water wears hard on wooden fixtures and swells the joints, he remembered learning from the Captain in one of their earlier meetings. He was getting more and more anxious, so he tugged hard. The contents of the drawer flew everywhere in a clatter. Feeling rushed, Alex bent to pick up the cooking ladle and the spoons now sprawled across the floor. A small ball of rubber bands bounced out of sight while about thirty different pens and pencils rolled every which way.

"Don't worry about them. Just get the pen and paper," the old man said. Alex had noticed in the past, during many of their talks, that anytime Captain Shovers got upset or agitated or anything, his accent would get heavier. The roughness and hardness of his questionable youth on the open seas would work their way to the surface. This time was no exception. Not wanting to upset the man in what was already shaping up to be a traumatic experience, Alex pulled a pen from the pile and returned with both it and a piece of paper in hand.

"Get all of this down, boy," the Captain said.

"Sir?" Alex said.

"Write everything you see on that paper," he pleaded.

"Oh, yeah, okay," Alex said and immediately began drawing every shape, every symbol feverishly, stopping only once in a while to ask the Captain for clarity on a particular scene. Every so often the Captain would belt out what he saw dancing across the ceiling.

"An hourglass. A beetle? Is that a sword?" he'd yell.

Random disconnected essays flashed across the dimly lit vessel. Triangles and human shapes and what appeared to be a bull with horns would appear scattered against what seemed to be words.

There were wavy lines, circles, and letters similar to our own, but not exactly; no rhyme and presumably no purpose. Alex noted strange pictures of animals like birds and dogs.

"Ahhhhhh-cheee!" screamed the Captain as he dropped the lamp. He'd held onto it too long, and his hand now reddened with swollen pain from the heat. Both symbol and scene left the room in an instant. Blowing on his hand, Captain Shovers raced toward a small sink behind him, still holding it from the pain. The pump kicked on with a twist of the knob, flushing cold water over his hand, providing instant relief. The necklace still sat on the table where he'd dropped it.

Outside, Alex could hear talking, and since he couldn't make out any of the words, he speculated it was the three sailors from earlier. Based on the level of the commotion, they must have seen some of the lights piercing through the small windows of the ship.

In those moments of the madness, Alex had managed to jot down almost three pages of scrambled notes and pictures, in the hope that they could decode them. He sat now staring at the pages, hoping something would jump out at him. But nothing came to him. None of it made any sense. Alex would sit for hours with his grandmother playing board games and solving puzzles, but that was no training for what was in front of him. Captain Shovers now sat next to Alex on the same bench seat at the table, leaning over him and giving it his best effort as well. No luck.

Despite dancing around the room only moments earlier full of life, these symbols, these scenes of ambiguity, sat lifeless on their pages. The two sleuths were discouraged and frustrated.

They talked for the next two hours trying to crack any hidden code of which they were sure existed. The Captain was a fan of watching late night detective shows on the bow of the Mermaid

41

with his thirteen-inch black and white, so this undoubtedly made him the expert of the two. They chose to focus on the individual signs and symbols rather than stringing them together. The determined pair believed that if they could determine what they were separately, they'd be able to figure out the bigger puzzle easier. They sat there, side by side, with little conversation between them.

The Captain was far less patient in his old age and, self-admittedly, had "seen it all," so if this intrusion into his quiet life were nothing more, then he would treat it as such and move on to something else. He was frustrated. "I give up. I'm a busy man. Things to do, you know."

Alex, however, had other plans. Noting the Captain's sudden disinterest, which he thought was absurd given what they'd just witnessed, Alex slid the necklace around his head and stood, tucking it away.

He wasn't sure what to do next in his investigation, but he knew he wasn't going to get much further here. Alex had seen Captain Shovers like this before and knew enough to leave. As he climbed the steep wooden steps up to the deck of the Mermaid, the Captain yelled at him, "You might want to check Trudie's place. She's got all sorts of things and such. She'll know. You go see Trudie, do you hear?"

"Trudie's! That's it! Trudie's Treasures. Why hadn't I thought of that?" Alex said with an insurgence of hope. "Thanks, Captain!"

He leaped from the boat to the dock, barely touching the plank that connected them. He was so intent on getting to the store, on getting some answers, solving the puzzle, that he'd forgotten about the sailors. They, however, hadn't forgotten about him. The two younger men of the group took off after him, around a stack of lobster pots, past the elderly ladies mending netting and back up the dock toward the street. They clamored over boxes and people alike. Alex hadn't seen them at first. They trailed him from a distance so they wouldn't startle their prey. It was by chance that Alex glanced over his shoulder and caught the thinner of the two duck down an adjacent dock and behind a small diesel fueling shed.

Alex walked faster, weaving in and out of a twisted maze of weathered dockage, past the *Jefferson Club House and Marina*, aptly named after its local benefactor, and back up to higher ground toward the street. Once past the marina, the sailors had little cover, and they knew theirs was blown, so without care they quickened their pace. The race was on. Despite being bigger, their foot race stood no chance against a thirteen-year-old boy intimately familiar with the docks and his surroundings and even more familiar with being chased by others.

It was then that Alex realized that he was in serious danger. He remembered yesterday's chance encounter with Jackson and his brood. He remembered the voice in his head. *Run.* So run he did. Faster he went, through the alleyways, behind the recycling bins and into a shallow doorway on a back street. He was slightly hidden by the stacked cardboard boxes that had accumulated there over the week. Alex knew this place. It was the back door to Trudie's, his destination. He'd made it. He was here. Safe. *Safe?* He laughed. He hadn't been *safe* in two days, he thought. The gasps of air burned at his lungs.

He turned his thin figure around in the narrow opening and slowly lifted the entire screen door up and in. He'd entered this place from the alley several times before and knew that the only way he'd get through was to lift before pushing. The salt air had swollen and warped the door over the years and forced it to drag on the floor if attempted any other way. He paused about halfway through, hearing footsteps toward the front of the store.

Holding his breath, Alex clung to the handle, ready to burst through and take off out the front, should his pursuers see him. Listening, wishing he were invisible now, he thought of his grandmother. Alex often thought of his grandmother when he was scared. She was the only one who'd always been there for him; comforting, holding, loving.

The steps moved on. As he pushed the door the rest of the way, he was greeted with a familiar sound. He cringed for fear he wasn't the only one who'd heard it. Alex had forgotten completely about the small brass bell perched above the door, alerting the proprietor of anyone entering through the back. He felt doubly stupid since he was the one who had mounted it there this summer. Alex was young, but quite the entrepreneur for his age. Every summer he would scour the town looking for odd jobs to earn some quick cash, repairing this and fixing that. "No task too small," he'd always tell himself. He tried mowing lawns, but that turned out to be a loss since the only real grass worth mowing in town was the Styers property, and they had a service cut theirs. He collected cans, anything to earn money. After all, he needed money if he wanted to travel someday.

Alex stopped dead in his tracks. He had one foot in the doorway and one inside the shop. That darn bell had given away his hiding place. He stood there long after the metallic ringing of the bell faded away, breathing slowly through his teeth. His head was darting back and forth, up and down the rows of old wooden display cases and shelving that lined the shop. Nothing. He saw nobody. He walked in grabbing at the bell to stop it from ringing again with the closing of the door. Looking around again for security measures and finding the shop empty, he whispered, "Ms. Trudie? Ms. Trudie, you here?"

Again there was nothing. Given her prized possessions, Ms. Trudie Dell always kept her shop closed up tight, and the resulting air inside was stale and dusty. Alex often wondered how anyone could see anything of value in what Ms. Trudie had on display.

The items under lock ranged from the curious to the bizarre. Most items were of the sea or had some sort of sailing connection. Some were items that sailors would trade with her from far off places. Simple seashells and colored stones lined the middle shelving, and even they, too, were locked under glass. Alex never understood why. He could find many of these specimens on his short walks across the granite rocks that lined the beaches of the town. He didn't see much value in them.

Ms. Trudie kept the special items under the main case in the front of the shop, but Alex wasn't too keen on making his way up there just yet. He wanted to make sure the coast was clear. The main display sat just off to the right of the two large glass windows that flanked either side of the door at the street entrance. Should he go up there to look, nothing could hide him from the men who chased him.

"Ms. Trudie? Hello?" Alex asked again. Still there was nothing. Slowly and methodically Alex began his search, not knowing what he was looking for. He moved silently, careful not to touch anything. He started left, toward the loft in the back of the shop. He gazed at each item, taking far more notice of things than he had in his past visits. This time something, *anything*, could have meaning. He wasn't comfortable in his recent thirst for this knowledge and even less sure where his uncontrollable drive for the answers was coming from, so he searched. Every now and again a trinket would catch his eye, but he'd move on, dismissing its relevance. The light here was poor and made for poor dissection and critique of the

45

wares. He caught himself laughing softly at times at the odd and even ridiculous things locked under glass. Alex questioned whether some of these items should have been left where they were originally found.

"Pssst . . . Ms. Trudie, it's me, Alex. Hellloooo," Alex said as he weaved in and out of the aisles, moving closer to the front. The closer he got to the door, the more concerned he got. He knew his curiosity had to move him toward the large glass case near the front door. But this would place him in plain sight. He also knew that it was this same large glass case that may likely hold the answers to his questions.

He heard a creak of the floorboards from the back of the store and ducked behind a row of shelving in response, turning toward the noise. Footsteps, above, on the loft. There was no hiding from anyone who may be spying down from that vantage point. It was useless to try, as they would be able to see the entire maze of shop displays. From behind a bookshelf appeared a figure. A light from behind the figure only cast the shadow itself in Alex's direction, making it difficult to see details of the person. His heart was racing, pounding harder than ever. His forehead and palms broke out in a sweat as he forced himself against the closest case.

"Alex? Is that you?" the voice asked.

It was weak and feeble, but he recognized the voice. His heart leapt for joy. It was Ms. Trudie, and boy was he relieved. Still whispering, he replied, "Yes, ma'am. It's me."

"What are you doing down there? Did you lose something?" she asked.

Realizing he was crouched only inches from the floor, Alex stood, stooping still, as he was mindful of the men searching for him outside.

"No, ma'am, I was tying my shoelace," he responded. Ms. Trudie had always been nice to him, and he hated to have to lie to her, but what was a small white lie if it meant his safety . . . and maybe even hers?

"How can I help you, my dear?" she said with a warm, motherly tone. She was sweet, and Alex had known her to be no other way, to a fault. Many times people had tried to take advantage of her kindness, none so much as Jefferson Styers. It angered Alex that people like Mr. Styers would be so underhanded and mean as to try to foreclose on Ms. Trudie. Jefferson Styers still maintained the mortgages on most of the small shops that had sprung up on his development. Alex believed it annoyed Mr. Styers even more that Ms. Trudie always seemed to make the payments just in time. This thought brought a smile to his face.

"I wanted to show you something I, uh, f-found, please," he told her. She was still able to make the descent down the steep stairs, but with great difficulty.

"Ahh, these bones . . ." she complained as she landed firmly on her cushioned shoes. She scuffled when she walked at about a half a knot faster than a snail. Ms. Trudie made her way toward Alex and sized him up.

"Well, my dear, what is it?" she asked as she motioned to a pair of chairs positioned off to the side. He was certain that Ms. Trudie sensed his edginess. Looking over his shoulder, Alex accepted and sat down, facing the front of the store. If he moved quickly enough, he thought, he could make it out the back before anyone got close.

"Alex?" she said, concerned.

"Yes, Ms. Trudie. I found a necklace and . . ." Alex said.

"Necklace? Necklace! Oh dear. It's time, isn't it? Oh dear! Oh dear! Oh dear!" she exclaimed, jumping up and frantically pacing in small circles. She reminded Alex of a toy robot whose wiring was short-circuiting. She began muttering to herself.

"What? What is it? Is something wrong?" Alex asked, worried about her sudden reaction to his news. She apparently knew something, which under normal circumstances would have made him excited, but the way she reacted only served to heighten his already elevated level of anxiety.

"You have it with you, don't you dear? You *do* have it?" she whispered imploringly.

"Uh, yes ma'am, I do," Alex replied meekly. They were speaking quietly now, neither sure as to why, but both sensing it was appropriate.

The front door burst opened. Their conversation stopped cold, and both snapped a look toward the front of the store.

"Tourist," Ms. Trudie surmised. How she could see from way back here, thought Alex, was a mystery to him. She slowly got up from her seat next to his and began the long, difficult trek to the front of the store. She took two steps and turned toward Alex,

"Alex?" said the old woman. He had disappeared, scared by the presence of a stranger in the store. A faint and muffled sound echoed through the quiet dampness of the room. It was Alex. He had slid beneath the table, hidden from sight. She bent over and gave him a look that implied how foolish he was being. But then, she had no idea what he'd been through, what he'd seen. These past two days swirled in his head. He closed his eyes.

"I'll get rid of her, my dear. Don't you worry anymore," she said, and with that, she rather rudely shooed the patron out the door and locked it behind her. Turning the *We'll be back at* . . . sign around, she pulled the shade. Alex was shaken, but by the time Ms. Trudie had returned to the table, he had collected himself enough to come out from hiding and sat, at the very least, on the edge of his chair.

Jittery and shaken even more now, Ms. Trudie watched him for a moment, then said, "You're like a nine-tailed cat in a room full of rocking chairs, aren't you?" Not exactly the comforting words he'd hoped for, but the words did serve to deflect his nerves briefly.

"Where is it?" she asked with a softer tone in her voice, hoping to calm him even further. Still somewhat bewildered at her apparent knowledge of the necklace, he slowly pulled the object out from under his shirt.

"Well, hmm, doesn't look like much. I've got a six-legged starfish over there under glass. Now that's impressive," she said, staring at the necklace from over the rims of her bifocals. Alex shot her a look as if to say *really?*

"Well, Camille said you might come for it someday. I suppose today's the day. Good as any, I imagine. Been holding on to it for years now," she said as she pushed her chair away from the table and stood again.

"Camille? Holding on to *what*, Ms. Trudie? Come for *what?* What's my gramma have to do with this? Does she know what's going on?" Alex pleaded.

"Now you stay put. Don't move. It's right up here. I think," Ms. Trudie said. She turned and began climbing the same steep steps from the loft she had come down from only moments earlier.

"Ms. Trudie? *Please*," said Alex anxiously.

"Tut, tut, boy. Patience," Ms. Trudie responded. It was difficult for Alex to endure her rather slow climb to the top and around the first row of upper shelving. Unaware of what he was doing, Alex, too, had risen from where he sat and began walking backwards, looking up and watching her every move. Afraid of being seen from the street, he was careful to not walk too far out into the shop. He edged against a large old metal table piled high with t-shirts, towels, and other tacky shop items. He could just make out her movements from gaps between the books on the shelves from which she stood behind. He watched her rifle through an old wooden schoolteacher's desk, drawer after drawer. It felt as if his heart had stopped. The anticipation was unbearable. He heard her muttering to herself, angry for not knowing where she had placed it.

"*Ahhh*, here it is," she said.

Alex's heart beat once again. He focused on her hands, although at a distance, he could see from his vantage point that she held in her hands a book. He watched her lift it high in the dimly lit loft. As she brought it down, he saw her blow away years of dust in a single huff.

She coughed twice, followed by one of those high-pitched *AH-squeak* type sneezes. It was the kind of sneeze that only dogs can hear; the same noise, he familiarized, that the girls in his history class would make by holding it back. His only comfort came in knowing that the resulting pressure from a teenage girl's sneeze only pushed out what little brains they had left through their ears.

As the dust settled, she tucked it neatly up under her arm and headed back toward her harrowing climb down to the first floor. Alex quickly returned to his place at the table beneath the loft so as not to be caught spying. He waited anxiously for what seemed like hours for Ms. Trudie to walk the five simple steps from the stairs. He was fidgeting and couldn't help it. The same questions from earlier began repeating through his mind. What *was* this book? What did it have to do with his necklace? More important, what did his grandmother have to do with all of this? Ms. Trudie said she'd been holding on to it for years. But how did gramma know? he thought. How *could* she know? And why were people chasing him? There's a connection, he knew it.

A cloud of dust thickened the air as Ms. Trudie dropped the book on the table. "Been a dozen years or so now," she declared.

"Wait. What? A dozen years or so. I've only just turned thirteen yesterday," Alex informed her.

"Yep. Seems about right then," she replied.

Alex's eyes popped out of his head in disbelief. "How could that be?" he asked. Ms. Trudie hadn't heard him, or at least pretended as if she hadn't. Alex was growing more and more frustrated the further along he got in this journey, and this was about all he could take. "Ms. Trudie, *please* tell me," he begged.

"All I know is that your grandmother, Camille, came to me some many years ago now and gave me this book for safekeeping. I remember that night. She was terrified. Not about something that happened, but about something that hadn't happened yet. Understand?" she began.

"*Nooo*," Alex replied in earnest.

Ms. Trudie continued, "She asked me to keep this book and said that you would come for it someday. Of course, I thought she had a screw loose. But no, I could see it in her eyes. Whatever she was telling me, she believed to the bone. Said it would help you find your way or something like that."

"Find my way? But I wasn't even born yet. How could . . . ? What did she . . . ? Why, but . . ." Too many thoughts, words, feelings, flooded his head. He couldn't get them out fast enough.

It wasn't until Alex dropped his head to his hands nearing tears that he noticed the book in detail. It was smaller than most books. In fact, it wasn't a book at all, but more like a journal. It was bound in thick, hand-carved leather and wrapped at the clasp with a small red ribbon. He reached over and turned the book to face him and, as he did, he could swear he felt his necklace getting warmer. It was tattered, and the spine was starting to fray, but that didn't interest him as much as what his eyes narrowed in on next. Carved deep into the leather, in the center of the book he noticed it.

Alex's jaw dropped to the table. He couldn't believe what he saw. "*No way!*" he exclaimed.

Three

Alex was an inquisitive, curious person by nature. He always wanted answers, in part because his grandmother had always taught him to ask questions. As he sat there with Ms. Trudie in the back of a dusty, unkempt knick-knack store at 320-C Kelp Drive overlooking the harbor, they puzzled at what lay before them. She was the frail proprietor of the establishment, too thin to stand long on her own two feet, and he was a boy whose life had only just begun.

They gazed at the small, thick leather journal that sat on the table in front of them, Alex more intensely than Ms. Trudie Dell. Although he was seeing the cover for the first time, Alex recognized right away what was carved deep into it. He pulled out his necklace and placed it cautiously against the front of the journal.

"A perfect fit!" he commented in disbelief, glancing up at Ms. Trudie. She nodded in agreement. Alex allowed himself to get excited with anticipation. This *had* to be an important piece of the puzzle, he hoped quietly.

Ms. Trudie asked, "Alex, what does it mean? Where did you get that necklace?"

"I, uh, that is to say . . . um, *found* it?" he responded. Alex had been caught off guard for a moment. His mind spun. How much should he tell Ms. Trudie? he wondered. How much did she already know?

In an attempt to avoid further questioning, he tucked the necklace back under his shirt and began unwrapping the ribbon that held the journal's secrets. Slowly he lifted the cover, as if afraid something would spill out. The spine of the book cracked open, and a dry musty odor filled the air around them. Thumbing through the yellowed pages, he settled upon the first entry. It was a series of strange lettering, in no apparent order, riddled with secondary notations along the margins. These, too, made no sense. Even more weird, he thought, was that each series was a combination of unfamiliar lettering mixed with symbols and shapes. He could recognize a few shapes, but had no idea what they meant. They were simple in form. Stick-drawings really, but that didn't help him any.

Then it hit him. His heart leapt again. It was doing that a lot lately. Briefly he feared a heart attack, but realized it was quite uncommon for someone his age. There in front of him were some of the same drawings from the Mermaid. They were the same ones that danced across the ceiling when the lamplight shone against his necklace. He noted a bird, the same drawing of a beetle, and an hourglass. They were moving, swirling inside his head, and seemingly having no connection to anything. Alex had been so focused on the pages of the journal that he hadn't noticed that Ms. Trudie had excused herself to the back part of the shop where she had a small kitchenette behind another door. She returned moments later with two cups of tea, piping hot, and placed them on the table next to the book.

"Oh, sorry. Thank you, Ms. Trudie," Alex said apologetically. He hadn't realized how long he'd been staring at the entries in the book and was somewhat embarrassed that he'd forgotten about her presence. She smiled reassuringly, seeming to sense his thoughts.

The style of the writings and drawings were all so strangely familiar to him, although he couldn't place why.

The shelves suddenly teetered and shook. The window glass vibrated against their panes. Years of collectibles wobbled on their overstocked shelves, clanking against one another. In the distance, the occupants of Trudie's Treasures heard something small fall high from its place on an upper shelf, hit the floor, and roll away to a muffled halt. Matilda had announced her intention.

"Twelve noon," Ms. Trudie responded simply, without so much as a movement. She continued to sip her tea and fixate on the object in front of her, her focus unbroken. Alex, on the other hand, jumped straight up at the sound, sending his teacup sliding to the other side of the table. After realizing that Captain Shovers and Matilda were merely exercising their daily routine, Alex settled back down and opened the journal once more.

"Ms. Trudie? Do you have any idea what this all means? The necklace? The journal? And how my gramma is involved?" Alex pleaded.

"No, dear, I'm afraid I don't. I *do* know that your grandmother told me it was important for you to have someday," she explained as she reached out and touched his hand. "Now naturally I wanted to ask her, mind you, but at the time I thought she was plum crazy. I kept it safe just as she had asked for all of these years. Only had it out twice, I think. Never opened it, mind you; never. Wasn't mine to open. Had it out once the day you were born and once when I was looking for something else," she said tenderly.

"Well, I can make out some pictures, but the writing is like nothing I've ever seen before," he said. "It's like random thoughts that someone threw down on paper."

"Maybe it only appears random to you," she added. "What if you look for a pattern?" she asked.

"A pattern?" Alex replied.

"Repeated thoughts or writings or symbols. Maybe the answer isn't in *what's* written, but rather *how* it's written," she continued.

Alex's eyebrows rose with that comment. Interesting; maybe she was right. Maybe. Alex had always been an avid puzzler. Every Sunday he and his grandmother would pull out the latest edition of *Tradewinds* and work on the crossword puzzle until it was completed. They would exhaust hours on riddles and brainteasers alike. He enjoyed those times when it was just he and his grandmother. They'd laugh all day long. But they always solved them. Almost always, he thought. Why was this one so difficult? he wondered.

He flipped a few pages into the journal and realized something straight away. There were different sections, or what he believed to be different sections. Each had different writings and symbols from the last. His head hurt. He flipped further in the hope of finding something familiar or at least by chance disproving his growing belief that this was unsolvable. Nothing. It was like the book was growing, even changing, or perhaps it was the mysterious author who was changing. All Alex gained were more questions.

"I give up," he said relenting and began to drop his head into his hands. It was at that precise moment that his eyes flitted over something familiar, something in the pages. It was something he'd seen before. His attention snapped back as he turned page after page feverishly. I know I saw it, he thought.

"There! There it is," he exclaimed, pointing to the two figures. It was a man and a woman. They were facing each other, not unlike the two figures on the necklace. But these were different somehow. Alex was growing impatient as he flipped back further into the journal. The text seemed to be changing with every turn. Another man and woman, different than the last, but similar enough for Alex to know they were related somehow. He moved back a few pages until he drew his eyes on an outline of something else vaguely familiar. Another figure. It looked like part man and part . . . *dog!*

His mind flashed back to last night. The creature on the front porch, the one who had left him the necklace; it was him! It had to be, and he knew it. Alex desperately needed answers and was certain it couldn't be mere coincidence.

This was too much of a coincidence and, considering all of the odd occurrences including his recent escape from the Greek sailors, he knew he was on to something big, and with that he closed the journal.

"Ms. Trudie, you've been helpful, but I think I need to do this on my own, whatever *this* is. I'm afraid that if I stay here much longer you may be in danger," he spoke bluntly.

A look of surprise came over Ms. Trudie Dell, proprietor of Trudie's Treasures. Alex was certain she had never been 'in danger' before, nor that she particularly liked the sound of it. He knew that she would try to dismiss his warning, but he desperately hoped she would listen.

Looking forward to the street and back to the right where the rear entrance was, Alex chose his exit carefully. He slid the journal into his back pocket with some effort, as it was much thicker than the opening of his pocket, and pulled his shirt down over the top. Stepping away from the table, the boy said, "Ms. Trudie, please say nothing to nobody. Not even my gramma. Least not until I figure some things out. I don't want to worry her." He smiled imploringly at her in the hope that she would acknowledge.

She stared at him, herself still trying to understand everything. Alex thought for a moment that it was a good thing he didn't show her what happens when he places light against the necklace. That would have freaked her out, he thought, and quickly dismissed the idea.

Alex worked his way back through the aisles of cluttered tables and disorganized shelves, past the stacks of boxes and overflowing bins. He took great care to not act like he was still hiding from what may be waiting out on the street for him, but his stooped posture gave him away. As he moved, he tried to come up with a plan. He knew he needed to do this alone, in quiet. But where? He no sooner asked the question and it came to him.

Alex was so caught up in his thoughts that he once again forgot about the brass bell above the back door. Wincing, he instinctively reached up and muffled the noise.

"Jeeeezzz," was the only response he would say out loud. He was taught better.

Sliding through the thinnest of cracks between the door and its jamb, he was in the alley once again. Alex was careful not to expose himself right away and decided to slither and slink his way toward the back of the alley and shimmy up the steel roof ladder of the adjacent building. He'd played here as a kid several times before, and it had always made for a great escape route from the likes of Jackson Styers and his lackeys. From his perch at the top of the roof, Alex could see the entire town. The buildings had been built with short parapet walls about three feet high, which allowed him to crouch behind them, hidden from sight. Alex thought it best to move up close to the front of the rooftop to try and locate his recent pursuers. Edging up close to the wall, he peered one eye first, then the other, over the wall. As he did, he heard a rustling sound from below.

His eyes turned and shot down to the alley toward the noise.

"Great. That's just what I need now," he said to himself. Jackson had turned down the same alley that Alex had just risen from and was heading straight for the roof ladder. Alex knew that the way Jackson was moving, the bully had seen him. Without any further caution, Alex ran toward the same ladder that Jackson was climbing.

"Hey!" he shouted down at him. This confrontation was so unexpected that it startled the big oaf, and he fell back off the ladder rungs and onto a pile of garbage bags and empty boxes. Sensing his momentary advantage, Alex wheeled around and took off running to buy himself even more distance between them. He didn't bother looking back. He could visualize the scene simply from Jackson's burst of explicit profanity.

From roof to roof he raced toward his destination with arms and legs flailing about. If I can just make it there without anyone else seeing me, he hoped. His desire was quickly crushed. Voices entered his mind, shouts more like. He stopped to clear his head and focus. From below he heard people yelling.

He had only to move slightly to realize that he'd been spotted. But this time it wasn't the school bully. This time it was *them*; the sailors from earlier, those from the dock, the same ones he was trying so desperately to avoid. His altercation with Jackson must have attracted their attention somehow. How, didn't matter; what mattered was that they were back on his trail, pointing and shouting up at him. He had been exposed.

Knowing all that stood between him and the safety he longed for was about five feet and some running was enough to move him from plain sight. Five feet sounded easy. The reality of it was that he needed to jump at least that to get to the next rooftop. Easy to do, *maybe*. But he was twenty-five feet above street level and had never made this jump before, never even attempted it. It was too dangerous. The pavement below was hard and flat.

He remembered a joke someone once told him about falling off a roof. Something about, "It's not the fall that'll kill ya; it's the sudden stop." Admittedly, this was no time for jokes.

A noise from behind made Alex spin his head. It was Jackson. He was back and looking much like a train barreling toward him, complete with billows of steam pushing out from his head. He was beet-red and moving fast. Alex took about three steps back and let off, running faster than he'd ever run. His arms were like pistons pushing, pumping. His legs were reaching farther with each step.

He was airborne. What a sight! There was no grace. No smoothness to his movements. Arms and legs went awry in every direction. Birds covered their eyes in shame. A gull even squawked in the background. It was as if time stood still simply to avoid this unnatural aversion to flight.

"Ooooff!" came the noise from deep inside his body. He made it! Well, sort of. He made it from the waist up. The rest of his body hung, dangling over the edge.

There he dangled, scared, his ribs in pain. His grip managed to have landed around a utility pole located near the edge. It wasn't helping much. Too scared to look down, he swung his legs from side to side, stretching for some ledge that he knew didn't exist. His grip was loosening, slipping from the pole.

"Well, well. Serves you right, Chronos. I hope you fall." And with that, the mug bent over and picked up pebbles off the rolled roofing where he stood. One by one he threw them across the gap between the two buildings at Alex, missing by inches most of the time. But those few, those that did land, did so squarely against his back and head.

They hurt badly. Jackson didn't have much athletic ability as Alex was aware, but what he did have was strength, so when a rock or a pebble met its target, even by chance, it stung.

Alex tried his hardest to put the pain of his pelting out of his head and focus on the real danger of not falling. He didn't want to die today. How would he explain that to his gramma? he thought.

"Ow! Cut it out, jerk!" he yelled at the brute.

"Jerk? I'll show you who's a jerk." He tossed an entire handful of pebbles at Alex. Alex found himself in a hailstorm. Sweat rolled down into his eyes from the fear. He tried to blow it away, but failed. He told himself he wasn't going to cry because real men don't cry. Fighting back the tears, he gave one herculean effort to pull himself up from over the edge. It worked, but not without its own offer of pain. He managed to cut and scrape himself, ripping his jeans down his right leg. The tear was about three inches long and enough to have left a deep wound of trickling blood soaking through the material. He rolled onto the roof and lie on his back, panting from his effort. Alex knew this was no time for resting. He had to get back up. He had to get away. He wasn't safe yet.

Pushing himself, still weary from facing his own death, he lifted himself and began running. The pain in his leg was a fierce reminder of just how real all of this was. He ran with a limp, out of breath and struggling to make sense of everything. Alex took comfort in thinking of his grandmother and her loving arms. He ran harder. His destination was close.

The voices of the men who chased him were still piercing his thoughts. They were still after him, and they sounded angry. They were getting closer; he could feel it. The intensity of the chase burst through every pore of his body. All he wanted to do was stop; stop and pass out.

Their commotion got louder. Their shouts suddenly turned to screams, and Alex heard what sounded like growling. The men were still yelling at him, or so he thought, but the shouts were now more like shrieks. There was fear in their voices. He heard more yelling, followed by more growling. What sounded like a bark caught him by surprise. He didn't have time to turn around and look, nor could he fit another thought into his head. It was already overflowing. The noises from the street below got more and more faint with each passing step. He only slowed when he was certain that he heard nothing.

"Finally," he said in complete exhaustion. He'd reached the edge of the last rooftop. There was a ladder on this roof leading down to the back of the building, much the same as every rooftop he'd crossed. The difference was that this particular escape route put him closer to his destination. He could see his house from atop the roof. Looking over his shoulder as he made his descent, Alex couldn't help but think that his destination looked miles away. He knew he couldn't lead them straight to his house. He'd be putting everything he loved and cherished in danger, and he wouldn't risk that.

Taking the last two rungs to the ground, Alex devised a route that would take him backtracking up the opposite side of Harbor Point and through some neighbors' yards, then home into his own. He carefully worked his way over fences and through the neatly manicured shrubs and bushes, stopping every now and then to survey his surroundings. He trekked past the recycling area, behind the bins.

At one point he heard laughing and turned to realize that two older girls from his school were pointing in his direction and giggling. He realized with a blush that he must have made quite a sight as he danced and tiptoed from tree to tree trying desperately to conceal his whereabouts from his hunters. But today, right now, he didn't have time for girls. Dumb girls, he dismissed with an air of annoyance. Who cared what they thought anyway? That is, if they could *have* an intelligent thought, he consoled himself, and dismissed them with a cold stare.

He was next door and was almost home free. He just had to move through the Moores' back yard without being seen or attacked by Mugsy or the two men searching for him. Now, Mugsy had always been pleasant to Alex. The dog had always given a wag and a short *Woof,* but Alex had always been on *his* side of the fence, too. Alex had seen Mugsy in action before and knew that if he caught him off-guard, the animal may just turn on him. So slowly, cautiously, quietly, he moved, zigzagging across the yard. When he reached about three feet from the shared fence line that dissected his yard from the Moores', he tossed his aching body over and landed with a roll. Mugsy hadn't seen him, nor had anyone else, and he was relieved.

"Whew," he said quietly. As he picked himself up, he saw his grandmother in the rear upstairs window of the house. He could tell from her movements that she was vacuuming the upstairs hall. Watching her, he was suddenly overcome by a wave of emotions. He was flooded with love for her. She had always taken good care of him. He felt guilty that he was putting her in danger. He felt scared of what may happen to him . . . and her. He longed for her to hold him and tell him that everything would be okay.

How could he be so selfish? he thought. He was angry with himself for not thinking his plan completely through. He was so wrapped up in escaping those who chased him that he didn't see. She *was* in danger, and it was his fault.

Enraged at himself, he brushed off and edged back toward the shed. He knew it wasn't going to be easy, but he had to open the door and hide inside. Easier said than done, he recalled. In the past it would take huge efforts, sometimes both himself and his grandmother, to simply open the door. He remembered having to use a crowbar last time. He didn't look forward to this task, struggling, making all sorts of noise out in the open. He was sure he'd be noticed.

As he approached the heavy door, he caught sight of scratches high above the frame. Not recognizing them, he stopped.

"Where'd they come from?" he questioned aloud. They were far too high for him to have caused them in the past, and he'd remember having put such deep scratches in the door. His grandmother would have remembered, too. Alex reached up to run his fingers across them and realized that, to do so, he had to stand on his toes and stretch his long arms to their farthest just to touch the bottom of the scratches.

Puzzled, he dropped flat-footed and grabbed the door handle. He'd been through this before, so he gave the door a considerable tug. It whipped open so easily that it forced Alex to tumble backward to the ground. He was tired of being on the ground so much lately. But why, or rather how, did the door open so easily? His leg was still bleeding, and the pain in his ribs from hanging several stories above the ground was still cinching his mid-section.

Although it was bright and sunny outside, all Alex could see was darkness coming from inside the shed. Shadows were cast across the inside, bending and contorting around everything in their path. At one point he thought he saw something move inside, then he heard a clash from the back corner.

"Mittens!" Alex exclaimed in a forced whisper. Out pranced the cat like it owned the world. Alex swore it smirked at him in defiance.

"Git!" Alex persuaded with a stomp of his foot. Mittens hissed and sputtered as she passed him.

Alex rose and once again approached the wooden structure. The wind was picking up and the sky was darkening. Must be a storm, he thought. The weather would often suddenly change where they lived, being so close to the sea. Closer he moved, his hand reaching out in front of him in the blanket of shadows, feeling for the flashlight he knew was on the workbench to the left of the door. He fumbled and knocked a glass jar full of screws over on the bench. Reaching to somehow capture the sound, he looked over his shoulder for any signs of movement as he entered the shed.

Alex squinted as his eyes adjusted from the light to the dark, moving and knocking into the old push mower in the middle of the floor. He winced with pain as the cut on his leg pulled against the mower. He didn't dare cry out. He was too close to any possible answers to chance getting discovered now. Feeling his way through the shed, somehow larger inside than out, he made his way toward the back corner and sat on an old discarded box of holiday decorations and fell half through. He decided not to move, as it would have been too noisy and cumbersome to get out; and besides, now that his eyes had better adjusted to the lack of light, he was anxious to crack open the journal he held so tightly against his chest.

He could see through the cracks in the clapboard siding of the shed that it was growing darker outside, and the impending storm was closing in. Pulling the journal away, he tilted it against the best reading light. Thunder rumbled in the distance, a flash of light.

Alex took a deep breath and flipped to the first page. Again he thought the writing was somehow familiar. Shaking that notion off, he redirected his focus to what was on the page before him. A code perhaps? He turned the journal sideways and upside-down. No luck. He mulled over some thoughts in his mind, a private journal, an important record of sorts? "*Naaahh*," he said softly, "my luck it's just a grocery list."

Then he saw the picture of the man and woman again. It was

similar to the scene carved on his necklace and engraved deeply on the cover of the journal, but not exact. This particular picture had them dressed in strange clothing with small branches and leaves woven into crowns on their heads. Instead of a tall thin tree, there was what appeared to be a stone pillar between them. No snake this time, but rather a bird was drawn in flight around their heads.

"Good," Alex spoke, "I hate snakes."

The text itself, if it was a form of text, was arranged in no particular pattern, nor was it written in anything that remotely resembled English. In fact, he thought, it looked much like the incoherent ramblings of a lunatic, newly escaped from his incarceration and on the run, pleading his innocence. Okay, Chronos, back to reality, he coaxed. His eyes were getting weary from squinting so hard without much light. He shut the cover of the journal and closed his eyes for relief. No luck. Too many thoughts were racing through his mind. He couldn't keep up with all of them. The questions, the gash in his leg, the men in pursuit; it was all too painful and cluttered. All of his senses were on overload. He shook his head hard, and opened his eyes.

There it was! Right in front of him! A clue!

"What the heck?" he asked curiously.

His eyes narrowed and focused on the spine of the book. There was something he hadn't seen before. He'd been concentrating too hard on the contents of the journal, rather than the journal itself. He ran his thumb over it, perhaps to confirm that he actually saw something. But it was there, in the smallest of print, cut deep into the worn brown leather of the spine, words had been written. He read aloud, *"Through time and space I will travel to mend the deed unraveled."*

His chest grew hot from the necklace. Lowering the journal, he pulled the necklace away to look at it. It was glowing. By this time, little light penetrated the shed. What little there was dappled in through the glass and bounced off the necklace. The shed was immediately filled with the same symbols and primitive writing that lit up the inside hull of the Mermaid. The pendant at the end of the chain began to spin as if some hidden force was manipulating it. Without knowing why, or perhaps maybe he did, Alex thrust the pendant deep against its resting place carved into the bound leather cover. The wind howled in protest. His body jerked straight uncontrollably, then buckled.

The room began to pitch and swim around him. Pictures, visions of other people, strangers in strange places warped in and out around him. The shed rocked and clattered, and the noise roared through him like a freight train. He recognized this noise somehow, but that fact didn't make him any less scared. There was only one thought; *what was happening?* The wooden floorboards heaved with a single great force, sending him into the air. Every muscle in his body ached as he twisted and writhed in pain. He tried to scream, but nothing came out. Beams of blue light burst through every crack and seam of the shed, outward into the darkened sky.

As the light around him pulsated more and more intensely, he saw his grandmother through one of those cracks in the wall. She was standing at the upstairs window staring down at the shed. She appeared to be . . . waving?

His stomach turned in disagreement. He was sure he was going to vomit any minute now. In a sudden climactic vision, the shed ripped apart and exploded into singular pieces of battered wood. They appeared to be floating, inanimate around him. It was silent. Beyond the pieces he saw space. It was a deep, black void riddled with stars, as if the very fabric of space had been torn apart. He suddenly felt calm, as if he were floating. All the pain was gone.

The stillness of space that enveloped him was split open with a powerful blast.

Quickly, before forming any thought, Alex was sucked downward. Everything disappeared, gone from sight. Alex had blacked out.

Four

What seemed like an eternity had passed before Alex moved and woke with an *"Unnngghh."* His face was pressed to the ground. Stirring slowly, he felt unusually warm. His mouth was dry as though he hadn't had anything to drink in days. Alex shook his head as he pushed himself up from where he lay and felt something strange beneath his hands, something hot and rough.

"What the . . . *SAND?*" he exclaimed. The shed was gone, and all that was left were the remnants of a blue light fading just beyond his reach; that, and one whopping big headache. He was still dizzy from the whole ordeal. Beside him lay both the journal and the necklace embedded in the sand. Sweat worked its way down his temple and across the outer corner of his eye, and it stung. As he wiped it away, the horizon focused into view.

Desert.

"What the heck," he spoke. The words were forced through his dried, narrowing throat, and he coughed uncontrollably at the feeling. He tried swallowing, but no luck. What lay before him was a vast sea of hot, dry wind-sculpted sand, beyond even what his eyes could see. How could this be? A large part of him wanted to believe he was dreaming.

"Where am I?" came the next obvious question. It was a space so enormous, and so void of anything else, except sand. The heat of the day's sun beat down on his head like a furnace. He sweated continuously. Of course, he *was* thirteen, and he didn't know of any other thirteen-year-old boy who didn't. He had always been a heavy sweater. Gym class was particularly brutal, and the resulting sneers and half-comments from his peers didn't help his nerves any, which, of course, made him sweat even more. But this wasn't gym class.

This was, despite the fact that his brain was telling him otherwise, a desert. He'd seen old movies of people stranded in the desert, some even dying. Not good, he thought. There wasn't a single noise. No animals, no birds, not even the wind spoke. He slowly turned and saw 360 degrees of the same thing. Desert. "Not good at all," he said.

They moved swiftly. Cautious and silent, they had done this before. From out of nowhere several men rushed at him, ready with pointed spears. They were shouting something. He couldn't understand them. This angered the men even more. Alex was surrounded. He had just enough time to notice the strange clothes they wore. No more than a fashioned headdress, what looked like a towel draped around their waist and a type of hand-made sandal on their feet. They were all dressed similarly, with no single man having any distinguishable markings or differences.

Then, in a flurry of shouting and excitement, one of the men to his right hit him squarely in the side of the head. Alex dropped to his knees immediately, clutching his head where the blow had landed. There was blood in his hands, trickling through his fingers. His eyes caught the journal, and he quickly snatched it up, covering his maneuvers with his slumped shoulders before the strangers rounded on him again. Feinting to his left, he rolled and missed the next blow, but was nimble enough to successfully grab the necklace in his hands and shove it in his front pocket in one decisive move. He was met with a long stick across his shins.

"Agghhhhh!" he cried, now sitting and grabbing at the pain. Four long and sharp spears pointed at his head.

Within minutes, he was bound at the hands and feet with rope. A leash tied at his hands led to one of his captors. At spear point he was persuaded to move farther into the desert emptiness, toward the unknown.

Whatever was going on, Alex knew these guys were serious. He was desperate for answers, scared and lonely. This unbearable heat didn't exactly help either. A large black scorpion scurried across the sand about two feet to his right. "Of course," he said to himself. Alex kept thinking that it couldn't possibly get any hotter, but it did. How he longed for the cool sea breezes of home, sitting on his bed with the windows open and the smell of the salt air wafting through the house. There was no end in sight, no apparent destination that he could see.

They had walked several hours, and every part of Alex's skin felt burnt and sore to the touch. He was thankful for what little protection his pants and loose shirt provided, although both had long since been drenched in sweat. But strangely the sweating had stopped a while back. His body was beyond that now, and the sensation of tingling came over him. He shivered, but knew he wasn't cold. He pressed on in fear for his life. He watched the men closely. Every move, every motion, was deliberate. They appeared to know where they were going. What's worse, Alex thought, is that they were relatively unaffected by the desert sun.

Slowly and without care, he was being pushed and prodded up and over each sand dune, tripping and falling every other step in the loose sand. "I don't understand!" he said. Desperation overwhelmed him. "Please, what did I do wrong?" he asked. There came no answer other than a foot to his back. He rolled down the next dune, getting tangled in his bindings.

They came upon a flat spot in the terrain with large dunes surrounding the entire basin. Wind had carved out this hollow over the years or, for all he knew, in a day. He had lost all sense of time and distance. Each dune was the same as the last. The sun was low in the horizon ahead, and when they dropped down into the bowl, it was casting shadows over the entire area, making it several degrees cooler.

Without speaking, the men broke up into groups of two, and each split up. One man reached into a cloth pack slung low over his shoulder and unfurled a large piece of fabric. His partner began driving stakes around in a square pattern. They appeared to be setting up a tent of sorts.

By this time Alex didn't care what any of them were doing as long as he didn't have to keep walking. The man nearest him drove a single stake into the ground. He was to be Alex's guard for the remainder of the night. When he tied the end of Alex's bindings to the stake, Alex knew he wouldn't be sharing any comforts that the tent might bring.

He dropped to his knees in exhaustion. Too tired and sore to even close his eyes, Alex watched as two other men ran off over the dunes, spears in hand. Shortly the tent had been set and camp had been made. The two men who had disappeared now returned carrying something.

It resembled something like a rabbit, only slightly larger. Within minutes two of the men had built a small fire. Alex had no idea how they could have built a fire. He hadn't seen anything but sand for hours. But still, there it was.

The sun had long since fallen behind the dunes, and darkness was settling in on the camp. It was cooler now in the darkness. His skin was starting to blister, and his wrists were reddened from the ropes, but at least he wasn't walking. There was that, he thought.

Alex's stomach ached for food. He would have begged for some water if he felt he wouldn't get beaten again. A man approached. He and the guard shared a glance and, with that, a piece of soaked cloth was thrown at Alex, landing in the sand at his side. It smelled foul, but Alex was too hungry to care. He snatched it up, protecting it as if some wretched animal himself.

He cared little for how he behaved at this moment. Alex had been given the drippings of what little grease was squeezed from some poor animal's meat, and he wasn't about to waste it. He sucked on the cloth, wrenching every last ounce of juice from its threads, sand and all.

The night began quiet, and Alex was tired. His captors had left him, save for the one guard who apparently didn't sleep. Alex briefly thought of escape, but then where would he go? He had no idea of where he was, and he certainly couldn't survive on his own in the heat. No, he thought, he was better off with these men. Alex slept.

By the time he woke, the sun was already high in the sky. He could feel the heat swelling up on him. "Here we go again," he said to himself. The men had already packed and were moving toward him. He was jerked up to a standing position, and the spears were upon him once again.

Up, over the first dune he trudged, slipping two feet back for every three forward. Progress was slow, even more so than yesterday. They marched him relentlessly. They stopped only once, drinking from a flask made of sewn animal skin. Alex waited for a turn that never came. They had been moving in the same direction for what he had guessed was about two hours when they topped a large dune. Before him was a great flatness, a plateau that reached impressively beyond the horizon.

"*Gi-ZAH*," one man spoke with a slit across his face that in some cultures may have passed for a smile. It was several more hours of limping across this great plateau that brought them to a stop. Alex was already tired from the day and welcomed the rest, albeit a short one. He had taken to walking with his head down, away from the sun's oppression in the attempt to eek out every last ounce of cooler temperature that his own shadow could afford him.

Upon stopping, he heard the men whispering. Understanding none of the words they spoke, but sensing something familiar from them, he looked up. He knew it immediately. It was fear in their voices when they spoke. He didn't know what they were saying, but he knew fear. He was all too familiar with it. What he really wanted to know was who or what they were suddenly afraid of? Just then, over the shoulder of one of the soldiers, his eyes caught at something.

What he saw next was the most unbelievable sight he'd ever laid eyes on. The sweat in his eyes blurred his vision, and he wiped again at it, smearing sand across his face. There, across a vast sea of hot, dry wind-sculpted sand were the shadowy casts of enormous structures, rising from the ground as if the sand and earth themselves rose up to meet the stars and sky. Complete disbelief consumed him immediately. He knew *what* they were. He knew *where* he was. What he didn't know was *how*. How did he get here?

"Pyramids? Egypt?" he asked in a stressed voice. His mind was racing again, searching for some sense of what he saw. Whichever way he sliced it, he just couldn't figure out how on earth he got to Egypt. But something was off, Alex thought, noticing slight differences in the behemoths from this great distance. He was too far to be sure, but they somehow looked different to him than the pictures in his history book. And there was something else, too, something odder still.

Alex was sure that this was their destination, a hot and long trip lay ahead. His shoulders slumped in near defeat.

He had learned about the pyramids in Ms. Flowers' class, while feverishly avoiding her icy glare. He honestly believed that if he were to look directly into her eyes too long, he'd probably turn to stone.

But these were nothing like the pictures he'd seen in his schoolbooks. They were larger than any other single thing he'd ever seen. And they were . . . different somehow. They looked incomplete. His mind wrestled with the notion. When that proved unsuccessful, he then tried convincing himself that the only possible conclusion was that he had heat stroke and would likely die soon.

But he could see it, more and more, with each passing step. As he pressed his eyes closer into the distance, he realized they *were* incomplete. There were three in all, each in various stages of construction. Despite having such a hard time in Ms. Flowers' class, Alex had learned a thing or two about history.

All that he could remember, however, was tucked away in a tattered history book back home in his bedroom by the sea, propping up one end of his safe and comfortable bed. He remembered thinking at the time that it was being put to good use. What he remembered next hit him like a hammer; three pyramids located on a great plateau. These were the Pyramids of Giza!

"Gi-ZAH . . . of course!" he exclaimed as he recalled the soldier saying earlier. He remembered reading about all of the different pharaohs and their reigns throughout history. He remembered how the pyramids were a great feat in construction that spanned over even greater periods of time, except these pyramids were all being constructed at the same time. The real Pyramids of Giza were constructed separately, over time, and not all at once. At least, that's what he'd read in his book. That's what he was taught. He was sure of it. Or was he wrong? Had he misunderstood what he had read?

It seemed so long ago to him now, and these were no longer the only questions flooding his mind. Wait, was history itself wrong? Were these the same pyramids? His thoughts shifted to his grandmother. What would she say? Was she okay? Did she know he was even missing? *Was* he missing?

Alex could see that there were roadways at the base of each ramp, twisting up toward the pyramids, dredged from the foot traffic of thousands. It was still too far to tell from where they originated. They seemed to stretch from the farthest reaches of the desert itself, but one thing was for certain; they all led to the pyramids. With each passing step, both sight and sound seemed to gather and pass with the winds.

They were now at the outskirts of an encampment of what he presumed were thousands of people, maybe more. Teams of people were lashed together with large ropes, three to four rows wide, hundreds in a row, pulling with backbreaking effort to try to move mountains of carved stone. They rocked in undulating unison. Their feet were bound to those behind them, making it increasingly more difficult to perform an already staggering task. Some wailed in pain, most bled. Almost all were beaten. Whips were cracking high above their heads, and many landed on their backs with the sound of tearing flesh. If one fell, the others would ignore him out of fear, and he would be removed and replaced immediately, disappearing with the guards. Alex wept in silence.

These people seemed to have a structure or a command. The men who found him in the desert appeared to be the same rank as those who provided the beatings on the lines. They were guards or soldiers of some type, he thought, but not much better off than the slaves themselves.

They were still several hundred yards away from the base of the ramps, but Alex was in awe of the structures. They blocked out the entire horizon. Their enormous size, built on the backs of men, seemed to defy reality.

Closer now, he could tell that they were definitely incomplete, the largest, being the furthest along in construction. Hundreds of men descended on it with crude tools in hand. Their goal was to chip and grind by hand, to otherwise smooth its still rough exterior. The second two structures, no less amazing by any standards, were still in their stages of rough construction, with whole sections of massive stone still missing from their precipices. Alex could just barely make out what he believed to be narrow passageways or rooms cutting through these masses of stone.

He remembered his history class yet again. According to the 'experts,' pyramids were constructed with a grand design, as if with purpose or reason. Believed to be for burial purposes or honoring their great rulers, the architects planned a series of hallways and chambers, some even for treasure and artifacts, connected but created by the precise placement of massive stones. Well, at least they got something right, Alex chided. His mind ripped back to the present.

All of what he saw was too much to comprehend. He was overwhelmed. "It just can't be possible," he said, trying to convince himself. The closer they marched him, the worse the atrocities appeared. He couldn't stand it, but he couldn't look away either. It was just past mid-day and at the sun's worst. It had to be 120 degrees, Alex guessed.

The enormous ramps were built of the same coarse sand from the desert and moved upward toward the looming pyramid. A single woman for each line ran up and down the ramp barefooted, carrying drops of water, lifeblood to the slaves.

The scene unfolded before him, stone grinding on stone, ropes stretching, whips cracking. This can't be real, he thought. Alex watched as two men, under the whips of a guard, loaded one of their fallen into a makeshift sled and dragged him down the ramp. He wasn't sure where they were taking him, but was quite sure it wasn't good. Some time had passed when the men returned, only two of them now.

To the right of the mammoth structures, cold and almost lifeless, spread a trench, Alex guessed about twenty feet wide that stretched for more than a mile. It was deep, perhaps two stories. Occasional stone-carved staircases, rising from the pit, were etched into the walls, narrow and steep. At the bottom lie the half-dead, or worse. They were faint corpses and scarce memories of what were once proud men. It wasn't just men. Women, beaten and worn, tended to their feet and backs. The only color he saw pressed from this horrific scene before him was red. Moans from the depths filled the air. It was too much. Alex covered his ears.

"Who could do this?" he asked out loud. And with that, he was forced to the ground, his face pressed against the hot sand with the point of a spear, a foot on his back. He lay in such a position that he could still see over the edge of the pit, and his eyes focused on the death before him. He squeezed his eyes so tightly shut from the atrocities in front of him that he could feel the sand underneath his lids scratching to get out. He wept again.

A sudden chilling quiet drew over the land like a thick cloud of dew, muffling even the most agitated of beasts penned up at the base of the ramps. Used for carrying the heaviest burdens, these strange animals had seemed to like the situation even far less than Alex, perhaps even less than the slaves. From what Alex could tell, at least they received food. They quieted.

78

The men, beasts of burden themselves, became hushed and silent, all dropping their heads as if bowing. Lying there on the ground, he felt it, faint at first, but growing. Something was coming, something big.

With a foot now pressed against his face keeping him to the ground, Alex's movement was stifled, but he was able to move his head just enough to see. Nobody was moving. All work had stopped. There was no creaking of the giant ropes, no cracking of the whips. The only noise was the growing rumble that seemed to come from the earth itself. Louder and louder it came. His heart pounded.

The loose sand in front of him rose and jumped about with every thunderous beat. Tools and equipment on a nearby table leapt against each other, falling from their perch into the sand below. Even the wind was silent, but growing in strength. It was a strange wind, as if generated out of thin air. It carried nothing with it other than the feel of the hot desert. The rumble became a roar; the roar became deafening. What could possibly be so massive that it could cause a noise like this? he thought.

He glanced up at the men surrounding him, his captors; they were bowing, and scared. Alex's body began trembling in anticipation. Something bad was coming. Alex couldn't help but think that whatever it was, it was the reason for the slaves, the horror. *Gi-ZAH,* Alex recalled, had been spoken earlier out of some deep felt fear. It was the same fear he sensed from these men now. It was the same fear also welling up inside of him this very moment.

Alex hadn't looked at his captors closely until now. What he saw only added to his terror. Their faces, weathered and darkened from the sun, were hollow and gaunt, almost skeletal, with blackened eyes set deep into their sockets. Their bodies were thin and lean. Nothing but muscle stretched across bone; there was no fat on these people. Scars from earlier battles etched across their bodies like ancient text detailing history itself. They were either expressionless or raging. There was no in between. They moved with purpose in everything they did.

The noise was beside him now, beating and grinding the sand; it filled the air completely. Alex could see the sandstone blocks, enormous at thousands of pounds each, giving way to the sound that came. Nothing he'd ever heard before compared.

His mind flashed back briefly to the *5th Annual Summer Regatta and Row* race in town, complete with grand finale of parade and evening fireworks; a big event for a small town, but it was what everyone looked forward to all year. There were street vendors and a carnival. They even blocked off the entire street for the parade. Not that they couldn't close down any street any time of the year; not much ever passed through his small town. But the parade, the fireworks, wow!

This sound, this shaking of the earth, was even louder than the score of high school drums that brought up the rear of the procession, much louder. It was louder than the evening fireworks that colored the sky. He knew. He was there.

Then it stopped; not just the noise, everything stopped. The wind, the noise, even the tiniest of sand grains dancing in front of his eyes stopped. He looked up again and, where nothing previously existed, they were there. *It* was there.

Some twenty feet or so from where he still laid, stomach to the ground and face against the hot sand, Alex gazed upon a sight so strange, so bold in its surroundings that he had to look twice to see if he was imagining it. There stood four men, gilded in gold-laden fabric. Each man wore a short cloth around his waist and solid gold bands around their arms and wrists. Their heads were covered in a cloth headpiece that ran down to their necks. Each headpiece was woven with golden lacings to allow them to rise above their heads at the front. No doubt in the strong desert heat these were for function as well as for show, Alex surmised.

The men stood, two by two, carrying a large golden cage supported across two long poles. The cage was draped with a sheer fabric on all four sides, covering, or perhaps hiding something inside. Several times Alex was momentarily blinded by the glint of the sun reflecting off that much gold.

The entire vision appeared to hover just out of focus as if they were floating. In fact, Alex could see that their feet were easily four inches above the sand. The heat; it's got to be the heat, Alex tried convincing himself. Something was telling him that this was only the beginning.

As the sun blazed high in the sky, it shone through the sheers just enough to cast a shadow of what was inside. Alex stared in fright. He couldn't take his eyes off from what he saw. It was only a shadow cast against the sheer, but it was real enough.

A tall figure was seated prominently in the center of the enclosure and looked as if it had two ears centered atop its head that soared another foot above and flattened out. A long rectangular snout jutted almost out of place from its head.

Whatever was inside, whatever was casting that shadow, Alex believed was somehow being distorted by the sun against the fabric. He guessed it may even be wearing a helmet or mask. It was like nothing he'd ever seen. At that thought, the shadow turned slowly and looked straight at him. It was as if this being, this *whatever* hidden inside, could read his thoughts. For the longest moment it stared back at Alex. It made no other movement. Alex's head was suddenly filled with an ear-piercing screech so painful it felt as if his brain had been torn slowly in half.

He struggled to cover his ears. No luck. Alex couldn't wiggle free enough from his position to provide any relief from what he heard. As he struggled about, he saw men dropping to their knees in pain, clutching their ears from the brain-splitting sound. The penned beasts all jumped and clamored in raucous unison, barking and howling at what they heard.

Alex felt something trickling from his ears. He smelled something familiar, something horrid. It was blood. Blood ran from his ears. As quickly as it had happened, it was gone. No trace. It simply vanished. Only this time was different. This time there was no noise, no rumble. Just the ringing and throbbing in his ears remained. The wretched souls surrounding him were still quivering as they struggled to their feet.

It took several minutes before anyone regained their composure, standing and shaking off the assault. Alex looked around as best he could from underneath the bottom of a foot. The spear had since been removed from its precarious position, and the men were reaching down for him. Tugging hard at his bindings, they jerked him upright. Even this didn't come without its own pain. They were walking again. Alex, feeling somewhat more confused than cautious, risked looking around for some evidence of what he'd just seen. There was nothing, no marks in the sand; not a trace, other than the blood from his ears drying in the day's heat.

As he was being pulled away from the scene at the base of the giant sandstone ramps, Alex struggled to make sense of what he'd just seen. His ears were still ringing like the bells from his town's church. He'd give anything to be in church right now. If it weren't for the horror in front of him and the pain he'd endured, he'd almost think it funny. Almost. He'd never been one for attending church, but always did so at the insistence of his grandmother. He'd frump around early every Sunday morning, taking his sweet old time, all the while his grandmother prodding, "C'mon, Alex. Young man, if you don't get a move on right now . . ." she'd always say.

The thought that the man inside the cage, the one wearing the mask, had something to do with all that Alex saw, slowly formed. Alex turned the thought over and over in his head. His blood ran hot as the desert sun.

They passed by a series of crudely fashioned tents pitched about a hundred yards from the ramps, yet still within the reaches of virtually everything bad he'd witnessed. All but one guard filed into a singularly large tent located in the middle of the encampment. Alex noticed that others, just like the guards, were scurrying about prepping the area for the evening. The remaining man continued on with him giving frequent reminders of exactly who was in control.

Alex noticed that the wails were getting more muffled with the passing distance. Soon the two of them were beyond the campsite, the men, the beasts, and the cracking of the whips. Alex was only pleased about the latter. The rest meant he was on his own again. The rest meant his chances for opportunity were probably less, unless he could overpower his single captor. Yeah, that'll happen, he dismissed. The man, in addition to being greater than a foot taller than he, was obviously much stronger and trained for battle. Oh, and of course, Alex reflected, he also held the ropes that bound him tightly.

His hearing was finally returning, and the confusion of what he'd seen earlier was quickly being replaced by the fear of his current situation. Alex wondered where they were taking him next. They were moving away from everything, back into the desert. But it was also getting late, and he surmised that the guard, even with all of his strength, wouldn't risk going too much farther into the desert at night.

Alex's question was soon answered when on the backside of the next dune he saw an opening. They were heading straight for it. The hot sand was loose under foot, but became harder as they approached the opening. The opening was crude, but not natural. Someone had purposely made this structure. But its purpose was exactly what puzzled Alex. It was cave-like in appearance, and the drifting sands had blown into the entrance over time. Alex speculated that it had been there in the middle of the desert for years, centuries even.

Alex hesitated slightly at the door, but was quickly coaxed through the opening with a shove. Stumbling inside the passage, he noticed the sunlight had quickly given way to darkness only a few feet in.

Just out of reach of the sun's rays, a huge intricately carved sandstone door met them. There were detailed carvings chinked into it with the remains of what was used for colored paint showing its weather from the years. Above the door, the stone archway that carried the weight of the dune above was further carved into a serpent-like creature, wrapping itself across and down, around the pillars that held it. The column itself was carved into a tree in full blossom. A bit out of place for the desert, Alex thought.

The man moved behind him, but Alex couldn't see. A dull grinding noise echoed deep from behind the door, and it slid open. Alex instinctively stepped inside, more out of curiosity at this point. He watched as the guard reached into his pack and pulled out two small stones. The man walked over to a bowl and struck them together producing a spark. Several attempts produced similar results until finally a powder inside the bowl burst with light and flame.

Within seconds, a trail of sparks and flame moved down from the bowl to the floor and into a series of troughs. The flames encircled the floor around them, revealing the grandest sight Alex had ever seen. The flames shot up from their trenches only about a foot, but just enough to disclose every magnificent detail before them.

The chamber where they now stood was easily one hundred feet deep and seventy feet wide. The ceiling soared above them several stories and was supported by mammoth stone columns, each intricately carved with different scenes. Color flooded the scene as Alex stood there in awe.

Stairs at their approach spread the entire width of the room and descended another ten feet to the main floor below. Carvings covered the entire wall surface. Alex guessed that it must have taken decades to complete. There were several statues built from the surrounding desert sands, each towering about thirty feet from the floor on which they were positioned, all in a row. They stood, seemingly passing judgment down on all who passed beneath them.

Alex feverishly looked around in a futile attempt to try to capture all that he saw. There was too much to take in. There were racks of weaponry stationed along the walls. Smaller artifacts on several stone perches throughout the chamber reflected the light of the flames, making Alex believe they were items of polished stone and gleaming . . . *gold!*

The guard pushed him deeper into the chamber, along a worn central path, moving around rows of flasks and stone pottery. Alex presumed each held some sort of offering or gift. As his eyes trailed along the statues in front of him to the opposite end of the chamber, they landed on a gathering of several smaller ones that appeared to be in the shapes of animals. The closer they moved, the more the picture unfolded. There ahead, at the end of the chamber, were two large stone boxes positioned side by side, as if being protected by the surrounding crowd of beast-shaped stone. There were roughly a dozen hardened protectors in all. Closer now, he could see everything. The larger, rigid statues that lined the great hall had given way to this more informal, haunting scene. It seemed out of place, like it wasn't quite connected to anything else.

It hit Alex like a brick. Of course, he reeled! These weren't just any old boxes, they served a purpose. They were coffins, sarcophagi. Dead people. Alex shivered at that thought.

There, scattered around these sarcophagi, were the vivid memories of someone's nightmare. Although Alex could see they weren't real, it concerned him greatly that they had been anchored into stone pedestals. It was as if it was necessary to keep them from attacking. Each at least six feet tall at their shoulder, Alex could now tell they were all carvings of dogs, ready to attack, teeth bared, surrounding, facing the sarcophagi. What *is* it with dogs lately? he thought. The flicker of the flames cast movement upon these rigid forms, giving them near life. He knew without question that they weren't here to protect, but rather to keep those from escaping.

His mind flashed back to his history book beneath his bed post. Sarcophagi held rulers he remembered reading, people of great importance. But not here, he reasoned. What he saw wasn't done out of respect, but more out of fear, even hatred.

The guard, whom Alex had almost forgotten, was growing more agitated and nervous at this point. Noticing, Alex could now tell that the man had been here before and didn't like it. He shoved Alex around the throng of devil-hounds, moving past the sarcophagi, and stopped. Alex hadn't noticed it before, but there was another doorway, less conspicuous than the previous one. It was quiet in this chamber where every little noise echoed. Alex could hear everything. The guard's breathing seemed like a freight train; his own heart pounded like an explosion. There was something else. He heard it faintly, but it was growing. It wasn't the same as what he'd heard outside earlier. It was muffled until, without warning, the air was split with what sounded like a ferocious roar.

Both heads snapped back around in sudden fear. The growl bounced and ricocheted off the walls from all directions, making it difficult to determine where it came from, yet both were looking in the same direction. Both stared, fixated on one of the stone creatures behind them. Alex caught his breath. Did one of these demon-dogs just growl at us? Neither the guard nor Alex wanted to know the answer.

In response, the guard snatched up a stick from a bundle, reached inside his sack, and pulled out a cloth. Wrapping the cloth around one end of the stick, he appeared to be searching for something just around the door's column. When he pulled the stick back, the cloth was dripping. He'd soaked it in something. Cleverly holding the stick under his arm, he removed the two stones from earlier and sparked the torch to life.

Moving through a dark opening in the stone no wider than his shoulders, Alex slid in sideways. The hallway he'd entered wasn't intricately carved like the chamber before it. It was almost forgotten, an after-thought. It twisted and turned so many times as they pushed on that he had long ago lost his sense of direction. The only light came from the guard's oil-soaked torch he carried in his left hand, a spear pointed at Alex's back in his right. Alex stopped suddenly as if he'd hit a wall. His head reared back in offense.

"*Aauugh*," he said, covering his nose with his upper arm. He felt the sharpness of his reward in his lower back. He took another step, cautiously. Keeping his hand in place, he tried desperately not to breathe. A stale, putrid stench had filled the corridor with a thickness that settled onto his clothes. It was all around him, everywhere, so heavy and disgusting that even the walls appeared to be sweating blood. Drops of reddened moisture ran down the walls of the corridor and had stained the sandstone with its hue.

Alex had no idea where they were going, but his senses were on full alert, and not necessarily by choice. His skin prickled at the sound of a strange noise ahead. It sounded like a . . . There it was again. His mind jumped. He swore it sounded like someone, or something, coughed.

As if knowing it was forbidden, the guard spoke cautiously. Alex couldn't understand him, but sensed he was scared. This was the second time he sensed this from these people, remembering how the guards had acted in the desert upon first sight of the pyramids. Alex had been sizing up these people and figured that it would take something great, something awful, to frighten them. The guard sputtered again. Alex got the point, literally. He moved farther into the blackness, catching only shadows of what was ahead. His imagination was getting the best of him. The stench grew stronger and the air heavier. Alex could barely breathe as his lungs were filled with this foreign odor.

"*Uff*," Alex said. It was only after Alex's face smashed against it that he realized he'd walked into something hard. He could barely make out a barricade in front of him. He instinctively clawed at it to gain a sense of what exactly it was. His eyes adjusted to the cast light from the torch. It was crudely built, but strong. The wall in front of him was bulky and made of stone, mostly, with a slit about eye level running its entire thickness. It was this slit that the deathly smell was coming from. There was a wooden lever of sorts protruding from the wall to his right. Alex stopped cold.

There were carvings chiseled on the barricade. They were barely visible in the lack of light, but Alex noticed they were worn almost smooth from age. From what he could make out, they were simpler in detail and design, but definite in their meaning. Alex didn't have to read ancient Egyptian to know what they meant. He shifted his stance uneasily and started to tremble. It was death. Ahead of him was death.

The guard pushed past him to reach for the lever. Alex saw an opportunity. Without hesitation, he pushed into the guard with all of his remaining strength and knocked him down against the barricade. As he landed, Alex followed with a powerful kick to his ribs. The guard was doubled over in pain when Alex spun on his heels and began feeling his way along the walls. The torch had lost its saving light in the scuffle. He was moving blindly through the dark corridor. There was no way he was going any farther past that barricade, no matter what was behind it. He'd had enough. He felt freedom coming closer with each passing turn.

Alex heard the snap just before the leash went taunt at his feet. "*Unh . . . ghah.*" Alex had bounced off the wall and hit the floor, landing squarely on his face. The guard had recovered quickly and was in fast pursuit. His familiarity with the corridor gave him the advantage, and he quickly gained on Alex.

He didn't wait for Alex to stand. He was angry now, with himself mostly. Alex had made about 200 feet toward freedom when it was snatched from him, and the guard dragged him, face-down, the entire way back to the barricade. Alex was still on the ground, scraped and bleeding, when the guard jerked the lever down and the barricade slid with a grinding motion into a slot in the wall that previously hadn't been there. Yanking and tugging at Alex's feet, the guard pulled him inside and dragged him to the edge of the stone underneath.

He was in a cavernous room, open to probably three stories and just as wide; not a traditional room, but more like an opening in the stone. Roughened stone jutted out from the surrounding walls and up from the floor. The floor beneath him gave way to a drop of about ten feet, and he nearly fell off the edge upon this realization. He jumped to his feet in defiance of the guard and was immediately taken by the sheer size of this room.

As his eyes darted back and forth searching, he wasn't quite sure if he was looking for a way out or for something else. Perhaps it was whoever, or whatever, he'd heard cough from inside. The room was filled with the shadows of his imagination. Alex had barely noticed the guard's movements toward the door when he realized what was happening. The guard was leaving him here.

"No . . . no . . . no . . . NO! WAIT! STOP! PLEASE!" Alex cried out in desperation. The guard hesitated, showing the only sign of compassion Alex had seen in days.

"*Please* don't leave me," he begged. Alex was momentarily relieved when, much to his surprise, the guard returned. Shocked at this, Alex froze. The guard pulled a knife, and Alex jumped, startled. This was it, he resolved. This is where I die. His mind flashed memories of his grandmother. He was afraid he'd never see her again. Would she be okay without him?

Alex noticed the guard seemed to be paying nervous attention to what hid in the cavern beyond, and watched the man fumble as he reached down to cut his bindings. He hacked at the ropes feverishly and with a final snip, stood, staring into Alex's eyes. Alex searched for life in this man's eyes, compassion even. All he saw was fear and sorrow. With that, the man heaved Alex over the side.

With bone-crushing force, Alex landed hard on the stone floor below, sprawled out in a puddle of what appeared to be brown water. His lungs deflated on impact. He gasped for air, clutching his chest, having no real way to filter out the scent of death. His body took over, and the air filled his lungs. Alex was breathing again. Coughing out the film he could feel covering the insides of his lungs, he wrapped his arms around his body to hold back the pain of his ribs.

"*AAAAGGHH!*" he screamed. His cry seemed to echo on for an eternity. The only thing lasting longer was the pain he felt in his ribs. Alex removed the remaining lashes from around his feet and forced himself up. As he did, he saw a fleeting glimpse above of the guard running through the entrance of the room and into the corridor. Alex limped to the wall in front of him, calling out. The barricade closed with a deepened finality. Any hint of light left the room along with the guard. Alex couldn't remember a sound so definite, so looming.

"Hey! Come back! *HEY! HELP! HELP!*" he shouted. Being free from his bindings after so long, one would think he would be relieved, even grateful. But his situation had not improved; in fact, it had worsened. Alone, bruised and battered, in a dark, unfamiliar place was definitely not better. Beating on the hardened sandstone walls of the room didn't help much either. His senses sprang back to life at the sound of something else in this place. Alex spun around to his left searching a hidden area no more than twenty feet from his location. It was quiet again. There was no movement. No, it was farther to his left. It's there. He shuddered, hesitated. Shadows teased in the absence of light.

Alex's pain was quickly being overshadowed by his growing fear. His mind was either playing tricks on him or else he wasn't alone in this room. For a moment, he wasn't sure which was more frightening. Another slight movement from just beyond his eyesight convinced him of which.

He turned back to the stone-faced edge and began groping around the dark like a man suddenly blinded and half insane. He pushed and stumbled. Hand over hand, he felt his way across the wall. He knew he was being watched. He could feel the eyes on him. Alex didn't dare turn around. There was no time, and if he had, he was afraid that whatever creature was stalking him would attack.

Alex's eyes strained to capture every available ounce of light in the room. They adjusted slowly, and with each furious blink, focused in on a crude staircase that led back up to the barricade from which he had entered. Alex was growing frantic as he clamored and crawled back up the stairs to reach the barricade. Something was moving in, closer and closer. He could hear it panting, grunting behind him, maybe ten feet. He could sense it gaining on him, smell it as it grew closer. He glanced back, over his shoulder. Nothing.

Alex reached the door in a panic. He ran his hands over it to find some sort of handle, pushing his mouth up to the narrow slit to yell in vain.

"HELP! *Please* HEELLLPP!" he yelled again. Quiet. On the tips of his toes he pressed his mouth even harder against the opening, this time in the hope to breathe in fresh air. Ironically, it was this same air that almost made him vomit earlier, but in comparison to the stench that filled the room behind him, it was like smelling a field full of roses.

He pushed hard against the stone door, trying to move it from where it stood. No man could move this. Alex recalled the wooden lever on the other side and decided that this side must also work mechanically, the same one the guard pulled to open the door. He looked around for any similar handle that would work from the inside. There was just enough light; not even light, really, just a lighter shade of darkness, streaming in through the slit that he could see there was no lever.

His hands again brushed over the door high and low. This time he felt something. He pushed back from the barricade. Squinting as if to further press out any light and redirect it onto its surface, Alex saw them. There were scratches carved deep into the stone, high above the slit, so high, in fact, he had to stand on his toes to reach them, and when he did, he remembered.

"I know these," he said.

They were the same type of scratches left on his shed back home. They were nearly eight feet up the stone in front of him. It looked like something was trying to claw its way out. The scratches were deep, so whatever it was, it was strong. Not strong enough, though. He *had* seen them before. He distinctly recalled seeing them just before the shed blew up and disappeared before his eyes. Back when reality was actually . . . *real.* But what creature could have caused these? He had little time to formulate the next question when movement behind him seemed to answer the first one all too quickly.

He wheeled around quickly and instinctively crouched at the sight of what stood before him. He'd probably not have seen it at all if it weren't for the gray that trickled in through the slit on the door and cast an outline of a hunched mass no more than four feet away. Alex could hear it breathing heavily. Even slumped, it occupied a good two feet of space above Alex's height.

93

Each sat facing the other, momentarily frozen, in an attempt to size up what they saw. There, a glint, an eye perhaps. Alex took a deep breath. He noticed it was buried under a heavy material that covered its entire body. It rocked impatiently. It moved only once, and Alex pushed himself backwards hard against the stone with his feet. The scuffle sent a stream of sandstone fragments over the edge, bouncing off the surface below.

Instantly, all sound left the room. All concept of time became warped and unreal. It was like being in a vacuum. Scared for his life, Alex believed that this thing was doing something . . . *to him?*

Alex noticed it began to stir, as if unaffected by everything happening. It began lifting itself, straightening its body. It rose another three feet or so into the air. As it did, the play of shadows across its figure gave insight as to what Alex was looking at.

Terror shot through his veins and replaced the blood that long ago forgot to pump from fright. Its face was dog-like in nature, being longer than it was tall. A toothed snout protruded from underneath a hooded veil. Cold, black soulless dots replaced what should have been eyes. As it rose, the cloak, which had previously concealed its form, slid off its back and dropped to the floor in a slump. The beast stretched backward. Every bone in its body cracked alive.

The figure appeared to literally unfold and rise above him, extending a thin skeletal hand with outstretched fingers far too long to be human. Alex winced.

The beast released a roar so loud that it pounded Alex's eardrums. The floor trembled like an earthquake. He could hear dust falling from every crack in the room.

Its chest was heaving. Its mouth was full of sharp teeth ready to tear at its prey. Alex hoped it would be quick.

"Who are you? *WHAT* are you?" Alex blurted out in fear. He had to know. If he was going to die, here and now, he had a right to know. Once again, silence filled the foul air.

"HUMANS CALL ME ANUBIS," it responded with a hollowed echo much like someone speaking from inside a metal drum. The voice seemed to bellow and shake the walls that surrounded them. It came not from its mouth, but rather from deep inside the being that towered before him.

Five

"*WHAT!* You can *talk?* I can *understand* you? But how can you speak English? *How* can you even *speak* at all?" Alex asked, scratching his head in bewilderment.

The fact that it spoke was far more than Alex could handle at the moment until, "Wait. *Humans?*" Alex said. It had dawned on him the extent of his immediate situation. He was locked inside this cavernous stone room with what was to be, as the drawings on the other side of the massive stone door had indicated, his death. This form, this creature inside the chamber, the great beast before him, this was his fate. Alex couldn't help but wonder if this was Death itself. He cowered at the thought.

It was then that Alex's thoughts traveled back home. He missed his grandmother. His mind crept, did she miss him? Did she even know he was gone? How he loved her, his safe house, comfortable bed, and that strange little quaint town. Heck, he'd even settle for the annoyance of Mittens right now; anything to remind him of home. Jackson; he didn't miss that lug, though, he determined. But he would gladly take another beating from him instead of suffering some horrific fate by some monstrous creature in a strange land. Being chased by those Greek sailors was even somehow more welcoming to him now. The only problem was that time had been of no service to Alex. He was unsure how much time had actually passed since.

It loomed, high above its prey, as if contemplating the attack. Then Alex saw it; a look, fleeting, then gone. Perhaps it was his own misperception or a trick of the shadows, but he could swear that he saw a look from this creature that appeared sympathetic, almost caring.

Still sitting, Alex lowered his arms for a better look. It was fixed, firm and unafraid. Alex's eyes had started adjusting better to the darkness, and he could finally see what towered before him in relative detail.

There it stood, not more than an arm's reach in front of him, on two thinly muscled legs much the same as a man; a nightmare that occupied a height nearly ten feet from snout to toe, and every inch was covered with black short hair. Its chest was nearly twice around as its lower body, forming an almost eerie V-shaped torso down to the waist. It was muscled, all right, but lean, with some obvious skeletal-like features that made Alex wonder if it was alive or some form of the walking-dead.

It was formed from both canine and man. Its arms were long and sinuous, with bony claws that were, according to the marks on the stone, extremely sharp and strong. If it had any resemblance of a man it certainly wasn't in its face. Its head was definitely all dog.

Alex had always had a particular interest in animals, especially those from faraway lands. This creature's face was canine indeed, but more closely resembled a picture he'd once seen of a jackal. At the front of its head extended a snout full of long, sharp teeth. Saliva dripped from its mouth as if it hadn't seen food until just now. Rising high above its head were two tall, pointed ears, perked similarly to the Moores' dog, only much, much longer. The only clothing it wore was a tinged cloth wrapped around its waist, hanging long to its knees.

Its eyes didn't move from Alex. Cold glints of reflected light pierced Alex's soul. He was frozen in terror. His back pushed up against the cold stone; there was no way out.

"AAARRRRGGGGGGG!"

The blood-curdling scream reverberated down the passageway and into the room, catching jagged stone along the way to change its direction. Alex immediately recognized it as the guard. It had to be; there was no one else. Alex had also noticed that this scream, which had turned his own blood cold, barely registered with the predator before him.

"SET!" came the thunder resonating from deep inside the creature standing before him.

The very walls trembled in fear of the voice from within. At this moment, Alex wasn't sure which he was more frightened about, the guard's terrifying scream or the beast before him, the one called Anubis.

"RELAX, BOY. I WILL NOT EAT YOU," the creature spoke again.

"Wh . . . wha . . . are you going to kill me then?" Alex asked meekly.

"NO!" came the howl. The question angered the creature.

This response didn't have quite the calming effect on Alex that it should. He remained guarded against any movement from the beast. Alex sat quiet and motionless for the longest time. Only the breath from the heaving chest of what stood before him made any sound.

Standing there on its hind legs like that of a man, it stared back at Alex, indignant. Alex had seen this look before on others, Jackson in particular, and knew enough to back off. He could see enough to understand that the beast was agitated, but not with him. It was like Alex didn't even register with the creature, like he didn't even exist. A great long silence froze the air, and the two remained caught up in the passing of time. Minutes, perhaps hours, had passed, and the beast had appeared to be contemplating some far-off thought. But the need for explanation overcame the beast.

"I DO NOT HUNGER BUT FOR ONE THING," Anubis said as it turned and walked away. It wasn't until it reached the bottom of the room that it returned to all fours and paced along the far wall in silence. It was obvious that the beast was wrestling with its thoughts, utterly unaware of Alex's presence anymore.

Now seated a much more comfortable and safe distance from the creature, Alex's mind began to drift. He was caught in a mental frenzy between analysis and remembrance. His mind jumped back and forth from flashes of his boring, mundane life that seemed so far away now to his current situation. He tried desperately to sort out all that had happened in the past several days. *Well*, it certainly *seemed* like days, Alex thought. His mind went into overload.

When Alex woke several hours later, the last thing he could remember was someone screaming. Wait, not someone . . . *him*. Alex choked. He sat up quickly to gather his thoughts and scan his surroundings for the first sign of movement. His eyes landed on the hulking mass in the far corner of the great room.

Alex wiped the drool from the corner of his mouth as he stood. His body was achy from sleeping on the hard, cold ground. It wasn't until that moment that he realized the pain was gone. He grabbed for his leg to feel through the hole in his jeans. The blood had dried long ago from the sun, but there was no wound. No pain. Nothing. If it weren't for the dried blood, it was like it had never even happened, like Jackson had never chased him. He remembered hanging on for his life, dangling stories above the ground from the rooftop. He remembered the gash, the pain, but no more.

"Freaky," he said softly.

Alex stood there thinking about what to do next and, as he did, his need for answers began to build again. He knew he was stuck here in this room. He knew he was still in danger. But what he didn't know was for how long. The one thing, or rather person, who could give him answers appeared to be asleep on the far side of the room.

Alex quietly and carefully moved down the same path that only hours earlier he had crawled up. His oversized feet slipped only once, but it was enough to send him back, and he slid hard the rest of the way down. He hesitated at the end of his ride, brushing himself off and glancing over to Anubis. He didn't stir.

He could hear him breathing from this distance and calculated that it would take an awful lot of air to fill this creature's lungs. Somehow, while watching Anubis sleep, Alex got the sense that he was far safer in the cavern with this beast than he was outside with all that he had seen, with those guards . . . with Set. But he knew he couldn't stay here forever, that he had to escape, to get back home where he belonged. He knew that they'd be coming for him soon, and he needed a plan. But what could a thirteen-year-old do against all of these odds? He also knew that he was going to need help.

"Excuse me. *Excuse* me, uh sir," Alex said quietly, half afraid of what might happen when one tries to wake an angry ten foot tall, possibly rabid, dog-man. Who wouldn't be scared? he thought. It's not like this happens every day. In fact, he was pretty sure this was a first.

"YES?" Anubis responded.

"Are you sleeping?" Alex asked.

"I DO NOT SLEEP. I AM ANUBIS. OVERSEER OF THE UNDERWORLD. GOD OF THE DEAD. MY PURPOSE IS ETERNAL!" Anubis howled with the full force of an oncoming freight train.

Alex was keen on watching his companion, secretly searching for any clues that may help provide answers. It was then that he noticed it. He wasn't sure at first, but he was now. Its mouth. It didn't move. He was sure of it. Not yet trusting his own perception of reality, Alex squinted in an attempt to detect any movement in the beast's snout. Nothing. A series of questions, doubts, ran through his head. *How* did it speak? How *could* it speak? Was it speaking or *thinking? Was Alex reading his thoughts?* Or, was it putting thoughts into Alex's head? Alex shuddered at the last notion and looked up at the beast meekly for some sort of answer.

"DO NOT FEAR ME, BOY. I AM NO ENEMY," Anubis exclaimed. Alex had to partially cover his ears from the percussion that came from within the beast. He could tell that as Anubis looked closer at him, frustration washed over the beast.

"WHAT DO YOU SEEK?" Anubis bellowed. "YOU ARE TOO YOUNG FOR MY HELP."

This last comment deflated the young man of thirteen who had spent the last several moments simply mustering the courage to even approach the beast. Alex believed that act alone made him more of a man than most. Slumped shoulders, he turned away in retreat. Appearing puzzled, Anubis stood, unfolding his enormous figure, and extended his long thin arm outward toward Alex.

"HUMMNPFFT. MY APOLOGIES. I DO NOT SPEND MUCH TIME AROUND LIVE HUMANS," Anubis explained.

When Alex turned back, he was shocked to see a giant clawed hand in his face. It took him by such surprise that he stumbled backwards about three steps, catching himself against the lower wall of the cavern.

"YOU DO THAT OFTEN," Anubis said.

"*No!*" Alex retorted, trying to sound tough in his broken voice.

"THAT WAS NOT A QUESTION, BOY," Anubis clarified.

"Not you, too? Look, I'm not a boy. I'm a *man*," Alex corrected him, slightly angered.

"AGAIN, MY APOLOGIES," Anubis said, further reaching out his hand to lift the boy up from against the wall. This was the first physical contact that Alex had with the beast and, although he recognized it for an act of kindness, he was frightened. He hid his fear well, forcing a look of anger that contorted his face, making him look like a wrinkled up old man.

The beast was strong, but then, Alex had already guessed that. Anubis lifted him with just one hand as effortlessly as a rag doll, far off the floor. Alex fought the grip by wiggling and thrashing about, but had no luck.

"Let go!" Alex demanded, much like an obstinate five-year-old and was dropped to the ground immediately, collapsing into a pile not all that dissimilar from the piles of dirty clothes in his bedroom back home.

"*Ssheesshh!*" Alex managed to burn a glare back up at Anubis. He knew he was pushing the envelope on what he dared with Anubis, and so deflected his anger to brushing the dirt off his clothes. His mood calming more out of his desire to satiate his curiosity than survival, Alex began explaining everything. Anubis didn't ask.

Alex started at the beginning of his long and difficult journey. He began with that fateful morning of his thirteenth birthday and how important to him it was to be a man. He focused a lot on this particular point and his own disappointment.

He described his home, his town, friends, and his grandmother, each with more and more longing in his voice. His eyes seemed to focus on something distant and unobtainable. He spoke of the pendant and journal with excitement, of the creature that left it and of all the misery it had brought him. He seethed on this particular point so that his captured audience fully understood. He detailed the pursuit given by the Greek sailors who chased him. He spoke and spoke and spoke. He couldn't stop himself. He remembered little of the shed experience, but did his best to describe what happened.

Turning to Anubis he asked, "Have you ever been to my house? My shed? The marks are, well, the *same*," while pointing up toward the barricaded door. Anubis ignored the query.

Returning to the story, he unfolded the remainder of his journey and laid it out in front of Anubis. His capture, the sun, the misery he saw, the pain, the suffering, even death, were all provided with the utmost detail. Alex's eyes watered as he recounted what he'd seen. Catching himself, as a *man* sometimes does at these moments, he cleared his throat and finished the account with his sighting of a man in the gilded cage, followed by his own imprisonment. Alex's shoulders slumped in exhaustion.

Anubis looked at Alex only twice during this epic story, once when Alex described his home and once when he mentioned the journal. Silence came over the two. His sunburned flesh cooled from his long desert travels and caused him to shudder. The dampness in the cavern was adding to the chill. Alex's mind drifted to more pleasant memories, distant still, but pleasant.

Lost in thought, he paced across the floor absorbed in the quiet of the space. He missed his grandmother. Her quirky way had been a nuisance to him at times, but easily overlooked because he knew she loved him unconditionally. They were, for the most part, inseparable. The pair did virtually everything together. They played games, did puzzles, and even read the Sunday morning newspaper together over one of his grandmother's enormous breakfasts. *Ahhhh*, crab cakes.

On Saturdays, when his grandmother could corral him, the two would shop at Mercer's Grocery Store together. They tried to get there before the hoards of out-of-towners would descend upon the store, pushing their carts the wrong way down the aisles. Don't they know they're screwing up the flow? It infuriated him. And please, if you don't know what you want, get the heck out of the way!

After groceries, the two of them would pass by Trudie's Treasures and say hello, if Ms. Trudie were in. It was sometimes hit or miss, as Ms. Trudie liked to travel. In fact, she *had* to travel to gather all of her collectables, even if *traveling* meant she was just walking the shoreline picking up more shells and driftwood. It was best to leave her alone when she was down on the shore. She'd well up too many lost memories of her youth, and they'd be stuck until almost noon before they could break away.

Ms. Trudie was family, too, though. Not in the strictest sense, but she was always there to help his grandmother, and that made her family in Alex's book. Same with Crunch . . . er, Mr. Crunch, he corrected out of respect. Now, other than school, Alex tried to avoid Mr. Crunch in public for fear someone, specifically Jackson, would light into him about being a teacher's pet or something stupid like that. After all, a guy had a certain reputation to protect. But Crunch would always tell his grandmother, "We old timers gotta stick together, eh, Camille?" and his face would beam like a light bulb glowing bright.

Alex often noted the special kindness Crunch afforded his grandmother, and he appreciated it. But it was Alex who was her only object of affection, and she devoted herself to him. Alex knew it, too. He never once took advantage of the fact.

His concerns would always land him back to his grandmother. How would she go on without him? Would she be okay? He missed her so much. She always had a wide smile, a comforting hug, and a reassuring touch. Now, school on the other hand, *that* he didn't miss at all, Ms. Flowers' class in particular. If the trip to and from school weren't dangerous enough, sitting anxiously in her class every single day could wear on a man, right down to his soul. It's no wonder people called him *skittish*. Why, even Captain Shovers told him he was like a "one-eyed cat watching three mice-holes." Alex didn't quite know what that meant, but he rarely ever knew what the Captain meant. Nevertheless, what he was sure of was that the Captain didn't have someone like Jackson Styers and his mob on his heels at every turn. Survival, *that* was the reason.

But still, he missed home. Until recently, it was all he knew. Everything else he had only read about. His ideas of worldly events, of history and far off places, came from books someone else wrote. Books were always a common outlet for his restless desire to travel the world. For someone who loved his home so much, he found it difficult to understand his yearning for travel. But these books, these windows into other worlds, were quickly becoming clouded. What he had always believed as documented truth from reliable sources was unraveling before his eyes. There was proof of that standing in this same room with him, living, breathing proof.

"Proof. *PROOF!*" Alex exclaimed as if he'd been bitten by sudden realization.

Anubis just stared at his animation, puzzled at the words, trying to digest their meaning.

Alex noticed the confusion on his face and clarified, "Evidence. I need evidence. It's all a puzzle," he added as he stroked at the pendant around his neck, unaware.

"Everything I've ever read about ancient Egyptians seems to indicate that they recorded everything. Of course, not much of what I read seems to be true anymore . . ." He trailed off, giving up on his fleeting hope.

As if understanding what Alex was seeking, Anubis spoke, "MY STORY IS WRITTEN HERE." He pointed toward the faint carvings etched across the entire wall.

"MANY STORIES ARE WRITTEN HERE," he added, and more of the ceiling cracked at the sound of his voice sending dust and sand into a cloud, filling most of the cavern.

Alex nearly got whiplash as he spun his head around to face the wall. There was something there, something covered in years of abandonment and neglect. The dust from the ceiling settled quickly, and he gasped at what he saw. Wonder filled his insides.

The wall ran nearly flat, except for the relief of the carvings, which continued on for almost fifty feet and well over twelve feet high. He hadn't noticed them until now, caught up in selfishness and preoccupied with his own misery. It had only been just a wall before. *Now* it was potentially a clue, an answer, perhaps *all* of his answers.

Was this what he was searching for? He grew closer with an outstretched hand as if in a trance, then hesitated. He knew he needed more answers than even this wall could provide. Disappointment set in.

Any disappointment was short-lived and ultimately replaced by his longing to get home. He needed a plan, and it all started with this wall. He could feel it. Without much thought on his initial assault, he began brushing away inches of dust.

His first touch was far too aggressive for the ancient wall, and sandstone crumbled in his hands and landed at his feet. He jerked back and hesitated once again. Wincing, he realized what he'd done and considered the integrity of his surroundings. They were ancient and obviously crumbling. Anubis' voice was a measure of that.

So again, slowly and with far more caution, he stepped up to the wall, gathered all the breath that he could muster, and slowly blew across the reliefs. A dust cloud was sent, hugging the wall toward Anubis.

"AGGGNEESTHHSSSPPTTT." Anubis sneezed, and more ceiling fell from the concussion of noise, snot running from his snout.

"Sorry," Alex spoke between his teeth.

As if possessed, Alex removed the journal that he had so carefully hidden all of this time inside his clothes. He was glad to extract it from hiding as it had been causing him a dull pain for some time. Now, he thought, he could put it to some real use. He'd recognized the style of drawings on the wall. They were similar to the journal. Some, but not all, appeared to have been drafted in the same context as the reliefs on the wall in front of him. This excited him. Unfortunately, there were too many scenes to take in and decipher all at once, so he decided to take a more systematic approach. He started by opening the journal to the first page and began searching for commonality between the sketches in his journal and those on the wall.

Having little luck recognizing anything at first, he began stroking the pendant while he surveyed the scenes in front of him, deep in thought. This subconscious action was ultimately becoming habitual, instinctive somehow, yet it felt soothing to him at the same time. It helped him think. He was, however, painfully aware of the heat it generated every time he did.

"That's it! Of course!" he cried aloud. "The pendant! I'll start with the pendant!"

Staring down at the scene carved into the ivory around his neck, he gazed at the man and woman while they in turn gazed at each other. Why he started with them and not something more obvious to his needs, something that could get him home, he didn't know. This scene was somehow drawing him in. He wondered why they were so important. Who they could be? The desire to know what they meant to him was almost unbearable.

Each couple in the journal was drawn slightly different than the others, as he remembered. Thumbing over the pendant in his hand, this particular couple was carved facing each other on either side of a tall narrow tree. They wore long ceremonial-type clothing. A serpent wrapped the tree. He shuddered at this. This was the second time the serpent gave him a chill up his spine. It struck him as odd that this particular carving of a snake would scare him so, but it did.

He searched the wall over. His eyes fell hard on a picture of two similar figures. His heart jumped to his throat, and it was only after he choked down a large gulp of air was he able to clear the mud from his head.

"These people, they're like those in my journal," Alex said aloud, more at this point to convince himself than to engage Anubis in conversation. With a shake of his melon to clear the cobwebs, he slowly ran the tips of his fingers across the carving. He felt it. He saw it. It was real. His heart was back up in his throat again. His usually glum expression was ripped through with a toothy smile from ear to ear. He was on to something here, something huge. It was the same as the pendant.

"Wait, no it wasn't," he realized. It *was* the same, just *different*, somehow.

"Crap!"

He raised the necklace up off his chest, and it sang through the air as he held it close to the scene on the wall. It grew hot in his hand, to a point that it was giving off a sort of white light. There

108

were indeed two people, a couple, or specifically a man and a woman. And *yes*, they *were* facing each other just like the pendant. But the similarities stopped there.

Their clothes were different, and the man had a beard, unlike the man on the pendant. The man depicted on the wall also had dark skin and was covered in an elaborate robe and wore a much larger headdress. Both men were obviously great leaders or at the least important, Alex considered. This man also held something in his hands; a type of tool or piece of equipment. They weren't weapons, not that Alex could tell; they looked much more like farming equipment.

The woman was of striking beauty, standing tall herself in a large decorative hat. She appeared to be covered in jewelry. It wasn't the cheap type of jewelry that the girls at PSA wore, or "bling" as kids call it nowadays. Most of them, those conceited enough to think the entire world revolved around them, would swoop down on Trudie's Treasures and mull through her collection of riches, fondling everything until they decidedly exhausted all of her assets. They traveled in packs, gaggles, like the geese in the harbor. He knew most of it was junk. They knew most of it was junk. But they didn't know that he knew, and that gave him great joy.

He had to look several times to make sure he wasn't seeing things. Rubbing his eyes, Alex's vision came into focus.

"Wings?" he shouted in disbelief.

Checking more closely a third time, that's exactly what they were. This woman had wings attached to her arms. How strange is that? he thought. But then, nothing seemed normal to him lately. Even her headdress was strange. It had a large circle or disk at the top attached between two horns. Odd.

"Who are these people?" Alex turned to Anubis, who had been

studying Alex as much as Alex had the wall.

As if having been distracted by the young man before him, Anubis let out a low gurgling growl that seemed to be uttered from somewhere deep in his chest. It was obvious to Alex that Anubis considered the question almost rudimentary, basic in nature.

"OSIRIS AND ISIS. MY KING. MY QUEEN," the monster lectured. The walls trembled with fear themselves, and once again dust was in the air. Alex shook it from his hair and looked back at Anubis inquisitively. There was still a sense of disconnect in the air, so Anubis attempted to explain.

"OSIRIS IS KING OF KINGS. GOOD KING. FAIR AND JUST. MEN FOLLOWED. RESPECTED. GOD OF LIFE AND DEATH. GOOD FORTUNE. GREAT RULER. GREAT WARRIOR. THE GOOD ONE . . ." Anubis trailed off again.

Alex recognized sadness in Anubis' voice. Despite the echoing roar that accompanied it, there was loss there, hidden. When the walls became silent and still from the reverberation of Anubis' words, Alex pressed on, anxious to find out more, anything that could give him the answers he so longed for right now.

"And her?" Alex asked, covering his real motives for pressing Anubis, pointing at the woman on the wall.

Fleeting waves of guilt came over him, coupled with a feeling of pity for this being before him. He felt guilty having put himself first, and pity for one who may well be worse off than him. But Alex was desperate to find out answers, desperate to return home.

Anubis showed no physical expression, gave no clue as to the pain he must be enduring, but continued,

"GOOD QUEEN ISIS. BEAUTY. KIND. MOTHER OF EGYPT. QUEEN OF OSIRIS. EGYPT LOVED HER," Anubis simplified. It was the kind of description that would have gotten lost in any amount of detail. His expression displayed his conviction of this fact. Alex got the picture.

"They sound like wonderful people, King Osiris and Queen Isis," Alex said in his best consoling type voice.

"YES."

"Uh, so what happened?" Alex quizzed further.

"TRICKERY. DECEIT. LIES," boomed the behemoth so loud that Alex had to steady himself against the wall, resulting in even more flaking of the sandstone wall, crumbling to powder.

Alex hit a nerve, and he knew it. Something about what had happened grated on Anubis, so he changed the focus of the conversation.

"Is this you?" he asked, pointing to a carving some several feet away. It was worn around the edges, but Alex recognized the creature. It was a different scene, one removed from the first, almost as if it were a different story altogether. Anubis was carved in a kneeling position. This particular carving also depicted him with what looked like a mane on his head that rode between his spiked ears and down his back. Looking at the real deal in front of him, Alex assumed that this was a hat or headdress that he no longer wore. There was a long staff next to him that curved at the end, much like the staff The Riddler had in the Batman movie, he compared.

Brushing and blowing as he went, Alex was careful to minimize the destruction. As he did, a scene unfolded before him, an unimaginable picture, even stranger than what was currently towering over him.

Alex had a certain level of acceptance. He was a young, uh, man who readily trusted his instincts, but was cynical enough at a young age, and he believed this trait kept him out of trouble on more than one occasion. Being cynical, he was having a tough time believing what he saw. His mind was about to crack from everything he'd already seen. His instincts were telling him that not only was all of this real, but that it was just the beginning. So he forced himself to just go with it.

The scene depicted his new acquaintance kneeling beside a large scale. It wasn't like the scale that his grandmother used in the kitchen. Every time she pulled that old thing out, Alex knew it was going to be a good day. Biscuits and cakes came from that old scale. This one was much older, a balance scale with two pans hanging from either end of a rod teetering in the center on a pole. It was the type of scale used to weigh items against each other for comparison. Recognizing the scale was easy for Alex; the rest, well, the rest of what he saw made his eyes sink to the back of his head in fear and his throat run dry.

There was an odd, treacherous creature poised, looking up at the scale, its tongue hanging to it side as if hungry for food and waiting for the scraps. This creature scared him far more than even Anubis did. This creature was definitely bad. He could tell. Upon closer examination of the beast, it wasn't just one frightening beast, but several. It had the head of a crocodile, the body of a lion, and the back end of something much larger. There were other creatures and items that made up the scene, but Alex couldn't move his eyes from this particular one. It was something nightmares were made from. But as frightening as the creature was, there was something even worse--its devilish stare. It hungered.

"Creepy," he muttered. He went to turn away, but there was something else. The scale; there was something on it. In fact, there were *two* somethings on it. Specifically, each pan had something placed on it. One had a feather. A *feather?* he thought. Undeniably a

112

feather. The other pan, for which the feather was balanced against, was . . . Alex blew softly against the carving to clear the heavy dust. "Something . . . what . . . was . . . tha . . ." He blew harder to see. "It's a . . . a . . ." He blew one last time.

"*A heart?*" he exclaimed in surprise, pulling his head back with a snap.

"A heart! What are you doing with a heart?" He reared on Anubis.

"Are you gonna eat it? Did you *kill* the person and now you're gonna feed on his heart?" Alex blurted without waiting for a response. "What's going on? Why do you have that heart? What's that thing?" he asked of the creature with the horrific expression. "Is this a sacrifice? I said . . . *Did . . . you . . . kill . . . that . . . person?*" Alex asked, further emphasizing his question by pointing to the heart.

"I AM NOT AN END. I AM BUT A JOURNEY," Anubis responded.

"What the heck does that mean?" Alex pleaded, feeling a little unsure of his companion at this particular moment.

"WHEN MEN DIE, I LEAD THEM."

"Lead them where?" Alex immediately regretted asking.

"TO TUAT," Anubis responded with an air of regret himself. "TO JUDGMENT."

Alex presumed what he meant was that this *Tuat* was where it was decided whether a person went to heaven or hell, whether they were good or bad. Judgment. He figured he didn't want to know what was decided in this particular scene, so he didn't ask. The discussion, however, did make him think of religion in general and what little he knew about the subject. It's times like this, Alex thought, when one finds himself locked away, imprisoned in a strange place with a big hairy dog-like creature that he wished he'd paid a little more attention in church.

"Wait, what? What am I thinking?" he interrupted himself. No matter, he still couldn't keep his mind from reaching back into his own memories. The inside of his church was overly decorated for such a small, outwardly-quaint appearance. Passing over its threshold, a person could easily get lost in thought by any one of the several stained glass depictions of heavenly bodies, of angels, and the traditional biblical scenes. They were beautiful.

The older section was just as ornate, but suggested a more earthly approach with more of a focus on man and God. Several glass panoramas depicted knights and soldiers, some even with cloaked figures. Alex preferred this section of his church, although darker, dustier, and much damper.

His grandmother would sing away while he would explore. She was never in tune and always slightly ahead of the rest of the congregation. She'd put every ounce of energy into it and expected everyone else to keep up. While she sang, he would occasionally slink off to the older parts of the church, curious to find his own version of truth. This adventure would invariably lead him to drift off to faraway places and distant lands.

It was a cold and sometimes scary place for someone of his age, and if it weren't for his overactive imagination, he'd probably have a different recollection of it. Of course, scary or not, he'd much rather be there than here any day of the week.

"I PREPARE MEN FOR THEIR DESTINY," Anubis concluded and stared off, as if lost in thought.

Alex snapped back to reality.

"So, then if you travel with dead guys to this place, this . . . Tuat, then are you dead, too?" Alex asked, perhaps a bit more boldly than

114

he should have.

"I CANNOT DIE. I DO NOT LIVE," Anubis explained.

"Yeah, right. Then why are you stuck in here? *How* are you stuck in here . . . with me?" quizzed Alex.

"I AM IMPRISONED!" The entire cavern quaked from Anubis' outburst reverberating off the walls. Debris and dust dropped from the ceiling. The piles were beginning to add up, Alex noticed.

"*Imprisoned?* By *who?* *Who* could imprison something, er . . . some*one* like you? *How* could they imprison you?"

"SET," came the singular response that shook the walls and scattered dust into clouds across the ancient floor.

"Okay. I'll bite." Alex cringed as soon as he'd said the words.

Anubis shot him a look of detest. Thinking it through a second time, Alex continued, "Who is Set?"

"YOU HAVE SEEN HIM. THE ONE YOU FEAR. YOU ARE WISE TO FEAR HIM."

Alex's mind flooded in an instant, his heart pounded. He did know who Set was. He *had* seen him before.

"You mean the man in the cage? The one responsible for all of that suffering and pain? He put you here? He's the one keeping you here? But *how* can he keep you here?"

"HE IS NO MAN. NO MERE MORTAL. HE IS A GOD. A RULER OF MEN. DESTROYER OF LIFE." The words vibrated every molecule of air in the room. The unintended result of his hatred for Set brought a stalactite crashing to the floor in an explosion. The effect was more of an annoyance to Anubis than anything, Alex suspected.

"HMMNFFT." Alex's suspicion was confirmed.

Anubis retreated on his words, turned, and slumped to the ground in the nearest corner of the cavern, covered in his darkness.

Alex had hesitated just long enough. The beast had settled a good bit. But like most teenagers, his patience was limited, and he approached Anubis yet again.

As he closed on the beast, he glimpsed a third scene on the wall. This, too, seemed to be of yet an even different event. It seemed somehow forgotten, almost purposely covered over and smeared with dirt and soot.

Anxious to learn more about everything, he carefully brushed away at the deteriorating sandstone. He immediately recognized the figure in this one. He'd seen this being before, outside. It was the man in the cage, the one Anubis mentioned. It was the god Set. A tall figure, it stood high on a mountaintop, one hand raised to the heavens, one pointing toward the earth, his jackal-like face sneering. Not a mountain . . . (Alex blew hard) . . . it was . . . bodies? It was a mountain of bodies! They were all dead! Each and every one was carved and intertwined into some grotesque distorted form of suffering. Alex recoiled.

"Okay. I get it. Set bad. Set *really* bad," Alex chided half-heartedly, then stopped, remembering the seriousness of the pain and suffering he saw earlier in the trenches outside. This man, this god, *was* bad. The hairs on the back of his neck stood higher than ever. A coldness came over him, and he crossed his arms around his chest for comfort, for security.

"SET HUNGERS. FEEDS ON WEAK. CRAVES POWER. EVIL. GOD OF EVIL," Anubis began. "WRITING OF SET BAD. MISFORTUNE. EVIL WIPED CLEAN," he continued, explaining the heavy smudges across the scene.

"But *please*," Alex pleaded, turning to Anubis, "what I don't understand is what does this have to do with *me?*" Embarrassed to have even asked, but desperate, Alex moved closer to the now silent beast. What Anubis said next was perhaps the quietest he'd ever spoken, muffled from the result of burying his snout under his cloak.

"NOW MEN DIE. I CANNOT LEAD. THEY WANDER SOULLESS BETWEEN WORLDS. BETWEEN THE NOW AND THE WHAT SHOULD BE," he explained succinctly, casting a longing stare upwards toward the ceiling.

It couldn't get much clearer than that. If Anubis led people to Tuat and Set now controlled Anubis, Alex deduced, then humans were stuck in a sort of transition between death and the afterlife. This *can't* be good, Alex thought.

The beast he currently shared quarters with had only spoken a few words to Alex, but already he had shattered not only his sense of reality, but also further shook his crumbling belief of self-existence and mortality. What he'd learned about the past wasn't as it was, or seemed to be. Nothing made sense to him now. This was far too large of a puzzle to solve all at once.

Anubis wrestled around in the darkness, then rose tall to properly herald the story about to fill the stale and foul cavern air. The glow of Alex's exposed pendant shone up at the creature, giving him an even more eerie appearance, if that were at all possible, Alex thought.

"GOD KING OSIRIS. FATHER OF EGYPT. TRAVELED FAR. GAVE GIFTS TO WORLD. KNOWLEDGE. MANY BATTLES WON. NO BLOODSHED. STRANGE LANDS. STRANGE PEOPLE. PURE. ALL WAS PEACEFUL. GREAT OSIRIS," Anubis said proudly, pushing his already enormous chest outward and up. A smile appeared to flash across his snout, the only clue to which was a trace of exposed white fang.

As Alex listened intently for some clue or hint from which to

117

hang on, the creature's smile turned to a growl.

"SET AND OSIRIS ARE BROTHERS."

"*Whhaaattt?*" Alex rejected in disbelief, his eyes now locked on the unlikely orator.

"SET WAS JEALOUS. *IS* JEALOUS OF OSIRIS. WANTS POWER. PLOTTED. OSIRIS TRUSTING OF ALL. EVEN SET." Anubis paused briefly, drawing in a breath as if cleansing his thoughts of the pain that Set brought upon him and those he loved.

"SET DECEIVED OSIRIS. ALL CELEBRATED RETURN OF KING. SET TRICKED OSIRIS INTO COFFIN WITH TALES OF TREASURE. TRUSTING OSIRIS. SET SEALED COFFIN FOREVER. TOOK COFFIN TO GREAT RIVER. THREW IT IN. THREW OSIRIS IN. BROTHER . . . FATHER. GONE." Anubis paused.

"ISIS SEARCHES. SET RULES." Alex heard sadness in his tone.

"HOUNDS OF SET RUN RABID. SET WILLS IT. MEN FEAR HOUNDS. MEN FEAR SET." Alex saw anger fill the beast's eyes.

"SET FEARS ONLY ONE. OSIRIS."

"And you?" Alex urged. "How did you get here?"

"I, TOO, SEARCHED FOR OSIRIS. SET SENT WORD THAT COFFIN WAS HERE. BURIED. I CAME. LIES. ALL LIES," Anubis explained.

"Yes," said Alex, remembering the two sarcophagi from the outer chamber. He figured they were placed there to lure Anubis, Osiris' faithful follower, into the trap. "That tells me how you got here, but *why* did he need to trick you, and *why* can't you leave?"

"IT IS WRITTEN THAT I ALONE CAN SAVE OSIRIS. WITHOUT ME, OSIRIS REMAINS LOST. SET WILL RULE."

Alex suspected that Anubis was avoiding this last question. He had asked it before and had yet to get a direct answer. Anubis had taken to pacing along the wall as he spoke, and Alex could tell this topic bothered him deeply. His breath quickened and his chest heaved. He was snorting with every other word.

"SET HAS BOUND ME TO THIS PLACE FOR ETERNITY. THE LOST ARE ABOVE US. PLACED THERE BY SET. HUNDREDS. THOUSANDS. TOO MANY." Anubis curled his massive claws into fists, forcing the muscles in his arms to bulge. "WITHOUT ANUBIS, MEN ARE LOST." A rage was welling inside him,

"*AAARRRGGGHHHHHH,*" Anubis howled, and the ceiling gave way, shaken from the blast of the sound. As it did, Alex saw flesh and bones drop from the ceiling like a heavy rain. His roar had loosened a layer of the oldest of bodily decay. The foul stench that had filled the room earlier now worked its way against every available molecule of fresh air and forced it out of the cavern. A putrid smell of rot entered the room.

Death had arrived.

Alex heard someone cry out in fear, and it was only after the settling of this unwanted guest did he realize that it was he who had cried out. The dead and dying had been thrown for years in a pile above the living tomb where they now sat, rotting in the desert sun. It was obvious to Alex that the desert scavengers had picked at the bodies, all the while they decayed. The excessive heat hastened the process, so a continual replenishment was necessary, and apparently Set was obliging. As if unaware of what had just happened, Anubis continued, "I FEEL EACH OF THEM. CALLING OUT. THEY ARE LOST. THEY NEED ME. I AM SUFFOCATED BY THEIR PAIN. TOO MUCH PAIN. SO MUCH SUFFERING."

Alex purposely looked away from the mass that sloughed off in a wet ooze of flesh, entrails, and organs. His arm once again returned to cover his nose. Both what was on the floor and what dangled from the opening in the ceiling gave off a steam from the decaying process. A wave of sickening warmth entered the cool cavern. Alex couldn't stomach it for long. It reminded him of the jars in his grandmother's kitchen, those high up on the shelves filled with all sorts of colorful oozy things; the same jars that would make his head spin and his stomach lurch. They would almost make him . . .

And it was over, literally. He had vomited all over.

Twice.

Anubis ignored his young companion, reflecting in his own pain, and for that Alex was almost thankful. Wiping his last meal from his mouth and chin, Alex strategically positioned himself with his back to the bodies.

Six

"We need to get out of here. How do we get out of here?" he pleaded to Anubis, knowing full well that if Anubis had known how to escape, he would have long ago. He was tired and couldn't remember when the last time sleep blanketed him.

Something was missing. Lots of things were still missing. The biggest gap was his journal. There was an obvious disconnect. Plus, he still had no idea how he fit into all of this. As near as he could tell, as a wise old man of thirteen, the main pieces of this puzzle were the journal, his pendant, himself of course, perhaps even Anubis.

His brain was on overload. How did all of this go together? He struggled with this question and, worse, what was missing. He knew the pendant and journal had similar figures. So did the wall behind him. They were all similar, but not exact.

His eyes were growing heavy as he settled down onto the floor. Leaning against the wall, he was careful to keep from dragging across it. He must have stared at the same page in his journal for hours, days even, or so it seemed. Nothing. He ran his fingers through his thick mop of hair. He saw strange pictures, symbols. Some things looked vaguely familiar, but only in style, and gave him nothing. These caused him the most grief. They danced around on the page and he couldn't focus. Faster and faster. More blurred. His eyelids were dropping. His head was swimming.

Anubis had since retired to his favorite corner, likely to avoid being near the dead. He wrestled with each falling piece of flesh. It made him twist in agony, as if somehow it was the bodies themselves that kept him prisoner here, wasting away. They were tormenting him. Each body placed upon the pile above was a tribute to Set's wickedness and a constant humiliation to the God of the Dead below who was powerless to perform his rightful duties upon these poor abandoned souls.

As Alex slid off to sleep, the room fell silent. He dreamed of familiar things, of home. Comfort came in the form of his grandmother baking in the kitchen, the posters in his room, the warm Atlantic breeze coming through his window, all the time he spent with Captain Shovers on the Mermaid.

Truth be told, he spent far more time with the Captain than with his peers. Most people would say he should socialize with people his own age, but Alex liked spending time with the Captain. The Captain did cool stuff. He taught him cool things; probably things a young man his age ought not to learn, but still cool. Besides, his grandmother knew. Well, she knew most of it; some, anyway. If they got close to trouble, the Captain would always say, "Now don't you go telling Cam about this one." Alex would spend hours every Saturday with the elder townsman.

He learned about manly stuff. The hardships on the open sea forced men to adapt, and he learned how. The Captain taught him what to eat if rations were low. He taught him how to spit chewing tobacco and showed him his tattoos. Many times Alex would watch in amazement and wonder as the Captain made Rosie dance upon his shoulder. There was even a certain way to load Matilda and ready her for fire. He learned this, too.

His knowledge of cussing was beyond most of his age, but he never used it, least ways not in front of his grandmother. In fact, neither did the Captain. The Captain showed him how to read the stars and chart a course. There were farts and belches flowing freely, with no apologies. A man could be a man around the Captain, and Alex liked that. Then he remembered,

Wait. Matilda.

Alex snapped awake.

Captain Shovers would always tell him, "Work with what you know boy. You need a plan."

"That's it!" Alex shouted, stirring Anubis. "Of course. Captain Shovers *is* the plan," or at least he'd given him the plan already. He knew if he could just sit and think about it long enough, he'd get it. Alex thumbed through his journal quickly.

"I know I saw it in here before. Where is it?" he spoke aloud, not expecting an answer.

"WHAT DO YOU SEEK?" came the response that caused more fleshy material to fall from the ceiling landing in a wet pile much like gelatin hitting the sidewalk.

"Aww, man, did you have to? That's gross," Alex complained. Anubis was indifferent.

"I need something like . . . like *this!*" Alex said as he held out his journal and pointing to a picture of a long tube-like stick, hollow from end to end.

Alex had a lot of memories he'd just as soon forget, but right now there was one he was glad to have remembered. The events of that particularly unassuming day were flooding back into his drowsy brain. The Captain was on deck, showing Alex not only how to load Matilda, but what could be used instead of gunpowder to fire her. He had all sorts of strange things laid out on a blanket on her deck. There were colorful powders and strange vials of liquid. He had cotton fabric and oils lined up next to what looked like salt. There were pellets, rocks, and minerals, all of which, if measured correctly and mixed in the exact right proportions, could create one heck of a convincing argument from Matilda.

Anubis retreated back to the area where he had laid, covered in darkness. Moments later he returned, edging out from the shadows holding something in his hands. The glow of Alex's pendant bounced off the object, and the reflection returned what looked to be a long rod.

"*That's it!* I need something like *that*," Alex retorted and, upon closer inspection of the object, "uh, no, actually that's *exactly* what I need. *Exactly!* That's the drawing in my journal! *But how? How* did your stick get *in* my journal? It's identical. Where'd it come from?"

"I HAVE MANY TOOLS."

Anubis unfurled his large pouch on the ground, and there laid the tools of his trade. As he did, a large ball of cotton rolled across the floor, slightly unraveling itself. There were oils and liquids, much the same as what the Captain had, secured inside by small pieces of animal hide fastened to the pouch. A red powder filled several small vials, whereas a much larger cask contained a type of oil. Another, filled with salt, was half empty and strapped next to other much smaller hand tools.

Anubis handed Alex the rod.

"What do you use it for?" Alex asked. A mere look was the only answer he received.

"You're right. I don't want to know."

"WHAT WILL YOU DO?" asked Anubis. Alex returned that same look which he himself had just received.

"HUMPPHT," Anubis snorted back his understanding.

Alex sized up the rod. He held it up to his eye lengthwise and peered down the center of it much the same as one would when looking through a telescope. He turned it over and even sniffed it once, although admittedly, this last part served no real purpose for his needs. Against his own better judgment, he grasped the rod hand over hand, walked over to where the bodies hung from the ceiling as if trying to escape their fate, and thrust the rod up into the decaying mass, causing overly rank organic material to land on top of his head. He was covered.

"Uhhgghh!"

Resolute in his task, he held his breath and didn't flinch. He released the rod and took two steps back, careful not to slip in the pile around his feet. Anubis watched in quiet confusion while Alex double-checked the placement of the rod. It was up there nice and firm. Almost immediately, the rod produced Alex's intended result, and they could hear the gas discharging from the end. It had worked.

"Quickly. We must move fast," Alex instructed, pointing to Anubis' possessions that lay on the ground.

Whereas Alex hated History class and hadn't paid much attention in it, a feeling he had only just regretted given his recent run of bad luck, he excelled in the sciences, particularly Chemistry. Because he actually paid attention in this class, he knew that it was ammonia that he smelled coming from the end of the rod.

"Oils. Yeah, they burn. And we can use this," he said as he snatched the cotton fabric. He was in the zone. Alex took one of Anubis' larger casks and packed it with a mixture of the Frankincense from one of the smaller vials and the ammonia that trickled through the rod firmly fixed overhead. It took everything he had to keep from vomiting again during his next task. Like a man possessed, he forced himself to . . . *umnpht* . . . reach into the sloughed pile of . . . *umnpht* . . . flesh and grab a handful of the most . . . *umnpht* . . . vile . . . *urp* . . . decomposed and . . . *ulp* . . . biologically active remains and shove them into the cask.

125

He'd learned from class that decomposing bodies, without the proper preparation, would decay quickly in this desert heat. The decaying process would break down the organic material and produce several gases and by-products such as the ammonia from above and something called acetic acid and another called ammonium nitrate.

He wasn't quite sure what the last two were, but had recognized the first one from a label on a cleanser his grandmother had used. The latter was a result of exposed bowels, just like above. *GROSS!* He also knew from his "out-of-class" experiences with Captain Shovers that each of these was dangerous in their own right and, if mixed together correctly, could give even Matilda a run for her money.

He wrapped the cask tightly with the roll of fabric that he had just dipped into the oil, stuffing the end of the roll into the open cask to seal it. Kneeling partially on the pouch, Alex picked up a nearby rock and brought it down hard onto the salt that lay spread on the pouch, smashing it into the finest of granules. He reached over and rolled the dampened sealed cask around in the powder.

"There," he said, holding up his creation, ooze dripping through his fingers and down his forearm. He was done.

His pride was short-lived. He turned his head just in time to vomit.

He set the creation down on the pouch, stood back, and admired his genius. He was *definitely* unappreciated, he thought. Wiping the hair from his face, he remembered just how disgusting he had become and frantically searched for anything to clean himself. Reaching down for the pouch to dry his hands, Alex was stopped short.

"NO!" Anubis roared.

"Sorry, my bad." Alex pulled back and decided that it was better to wipe himself off on his own clothes. Not that there was much in the way of dry clothing hanging on his thin frame anymore, but he managed.

Alex carefully picked up the cask, half-wondering if it would work. He ran the mixture through his mind. If this did work, he'd be free, he thought, they'd be free. He took a deep breath and walked up the ramp to the platform in front of the stone door. His eyes searched. The most likely place for this would be, no, not there . . . *there!* The upper right corner of the door, where it met the cavern wall, looked to be the most likely of places to him. It had a slight curve to the stone from wear which not only gave up a place for which to set the cask so it wouldn't fall, but also implied the door was thinner there, too.

"Can't quite reach it," he spoke under his breath as he struggled on the tips of his toes. Alex stretched and strained with no luck. He felt a warmth behind him, close, and a long-fingered hand reached over his shoulder, grabbed the cask, and placed it firmly in its intended resting place.

"Thanks," Alex said quietly without turning around. He was a proud young man and hated it when he had to ask for help, but his grandmother raised him right, and he knew when to thank someone.

"HUMMPHHTT." Wetness landed on the back of Alex's neck.

"Awwww, dude. *Really?*" he complained as he wiped it away.

"*DU-DUH?*" Anubis looked puzzled.

"Not Du-*DUH. Dude,*" Alex explained, thinking this cleared everything up.

Anubis still looked puzzled.

"All we need now is something to light this puppy with," Alex commented. Seeing the change in Anubis' expression, Alex knew his

127

large roommate was processing what he'd just said, so he attempted to further explain,

"I don't mean a *real* puppy. It's just an expression. Never mind. We need something to make a flame, an igni . . ." Alex had kicked something. He looked down around his feet. They were there.

"You've got to be kidding me," he muttered in disbelief. Alex bent down and snatched the same two stones that the guard had used earlier to light the outer room, and gave life to the passageway. They were here, at his feet. The guard must have dropped them when he shoved Alex over the edge. Good, he thought, serves him right, the jerk. Alex remembered the scream that came from the outer room before. He believed that same guard had met his own fate. He shuddered and immediately diverted his thoughts back to the task at hand.

"Boy, the gods must be smiling on me today." He laughed, bouncing the stones in the palm of his hand and looking up at Anubis. "Well, they're *sneezing* on me anyway." He reached to the back of his neck again, wiping it for effect.

Alex peeled the remaining cloth into a long strip, had Anubis tie one end to the cask, and let the other drape to the cold floor. From there the two walked hunched over and backwards down the ramp, carefully stepping while pouring out the remaining red powder in a thin line which led from the end of the cloth. This, Alex deduced, would give them more time to seek cover from the blast should he have, well, uh, overestimated his potion. They ran out of powder at the base of the ramp. Wishing he had more, Alex removed the two stones from his front pocket and took a deep breath. Anubis stared intently. Alex wasn't sure if his partner grasped what was about to happen. He stood at a distance and chipped the stones together twice and got nothing. Decidedly too far away, he moved closer and stooped directly over the end of the powdered trail banging the two pieces of stone together, trying to create a spark. The guard had made this look fairly easy. Doesn't take a genius, so why couldn't he? A flicker of light flew from the stone.

The powder flashed.

"Whoa!" he said as his head kicked back out of harm's way.

Flames danced from the powder, throwing light into the room. Shadows immediately joined in, jumping off the walls and across the floor. They both stared in wide wonder. For centuries, nobody could explain the attraction that man has had with fire, but these two, here and now, were a part of that cosmic question. Recovering from his near comatose stare, it dawned on Alex, "Oh, Craapppp!" and he took off running as fast as he could. His senses had just now kicked in. He quickly questioned his own sanity and concluded that this was indeed stupid, even for him. Anubis had apparently come to the same realization because he was right on Alex's heels. They both dove behind the same large outcropping of stone, nearly three feet high and just as thick. The powder sizzled for what seemed like an eternity. They heard a loud crack followed by an eerie silence. Alex was about to look out from behind the stone when the cavern erupted.

They both covered their ears, but it didn't help. The sound of the blast was followed by the sound of the ceiling crashing in on them. Sitting blindly in the mix of dust clouds and darkness, they heard the unwelcomed sound of moist bodies falling everywhere. The blast must have removed whatever blockage that held the dead back from entering the room. But now they were here, sharing close quarters with the two of them. The already rank air was stirred once again and filled the room. It took minutes for it to settle and grow quiet again.

Peeking up from their hiding places like rabbits in a garden, both Anubis and Alex struggled to clearly make out the scene. The noise, the blast, everything, had shaken them both senseless. Their ears still rang. Believing he was successful, Alex jumped up.

"Thank yyeeewwww, Captain Shovers!" Alex said, throwing his hands in the air like the winning boxer after the final count.

He tried to focus his eyes, but it was difficult with all of the dust in them. Rubbing them, he saw the results of his genius. Across a battlefield laid with waste and destruction, a huge stone door still stood where it had always been. Disappointment washed over him instantly. The cask had blown up and caused damage as Alex had hoped, but it wasn't enough. A large crack about an inch wide ran almost the entire length of the massive stone door. But the door still stood. Alex knew they didn't have enough material for a second attempt. His shoulders dropped as he looked at the floor.

Anubis, distraught himself, ripped a large chunk of sandstone from the floor of the cavern and lifted it high above his head.

RAAARRRRGGHHH! And the stone was flying through the air at the door, landing solidly in a thunderous blow on its mark. Again, stone flew everywhere, and dust billowed out from the impact like a mushroom cloud.

Light dappled through the dust. He'd done it! They could hear air pushing in through the large hole now in the stone door. They each took about two steps toward their freedom and stopped cold.

They froze, listening in the quiet aftermath. Had anyone else heard the noise? Nothing. Nothing, that is, except the warm fresh air now rushing in to fill the cavern.

"I loosened it," Alex muttered to himself. Anubis scooped up the tools of his trade and rolled them into the pouch. His crook was leaning against a corner of the cavern.

Only when they were certain they hadn't been heard did they approach the chaos left behind from the impact, carefully stepping over the fleshy hurdles and piles of debris. There were so many obstacles in their way that it reminded Alex of his own bedroom back home. Heading up the ramp, Alex comforted himself by tucking his journal back into its hiding place behind his back.

They stood at the large stone door now partially reduced to rubble, both inhaling the scent of freedom that wafted in through the opening. The hole was large enough for Alex to wiggle through, but too high for him to reach. As if reading his mind, Anubis lifted the young man up by his waist with one mighty claw and shoved his head through the hole.

"*Owwww!* Hey, watch it, would you. At least tell a guy when you're going to do something like that," he hollered, hanging half in and half out of the door. Alex squirmed and wiggled his way through the tight opening only to land on his back seven feet below.

"*Unngghhh,*" he uttered as the air left his lungs.

After a moment he finally stood, glad to be free of that place, and took a man-size breath, filling his lungs with the fresh air. Well, fresher than the foul stench on the other side of the door. Achy from the fall and brushing himself off, he almost lost track of the fact that there was one other who needed to be freed. A blind paw landed on his head as an instant reminder.

"I know. I know. I didn't forget you," Alex consoled.

"THE DOOR," Anubis barked back.

Alex pulled away from the grip on his head and turned as he did. What was that? He gasped. He was certain he'd seen something ahead. The passageway seemed somehow narrower than he remembered. The tightness of the curved path cast shadows in some unlikely places, but this was no shadow that he saw. It was just

131

ahead laying across the path. Alex stepped closer.

"THE DOOR," Anubis barked again.

"*Ssshhhhhh!*" Alex blasted back, holding his index finger to his lips.

He moved forward, creeping slowly, unsure of what it was. Whatever it was, it wasn't moving. Closer and closer he pushed, slowing as he approached. All was quiet except for the heavy breathing of Anubis' large chest. Alex could tell he was getting frustrated with him.

"Just wait a minute," he whispered. Closer. Only a few feet. His eyes trained on the tangled mass just ahead. Closer.

"*Huuunnhhh!*" Alex gasped, stumbling backwards. It appeared what blocked the path was the guard who had screamed earlier upon his retreat; the same guard who had put him here in the first place. Suddenly Alex felt alone. No, not alone, exposed. He looked around frantically. At least when he was stuck in the cavern, Anubis was there. His thoughts immediately took him back to his last known comfort. Anubis. *Yes*, Anubis, that's it!

Then he heard it. Unsure, it sounded like a scuffle to him, faint, like someone or something ahead shifted on its feet. Alex froze silently, hidden in the shadows himself. He held his breath, feverishly listening to confirm what he'd heard. Anubis' breathing was getting heavier.

"He *needs* to learn some patience," Alex muttered anxiously to himself. It was getting too loud. No, wait. He paused. Not Anubis. Something else was breathing, something closer to him. That's why it sounded louder. He lifted his head away from the wall he so desperately clung to and saw movement. It was slight, but it was there, hidden even deeper into the shadows. What now? he thought. He was beginning to panic much as he had when he'd broken the shed window, only this time it was no window.

"This isn't good. More movement. What the . . . ? Two eyes? Man, this sucks. Two eyes. Why'd it have to have two eyes? Well, I guess it's better than some other number, like one or three. Man, this *really* sucks." Alex's rants were broken with a sound so horrific, so penetrating; he knew only to be one thing. Terrified.

Seven

That was all Alex needed. He was off, bouncing down the hall at breakneck speed, back toward the cavern from which he'd just escaped. Anything was better than getting attacked, or worse. He knew he at least stood a chance with Anubis.

He glanced back over his shoulder at the sound of crashing noises. He wished he hadn't. A massive beast with long teeth and huge sharpened claws was gaining on him, filling the passage. It was strong and muscular, crushing the floor beneath its large paws. In the seconds that Alex had looked at it, he saw a dog-beast of giant proportions, with all of the wrong parts oversized, wrong for Alex anyway. Alex had the fleeting notion he'd seen a beast like this before.

Saliva stretching in the wind, dragging across its face, it was mad with the intent to kill. The mere stone walls were cracking each time it collided with them.

"*Waaaaaahhhhhh!* ANUBIS! HELP!" Alex was running blindly, his long arms flailing in the cramped passage.

He'd reached the door, knowing he couldn't crawl back up through the hole in time. He scrambled into the corner, tight against the door, covering his eyes. He was frantic and near insane, not knowing what to do. The beast slowed and growled smugly. It somehow knew its prey was cornered, trapped. Its prey knew so, too; an easy kill. He paced back and forth just yards from where Alex stood trembling.

"GET THE DOOR. THE LEVER. PULL IT," Anubis instructed the hysterical young man.

"PULL IT NOW!"

Alex reached up with both hands and gave a hard jerk. Nothing. He tried again. Nothing. The hound inched closer, running its long tongue across its snout, then stopped. Raising its head, it sniffed the air as if it recognized something familiar.

"THE LEVER. PULL THE LEVER!"

"I am! Nothing is happening. It's broken. The blast must have broken it!" Alex cried. A bloodcurdling roar filled the air once again. Alex's body went cold from fear.

The hound sprung.

A loud noise crashed through the air and ricocheted down the passage. Stone went flying, and a howl pierced his ears. This was it, Alex thought. He braced himself. He'd always heard that when facing death down, a person's life would flash before his eyes. He had nothing. The only thought that he had was that he was too young to die. Alex looked up at the last second through the thick cloud of dust; everything around him seemed to move in slow motion. What he saw was pure poetry.

Anubis met the beast squarely in the chest during mid-flight. Grappling in the air for what seemed like seconds, they tore and batted at each other with their massive claws before landing, still locked in battle. It was a lot like watching professional wrestlers in the ring, each taking his turn for the attack. They released, then circled each other. Hair and blood was flying everywhere, splattered across the walls. Rebounding off the wall, the hound had Anubis around the throat with its snout, clamping down; he had his friend pinned to the ground. Alex had seen dogs fight before, and this was a common maneuver to establish the alpha-male and demand submission or, in some cases, in this case, the precursor to kill.

The beasts rolled in and out of the shadows, clawing and

scratching. A solid blow was laid flat against Anubis' face. His head twisted, and he fell hard against the stone floor. He didn't move. A moment passed, and the hound looked confident he'd won. It turned its attention back to Alex, took one step, and let out an unexpected yelp.

Two razor sharp claws pierced out of the darkness and clutched around the narrow, soft part of the hound's waist, dragging it back into the shadows. A look of surprised fear washed over its face as its claws desperately tried to dig a foothold into the stone floor.

Bodies thrashed and jaws snapped. They were both at their most primal, protecting and attacking. They knew this was to the death. Alex could hear bones crunching and stone falling. The shadows made it difficult for Alex to tell which was friend and which was foe.

A triumphant roar vibrated through the air. Alex wasn't sure which one had howled. He strained to hear more, to see more. What he heard next sounded like a large tree branch crack in two, followed by a loud yelp.

It was over. Silence crept through the passage. The two beasts lay in a heap on the cold floor only feet in front of Alex, half in darkness. Each was lifeless. Hesitating, Alex spoke, "Anubis?" Alex whispered.

Something stirred. A breath. A moan. The hound began to move. Alex stepped back in terror.

"Oh No. No . . . No . . . NOOOO!" Alex cried.

With one final effort Anubis pushed the devil hound off and slowly rose before Alex. Staggering against the wall, too tall to stand up straight in the passage, Anubis panted. It was a hard battle.

Alex wiped tears from his eyes and ran to him. He grabbed his friend around the waist and hugged him hard. He hugged him like he used to hug his grandmother when he was just a boy. He hugged

136

him for warmth, for comfort, for security. He cried. It was all too much.

"DU-DUH," and he patted Alex on his back.

Alex looked up and broke his tears with a light chuckle.

"We'll work on it," he said with a sniffle and a smile.

It was dark, but grew lighter with every step they took toward their freedom. They worked their way down the passage toward the outer room. The first thing Alex noticed was the flicker of light dancing on the walls at the end of the passage. Good, he thought. That meant the troughs were still lit. Alex quickened his pace, anxious to break free from his confinement, but Anubis grabbed his arm,

"HOLD." Anubis seemed to sense something and raised his snout in the air, stretching it ahead.

"What is it?" Alex questioned, knowing by now that his companion must have a good reason to be cautious. "I don't hear anything."

"I WILL LEAD." Anubis pulled Alex behind him, and the two walked ahead carefully.

They peered into the outer room safely from the edge of the shadows. There didn't appear to be any movement. He hadn't taken a good look around the last time he was in here, but then, he was in a bit of rush. Of course, he was also bound and a prisoner, but that didn't matter now. These two strange figures, one man and one beast, slinked their way across the floor to the first column, safe from exposure. Their eyes darted around, trying to see better from this vantage point. The large room was quiet.

Anubis was the first to step out from hiding. He immediately walked toward the two sarcophagi laid to rest near their position. Alex was much more hesitant and followed slowly. There were still

137

too many strange things in this strange land that were, well, strange. His head was twisting around every which way, just to make sure. He was taking no more chances. If he was going to be attacked, he was going to see it coming.

As he approached Anubis, he noticed his friend softly stroking the lid of one of the sarcophagi. Alex knew this stone carved box was more than an empty coffin to Anubis. To him it represented Osiris, his leader, Egypt's father, a lost friend. But, as Alex stood next to him, he realized it meant far more than that to his overly large companion. It meant there was still a chance. *He* was the chance. Alex knew at that point that some things in life are more important than others. Friendship. Loyalty. Love.

Seemingly rejuvenated by his freedom, Anubis stepped back away from the sarcophagi and uncloaked himself from the ragged cloth that covered his body. The shabby hood cascaded off his large frame, dropping to the floor to reveal his figure in all of its glory. Alex stood back in amazement.

This great creature, with the full embrace of the room's bold light wrapped around his body, stood in defiance of all that had happened. Alex was able to take a good long look at the strange figure. His estimates in the dark cavern had been fairly accurate. His friend was easily four to five feet taller than he and had a hulking chest.

Discarding the cloak had revealed that Anubis was decorated with a golden hilt around his waist that dropped several golden plates to the top of his knees. A semi-circular golden chest plate wrapped around him and hung from his huge neck.

Anubis reached around to his back, pulled forth his headdress, and placed it on top of his head. The mane that had been carved into the wall in the cavern didn't do it justice. It, too, was laced with golden strands and gleamed in the light. Each muscular forearm had long golden bracelets covering from wrist to almost elbow. There were wide golden armbands around each massive bicep.

Standing there, holding his golden crook, Anubis was ready, not for his duties, but for his destiny. He was ready for battle.

Anubis released every ounce of pent up anger and reserved energy into a singular fearsome battle cry, and the walls shook with fear. No one, nothing dare stand in his way, Alex thought.

"WE MUST GO," Anubis said, turning to Alex. As they walked past the surrounding statues, Alex noticed how familiar these carved creatures looked to the one that killed the guard; the same one that Anubis killed only moments earlier in the dark passage.

"HOUNDS OF SET."

"*These? These* are the Hounds of Set you mentioned earlier? *Sheeesh.* They're *real?*" It was only just now that Alex realized the debris at his feet. Rubble? He turned quickly to see that one of the statues had been broken. Someone had destroyed it since the last time he'd been here. He looked harder.

"Someone didn't break into this; some*thing* broke *out*, didn't it?" he fired at Anubis. Anubis stood expressionless.

"These creatures are *real?*" he cried, looking up at Anubis in desperation. "Are they *all* real? Right here? Right now?" he asked anxiously.

"YES. WE MUST LEAVE," Anubis commanded.

"You don't have to tell me twice. I'm out of here." He headed for the wide stairs at the other end of the ornate room.

The two of them walked briskly toward the door when Alex's curiosity got the best of him and he asked, "What's with the columns? Who are all of these people?" Alex remembered his journal. He pulled it out, opened it in one hand, and began tracing

139

over the walls with the other. His eyes darted between book and stone, feverishly looking for similarities, something, anything familiar.

"A simple clue would be nice," he whined into the air, not expecting anything in return.

"THEY ARE GODS."

"And the snake? The one around the door," he continued. "I have a drawing of him in my journal, and he looks kind of like the one carved into my necklace. What's up with him?"

"HIS NAME IS AAPEP. NOW COME, WE MUST GO."

"But who is Aap . . ."

"I SAID WE MUST LEAVE."

"Okay, okay," Alex conceded.

A low cracking noise from behind stopped them dead in their tracks. They both turned in unison. They stood staring as the next gruesome hound broke free from its stone confines. It roared to life, shaking the stone from its coat. One by one they emerged, each howling and snarling, awaking from their slumber.

The pair didn't wait around to see the outcome. In fact, they *were* the outcome, if they didn't get moving.

The fearsome creatures sprang from their perches one by one and crushed the stone floor beneath their giant paws. Immediately they began growling at each other, not yet aware of their surroundings. Alex originally remembered twelve in all, cast in stone, including the one Anubis had killed.

Looking back as he ran and not paying attention to what was ahead, Alex tripped over a gathering of small clay pots, kicking and sending them scattering everywhere. He stumbled through them and fell face-first into a shallow wooden bowl full of red powder. It was the same red powder that the guard had sparked, illuminating the grand interior of the enormous room. His face was covered, and it reminded him of that time when the carnival came to town and set up their tents on the piers. He had entered several of them, wandering around by himself, coming and going as he pleased. One of the carnival people painted children's faces, and he had to sit still for about an hour waiting to look in the mirror. A thick red paste covered him then. It covered him now.

Alex felt that familiar itching deep inside his nose. It twitched, and before he could contain it, he'd sneezed back into the bowl, sending red powder everywhere. For the third time that he could remember, a large claw reached down and lifted him back up.

"NO TIME," Anubis said hastily.

The hounds gave chase, breaking from their stone encasings as if free for the first time. They were frenzied and ravaging, barking and nipping at each other as much as their surroundings. Scurrying over each other, they were establishing a command or hierarchy; then, as if possessed, they pursued relentlessly.

Their claws dug into the stone floors, leaving crushed stone in their wake. Some jumped to the walls and ran along them, gripping with their massive claws. Destruction and waste behind them, their path clear. They knew their objective now, and it was in the form of a small boy and the one called Anubis. Froth and rage covered their faces. They were crazed. Jumping, bounding over artifacts and each other, leaping from one vantage point to another.

Alex looked behind him and saw one running full throttle along the wall and leap across to one of the huge stone statues, crushing the neck of the carving with its grip. Stone fragments fell and destroyed several stone vases below. Each emitted a billow of green-colored powder as a result. Alex didn't wait to see the outcome. Another massive beast in crazed pursuit bound down the flamed

141

troughs that encircled the room, seemingly unscathed from the fire. Two more were bouncing off each other down the main pathway, snapping and biting as they ran.

Run.

Alex heard it. A quick glance at Anubis by his side and he knew. Anubis was the one. He'd been there, in town. That morning seemed so far away to him now, like centuries had passed. But he was confident now. Anubis had saved him from Jackson. He was the strange dog that had jumped between the two of them.

No sooner did Alex digest that thought when the lead hound leapt at him in one massive bound. As it did, Anubis instinctively shielded Alex with his own body, ducked, and skidded to a stop. The hound was taken unaware and hurdled through the air just inches above their bodies, crashing against the stone steps still several yards in front of them, pulverizing the second step to powder. The hound yelped from its landing and scrambled to regain its footing. It shook off the dust that now covered him completely and turned to attack.

Anubis was on him in two steps. Grabbing the hound around the throat and hind legs, he lifted the monster, then spun and threw the stunned animal against the nearest column. Alex heard something snap, and the animal collapsed without movement.

Another was keeping pace with them to their right, then suddenly veered off aiming directly toward the weaker of the two prey, toward Alex. Anubis reached the end of his long handled crook over Alex's shoulder and caught the demon hound around its neck. Stopping quickly, he gave it a yank, and the animal was pulled backward by its throat. Anubis howled and spun the gasping beast around in a circle over his head, then with a flick of the shaft, he released. The hound went sailing clean through another column and landed hard on a table behind it. The upper portion of the damaged column hung dangerously for a moment, then came crashing down, pulverizing all the artifacts below. Only boulders remained. Alex knew they had to keep moving. They couldn't hold off the attack in here, not for long.

The remaining hounds were closing fast and snapping at their heels. Alex's lungs were ready to burst. He was moving purely on adrenaline now. His only thought was of survival. If he could just get outside, into the open, he'd stand a chance, he thought. He had to reach the doorway. He had to get out. Faster, closer, with Anubis behind him, they dove under the collapsing archway, missing being crushed by the falling head of the carved serpent that slithered up the supporting pillars. They burst through the door and rolled out into the vast desert. The sand was raining down into the opening, filling it fast.

Lying there in the hot sand, it wasn't too long ago, Alex remembered, that he had admired the intricate carvings around the archway. Now it seems it will be lost forever. All of it, lost. Alex feared there might still have been an important piece to his puzzle inside.

Anubis stood facing the opening in the sand as if waiting for the onslaught, ready for battle. Each predator penetrated the opening, anxious for the kill. When the last of the hounds was free from the flowing sand, they circled their prey, pacing and foaming. Growling low, they tightened the perimeter. They surrounded the two, and at the first sign of an attack, Anubis simply and confidently raised his hand.

The air around them jumped, and the demons were gone.

Eight

Alex had closed his eyes at the impending attack, but managed to slit them open just long enough to have witnessed one of the most amazing events he'd ever seen. His jaw dropped well below his knees, and he could've used a forklift to raise it back up. His eyes were open wide in awe.

"Awesome!" a relieved Alex uttered. Alex had enough of being chased by virtually everyone and everything on the planet. He was mentally still trying to wrap his brain around everything and thought that devil hounds were a bit over-the-top, but was glad to be rid of them nonetheless. He wasn't sure what had just happened, but let's face it, it wasn't the strangest thing to have happened to him lately.

Recognizing that his response may have come out as a bit juvenile, he felt he needed to man-up quickly and said, "I mean, uhh, kind of anti-climactic, wasn't it?" His obvious attempt at being cool was too late, and he knew it.

"THEY ARE NOT GONE. I CAN ONLY MOVE THEM. TO STOP THEM, WE MUST KILL THEM," Anubis clarified.

"How on earth do we do *that*?" Alex shot back.

"WITH GREAT PLEASURE." Anubis sneered with a hint of vengeance in his thunderous voice.

Alex looked into his eyes and saw a thirst growing. Revenge.

Something had changed in Alex, too. He'd traveled through space and time, been beaten . . . several times, locked away in a dark cavern with a strange beast he'd never seen before, made friends . . . uh, kind of, he clarified . . . with that same beast, seen more death than any one person should, been chased by dogs on steroids, and

144

was now readying himself to fight an evil and powerful god. *Man,* Jackson sounds like a pansy right about now, he realized.

His mind drifted to his last confrontation with the bully. Would things be any different now? he wondered. He knew the answer. He wasn't afraid of the likes of Jackson anymore. He knew there were much bigger and scarier things out there than simple-minded Jackson Styers. Besides, he had Anubis now. The earlier memory flashed back into his head.

"It was you, wasn't it?" Alex began as sudden feelings of resolve flooded his body. His face felt warm at this realization.

No answer.

"In my town. The Moores' yard. My shed, *my house?* It was you," Alex pressed, feeling desperately close to an answer.

"YOU TIRE ME," came the only response.

They were a good distance from the ramps, at least several miles, Alex guessed. These were the same ramps that lifted the near-dead up to press on at the will of Set. The distance between where they now stood and where the pyramids loomed on the horizon seemed much farther than he remembered. When last he trekked across this part of the desert, bound and lashed under the watchful eye of a guard, he was sure it was a much shorter distance. He must be confused. He'd been through a lot recently and wondered if perhaps he was just turned around.

It had been days since Alex had laid his eyes on this sight, days since he'd seen the sun, felt its rays upon his back. It was still hot. Nothing had changed there, he chuckled in despair. But he stared at this sight in the distance with different eyes now, with contempt, with hatred not toward the innocent souls who toiled endlessly, but rather toward the one responsible for the pain, toward Set.

He glanced up at Anubis, standing tall on his hind legs casting a

145

shadow in the sand easily twice his own, and now felt what Anubis did. It was at this moment that Alex knew exactly what he must do. He simply spoke, "Let's go."

"HMMPPHHTT," Anubis responded in agreement.

And the two were off. Neither knew what the plan was, but both headed on, determined. They moved quickly toward their destination, toward their future. Alex wasn't sure what was in store. The two warriors, friends forged in battle, were prepared for the risks. Each knew it had to be done. Neither spoke of it. They moved on, silent in their thoughts.

The desert sand was soft and made for harder travel. It seemed to slough away with each footstep. They had no water, no food, and Alex couldn't remember the last time he had either. None of this affected his companion in the least. Alex both hated that fact and admired it at the same time. His new friend amazed him. Staring up at him, studying him, made the time pass quicker.

The sun was still hot, but setting quickly, and soon dusk was upon them, providing better coverage from those who may be seeking them out. Alex was growing less and less confident that they had escaped without notice, unaware to Set and his guards, to the hounds that gave chase only hours earlier. They were cautious and dared not start a fire for fear of being discovered, but soon regretted it when the sun dropped below the horizon. The desert heat blew off almost instantly and gave way to the night cold. They decided to take refuge in the cover of the night and sat opposite each other for some long awaited rest.

It was a clear night, and the moon sat high, full in its presentation. Alex was tired from hours of trudging through the hot sand and welcomed the rest. Reaching down to pull off his tattered sneakers Alex said, "Oooohhh, my dogs are tired," and rubbed his feet. His lankiness allowed him to pull his feet up to his nose and take a deep whiff. *"Whheeeeww!* Not so sweet smelling either," he said, pulling his feet back away.

Anubis popped his head up and frantically twisted it left to right. He was ready for a fight.

"DOGS? WHERE?" he inquired, searching intently into the darkness of the night.

"Oh, sorry," Alex said, hesitant to explain. "I meant my feet. My feet are sore and tired. You know, from walking."

"WHERE ARE THE DOGS? YOU SAID DOGS," Anubis shot back, still searching the distance for movement.

"I'm sorry. I made a mistake. There are no dogs." Alex had decided this route would end the conversation faster than if he tried to explain his comment.

Desperately wanting to change the subject, Alex pulled out his journal and decided to leaf through it for more clues. Reaching under his shirt, he took out his pendant, exposing its light. The dull glow was just enough to reach Anubis and light the pages of his journal clearly. He flipped to the page where he'd recognized the familiar hollow rod he'd shoved up into the dead, necessary for their escape. Next to it were the drawings of several smaller items, all identical and in a row. Upon closer examination he believed them to be the vials and the larger cask he used in his explosive concoction only hours earlier.

His heart pounded, his head felt flush. He figured this was too much of a coincidence to mean nothing, to be random. But he couldn't help but wonder who drew them or how they could have possibly known. More to the point, he was angry at himself for not figuring it out sooner. He desperately wanted to share his findings with Anubis, but like most young people, his curiosity got the better of him, and he continued flipping through the pages, eager for more.

There were a few symbols he remembered seeing on the cavern walls that were now spread out before him under the dim light. He had no idea, of course, what the strange bird-like creature was, but the drawings of the dogs, he knew. Oh yeah, he knew them well. They were monsters, vicious and hungry. Not very bright he thought, but strong.

"We can't forget about the dogs, now can we? What the heck is up with dogs lately anyway?" he asked himself quietly.

There was a familiar drawing of the serpent god similar to the one that had almost crushed them during their harrowing escape. This particular one intrigued him, although he didn't quite know why. He ran his fingers over a drawing of a balance much like the one he saw carved into the wall of the tomb as he tried to figure it out. There were many snakes drawn on the pages, too. He was eager to find out more, what this all meant, curious still about the connection between them. People usually think of snakes as bad, almost evil. If there was one thing Alex was sure of in his relatively short time on earth, it was that human nature is consistent. That's assuming he was still on earth, he thought. But likely, if people from home think snakes are bad, then here can't be much different. What does this snake mean to them, though? It can't be good.

"Tell me about Aapep," Alex asked, breaking the night's silence.

"TO KNOW AAPEP, YOU MUST FIRST KNOW RA. TO KNOW RA IS TO KNOW US ALL."

"Look, *yeeeaahhh*, I'm not too sure what you just said, but *aahhh*, I need some answers," Alex replied.

"WE ALL NEED ANSWERS."

"Yes, but I need them *now*. Who's Ra?" Alex implored.

148

"WHEN SUN IS HIGH ABOVE OUR LAND, IT IS RA WHO WATCHES OVER US. RA DISAPPEARS BELOW EARTH AT NIGHT. BATTLES AAPEP."

"Why? Why do they fight?" Alex interrupted.

Anubis shot Alex a look eerily similar to the one that Ms. Flowers would whenever he interrupted her in class with a question. It wasn't his fault. After all, he *was* there to learn, wasn't he? Anubis continued,

"RA IS GOOD. GOD OF EVERYTHING. AAPEP IS EVIL. TRIES TO STOP RA FROM HIS JOURNEY. TO STOP LIFE FROM CONTINUING. EACH NIGHT THEY BATTLE. MOST NIGHTS RA WINS. HE RETURNS NEXT DAY. RA IS HIGH OVER LAND AGAIN."

"Uh, *most* nights?" Alex questioned this particular statement.

"YES. WHEN THERE IS NO GRAIN IN THE FIELDS. NO MEAT IN EGYPT'S BELLIES. DARKNESS WHEN THERE SHOULD BE LIGHT. FAMINE WHEN THERE SHOULD BE FEAST. AAPEP HAS WON," Anubis spoke as if he'd seen each of these. Alex supposed he had at some point or another. Alex had never had to experience real pain until recently. He'd always had the safety and comfort of home, of his grandmother. There was always food, always shelter and warmth.

He realized at this moment that he might never fully understand the suffering that Anubis or the people of Egypt had felt . . . were feeling. True, he'd been beaten and clawed at, attacked even. But it wasn't until he lay beneath the foot of an angry guard not too long ago and witnessed the horrific scenes that played out in front of him deep within the trench that he got his first real glimpse of suffering. This is what Anubis knew. This is what Egypt lived.

Alex shifted in the sand, trying to avoid eye contact with Anubis for fear the tears he was so desperately holding back would come flooding out. He redirected his focus back into the journal and its secrets.

Alex had seen the human shapes drawn throughout the journal, and these particular sketches frustrated him most. He believed that out of all of the drawings, these were the most significant, but he knew he didn't have much else to go on. He was pretty sure the first two were Osiris and Isis, as Anubis had explained them, but he didn't know who the others were. They were all similar, yet different. His heart was telling him that they were all connected somehow; if only he knew how.

Random thoughts were flashing through his head like a computer processing streams of data. He was sure the triangles, three drawn in a row, were supposed to be the pyramids. Okay, so we got that, he tried convincing himself. But the other pictures, like the one of the bull, he had no clue what it represented.

"*Humnft.*" He shrugged and moved on.

"An hourglass?" he spoke out loud. "*Time*, maybe? Time for *what?* Out of time? Time is of the essence, perhaps? Time *travel?* That would be cool, wouldn't it?" Alex thought quietly for a moment, then, "*Hhmmm*, I guess I hadn't thought about it until now. I *did* go back in time, I think. It's a screwed up time, but I *am* here, aren't I?"

Alex strummed through several more pages until, "Heh, I recognize this Du-DUH," he said, pointing and laughing at a crude drawing of what he believed was Anubis. He turned the journal around and showed him. Anubis seemed distant and only gave the drawing a quick glance. He was thinking of tomorrow and Set, Alex determined. It was probably best to just leave him alone.

These three wavy lines he'd seen referenced in other books and recognized them to be water. He mulled its meaning over in his mind as he ran his fingers through his mop of a mane. He was certain of one distinct fact; there was certainly no water here in the middle of the desert. Not that he could see anyway.

"It's a desert, *hellooooo!* Who wrote this journal, some idiot?" he questioned, sounding quite discouraged.

Alex flipped to the inside of the back cover. It, too, was faded from years of use. His eyes popped. He hadn't seen it before, but it was certainly there now, an inscription of sorts. He'd spent all of his time focusing on the pages of the journal and had missed it. Admittedly, he would get like that sometimes. His grandmother had warned him in the past about getting "too caught up in the moment" or "too focused on the little things." She'd say things like, "You need to stop and smell the roses." His typical response was an adult's worst nightmare . . . a teenager with an attitude.

The inscription was worn down almost to the leather itself, but it was there, faint and ghostly. Actual letters and words that he recognized. It was finally something familiar to him. Some letters were missing altogether, but it read:

Ma   is gu d you n you journ   -GM

"Ma is gu d you n you journ? *Whhaaatt? Whose* mother? Who the heck is GM? Journ . . . *AL?* Journ . . . *EY?* Come on man, give me a break!"

Well, he conceded, at least now he had *some* correlation between the carvings and his journal. They all had meaning, just nothing he could use. Great, he thought hopelessly, just great.

"How is a picture of a beetle, a sword even, gonna help me get back home?" he fretted.

"Actually, a sword would've helped," he quipped.

"A SWORD WILL NOT HELP AGAINST SET," Anubis rang.

"Then what do we do?" Alex asked, looking up, startled at Anubis' booming voice. At least now, Alex thought, every time he talks I won't get sand in my hair.

"I MUST GET CLOSE. I MUST ATTACK."

"But how? How do we do that?" Alex said, concerned. In the past several days, though he had actually lost track of time at some point, Alex had been attacked by Jackson, chased by strange men, catapulted through time and space, sunburned, beaten by half-dead guards of some crazed god, beaten more, chased by way too many dogs to count, had no food nor water, and witnessed way too much death. He just wanted to go home. Quite frankly, he didn't want to *attack* anything. He was tired, and all he wanted was to sleep and get home, not necessarily in that order. His eyes began to droop.

"*WE* SHALL DO NOTHING. I MUST FACE HIM ALONE," Anubis demanded.

"Ooohh no, you don't! I don't think so. I'm coming with you. We're in this together. I can help. I *want* to help," Alex pleaded.

"YOU CANNOT HELP. HE WILL KNOW."

"Look. So far, this dude has had me captured, marched me clear across the desert under the hot sun by guards who beat me, then had me thrown into a dungeon, only to be attacked by killer dogs. I'm *so* gonna kick his god-butt, and you're not stopping me!" Of course, Alex realized that saying it and doing it were two entirely different things. He sounded tough and hoped Anubis thought so, too. He just didn't want Anubis to think he was afraid and have that fear be the one reason why his friend wouldn't let him go.

"I WILL GO ALONE. HE CANNOT SENSE THE DEAD." Anubis eyed his new friend, waiting for the next argument.

152

"What do you mean?" Alex perked back up, his attention heightened again.

"ONLY THE DEAD CAN GET CLOSE. UNDETECTED," Anubis explained with the faint glimpse of a twinkle in his eyes. This look made Alex nervous, although he didn't know why, and he looked away.

"SET HAS POWER OVER THE LIVING. HE CAN CONTROL THEM. YOU."

"So, you're saying that the only way I can get a piece of that howling hypocrite is to be dead? That sucks," Alex said, barely loud enough for Anubis to hear. Anubis chose not to respond, and the lengthy silence that surrounded them ate away at Alex. He fidgeted where he sat and poked at the sand with his fingers, stirring it around. He waited as long as he could.

"Too bad I couldn't die, without pain, of course, then come back to life again after I kick his butt," Alex thought aloud.

"NO. IT IS TOO DANGEROUS," Anubis responded in defense.

"I was *JO-KING! Duuhhh!*" Alex blasted back, anxious to quickly take back his remark for some strange reason.

Anubis bared his sharp teeth, and for a moment Alex thought he was grinning. Hopefully it was just gas, he thought.

"THE JOURNEY IS PERILOUS. THE RESULT IS ONLY DEATH." Anubis was almost feverish in his words, hungry somehow. He had one goal right now, to save Osiris. Only Set was standing in his way, and it was obvious Anubis was looking forward to their next encounter.

"You mean it *is* possible to die, then . . . *and then . . . come back? No way!* No way is that possible. But how? *Like zombies?*" Alex's voice crackled.

"ONE WOULD BE DEAD. BUT NOT," Anubis tried explaining.

"Yep, zombies. That's how *we* define them. Well, that certainly helps, doesn't it?" Alex cracked. His head reeled with thoughts of strange creatures, their attack on Set, and, of course now, the walking dead. The drawings in his journal were distant memories now. When did real life become so, well, *real?* he pondered. He liked his sheltered life back home, especially right now. There were no demons back home, no bodies falling from above, no sand in my pants, and certainly no zombies.

The closest thing to a demon he'd ever dealt with back home was Mittens, his grandmother's cat. "Man, I *hate* that cat," he recalled solemnly. That miserable feline was probably curled up in his blankets at the foot of his bed, sleeping. I wish I could sleep, he hoped.

Alex must have dozed off for a moment or two . . . or five. When he woke some time later he noticed the temperature had dropped, and the stars in the sky, constellations he had recognized as a result of spending way too much time with the Captain, had moved on across the horizon. Hours had passed and, when he sat up, somewhat rested from his sleep, he noticed Anubis still sitting in the same place and in the same position. Alex guessed that he hadn't moved at all since their earlier conversation and was happy to see that his friend hadn't left him. He'd been sitting there these many long hours, thinking.

Then he remembered their earlier conversation. Turning to Anubis and brushing the dad-blamed sand from his hair, *again*, he relented, "How can someone . . ." He was cut off.

"YOU MUST COME WITH ME TO TUAT," said Anubis, staring across at him.

"Tuat? Me? *Why?*" Alex wasn't taken totally by surprise, but did hope he'd never hear those words spoken, ever. He was generally much more perceptive. He had an almost uncanny sense when trouble was heading his way, and it had always proved accurate in his encounters with Jackson. But he was dumbfounded by this one, somewhat blindsided and suddenly very much scared.

"YOU WILL BE JUDGED."

"Judged on what?"

"TO SEE IF YOUR HEART IS PURE AND TRUE."

"*It is! It is!* We don't gotta go *an-y-where,*" Alex cried, shaking his head back and forth.

"IF IT IS PURE, WE CAN ATTACK."

"How *pure* is pure?"

"YOUR SOUL MUST BE WITHOUT CONSCIENCE. FREE OF ALL THINGS BAD. YOUR HEART MUST BE AS LIGHT AS THE FEATHER OF MA'AT."

"As light as a feather? *Who?* Look, I'm no scientist, but I'm pretty sure my heart, anybody's heart, weighs more than a feather," Alex tried to reason, but it was plain to see that Anubis wasn't listening.

"ONLY THEN WILL YOU PASS. ONLY THEN WILL YOU BE JUDGED TRUE. YOU WILL TRAVEL TO THE FIELDS OF AARU. PARADISE. IT IS A LONG JOURNEY. MANY DANGERS. MANY DO NOT SURVIVE."

"Oh, sounds lovely. Can't wait. *Uh,* what's behind door number two, please? What the heck happens if I fail?" Alex responded dejectedly.

"IF YOU FAIL, YOUR HEART AND SOUL WILL BE DEVOURED BY AMMIT."

"*Whhaaatt?* DE-who? Who's Ammit?" Alex stammered, not sure

155

if he wanted to hear anymore.

"GODDESS AMMIT IS THE DEVOURER OF SOULS. SHE FEASTS ON HEARTS WHO ARE NOT TRUE. THOSE WHO FAIL."

"Uh, define . . . *true*, please." Alex's mind immediately flashed back to the carving of the creature in the cavern. Ammit must be the horrible beast that stared eagerly up at the heart on the scale, licking its lips. He was pretty sure he didn't want to meet that thing anywhere at any time. Who comes up with these things?

"TRUE IS GOOD. NOT TRUE IS NOT GOOD."

"Of course."

"THOSE WHOSE HEARTS ARE HEAVY WITH THE PAST. WHO HAVE DONE WRONG. THEY ARE NOT TRUE AND WILL BE JUDGED HARSHLY," Anubis continued.

Alex didn't like this, not at all. Now frantic, his fear was getting the best of him. Why do I have to get judged? He was confident that he didn't have anything to hide, but still.

"Oh no!" he said, remembering that Anubis mentioned something about past deeds. What does that mean? It's not like he'd ever killed anyone before. He considered the shed window, even Mittens, and wondered if these would count against him. He did have unusually large piles of dirty clothes all over his bedroom. But he's a good person, right? They can't count dirty clothes, can they? He felt the sudden need to justify his good deeds.

He was always helping his grandmother around the house with cleaning, dishes, and taking out the trash. "Oh snap!" he exclaimed, remembering that he'd complained the last time he took out the trash. If I ever get back home, I'm so going to do what I'm told and keep my mouth shut, he thought.

He was working himself up into a twist and becoming more and more nervous with each recollection of past deeds. He knew deep down that no matter what, it's too late to change them now. The fact that it was too late was what worried him. Remorse began to set in as he pulled his knees up to his chest, buried his head, and started rocking where he sat. Anubis watched him closely. He was a god and had never experienced such emotions. It made him curious.

"If we're gonna do this, then how do we get there?" Alex asked meekly. He'd quickly come to realize that when asking Anubis a question, he generally didn't want to know the answer. He didn't blame him. After all, Anubis had nothing to do with any of this, and he couldn't help his delivery. It's the way he was. He was always short, to the point, and had little to no emotion. He didn't have time for it and, even if he did, he wouldn't know what to do with it. There was no beating around the bush with him.

"YOU MUST DIE."

"Whoa! Unh-uhh. Not me. I knew it. I just knew it. I knew you'd turn on me as soon as you could. I don't think so. I'm too young to die. In case you didn't know, I'm only thirteen years old." Alex had been so focused on what happens once he arrived at Tuat, he completely forgot about how he was going to get there. "What do you mean *you must die?*" he asked mockingly in his best Anubis-like voice.

"SILENCE," Anubis roared, catching Alex off guard.

"Hey, watch it. Shouldn't you try to convince me, instead of scare me?" Alex asked, his eyebrows lowered.

"YOU SHOULD BE SCARED."

"Look, you, you better explain yourself right now or else." Alex didn't have an *or else*, but he wasn't quite sure how to finish his sentence as he often led his conversations with more emotion than thought.

157

"I MUST PREPARE YOU FOR YOUR JOURNEY."

"Uh, *prepare?* What am I, a roasted turkey? What're you going to do, *stuff* me?" Alex laughed uneasily. Anubis just stared back at him. Alex didn't like the look.

"Uh, *that* was a joke. *Hull-oooo!*" Alex's eyes bugged out of his head. He was shocked and pretty certain that this was the first time this discussion had ever been had by anyone before. "This *can't* be real," he assured himself. Alex was sure that any moment now he'd wake up to the warmth of his blankets and his grandmother singing down in the kitchen along with the smells he so longed for right now. No such luck. Before he could say anything else about the matter, Anubis spoke.

"NEED MORE SUPPLIES."

"Sorry about that. But where do we get more supplies?" Alex asked as he careened his head in all directions. "There's nothing here. Nothing but sand and, oh yeah, more sand." He further emphasized by lifting a fistful of the loose stuff high into the air and letting it sift through his fingers.

"WE MUST GO TO MARKET," Anubis answered definitively.

"Market? What market?" Alex looked around again. Still nothing.

"WHEN RA NEXT RETURNS, WE GO. NOW YOU SLEEP." And with that the behemoth laid his head down, pulling the sand up close to him for its remaining warmth. Alex stared in wonder as his giant friend settled in for the night, kicking up miniature dust storms as he did. It still amazed Alex at how large this being was. Anubis was everything that wasn't soft and gentle. He was loud and raw in everything he said and did. Even his thoughts were bulky and rough. Alex ran his fingers through his own dusty mane and shook his head in disbelief. Lying down facing this goliath, he drifted off to sleep repeating the words, "It's not a good idea. It's not a good idea," and the gentle wash of sleep approached him like the cool shallow currents in the familiar harbor that was his home.

Nine

There was still a long night ahead of them, and Alex needed to get some decent sleep. He twisted and turned all night while demons shared nightmares in his head. It was about all a young mind could handle. The sights, the sounds, were real. He could even feel them. His whole body felt the vibrations of his dreams. It was so vivid, so real, that his eyes were forced open.

Anubis was standing tall when Alex woke from the rumble. His back was facing him, ready for the attack. He had placed his crook on the ground beside him, freeing up his gigantic claws for battle. Alex's eyes no sooner opened when he saw something explode up out of the ground in front of Anubis, sand flying everywhere. The moon provided just enough light to see. Alex watched as Anubis caught the airborne hound around its front two paws, rotated, and slammed it to the ground. It yelped as the air left its lungs.

Something else was heading directly at them. The sand mounded as it burrowed toward them just below the surface. It was moving fast and locked in on them. At the leading edge of the burrow, the second hound broke the surface and arched high up overhead, clearing the two already locked in battle. It twisted in flight, then dove back under the sand, disappearing. It reminded Alex of the time when he and the Captain had gone whale watching; seeing the whales propel themselves up out of the water, easily clearing several feet, only to descend back down, piercing the surface and vanishing out of sight. It was impressive; although Alex would much rather see the attack coming. He didn't like the hound being underground. He couldn't tell when or where it was. He watched intently for any movement, readying himself as best he could in the moonlight. Dawn was coming soon, and he'd have more of an advantage, or so he thought.

Glancing over at the others, Alex could see Anubis clearly had the upper hand in this battle. This time it was Anubis who had his opponent around the neck clamped in his teeth. The sand was stained red from the struggle. Feeling desperate, the hound pushed up off all fours and landed his weight against Anubis' lower chest, knocking him back, loosening his grip. The beast reared on him and attacked. Anubis was quick and clutched the open jaws of the hound in his grip, inches from his own throat.

Another hound broke free of the earth in a rush of air and sand. It had eyes on its next meal. Alex had only a split second to dodge the attack. He rolled to his side, then back to a crouched position, poised and listening.

He was aware of his friend's struggle, but could only hear his own chest breathing. Then he saw it. It was heading for him again. The loose sand swayed from side to side as if toying with him. Alex turned and ran out into the darkness. He stumbled several times in the soft sand only to regain his footing and stumble again. The beast was playing with him.

Alex feared running too far from Anubis, so he circled back toward his friend. A few yards from the safety of Anubis' presence, the second hound surfaced again and landed on all fours, still heavy in his pursuit. It was closing on Alex fast. Alex was now only feet from the protection of Anubis when the fierce hound batted at his head, sending him rolling through the night.

Spitting out the sand, he could taste it. Blood. The beast must have cut his head, and a raw mixture of blood and sand was trickling into the corner of his mouth. He sprung up and spit again, this time wiping his mouth and the side of his head. He confirmed the cut when he pulled his hand away, and it was covered. From the amount, it looked to be pretty bad, but he had no time to worry about that.

Alex looked around feverishly, expecting the onslaught. The hound was gone again. He was beginning to feel like a toy mouse, and didn't much like it. His senses heightened, Alex heard the now familiar echo of it breaching in the still night.

The hound sailed through the clear sky at Alex. This time Alex was ready. He slid his hand behind his back, groping at the sand. Got it! As the rabid beast's eyes locked onto Alex, it was too late. Alex had snatched Anubis' golden crook from behind him and jammed the rounded end of it into the soft sand, propping up the other end, meeting the beast in flight. The hound landed, impaling itself through the chest as the pointed end of Anubis' crook pierced its heart. Its full weight landed on Alex, pinning him to the ground. Alex had killed it.

He pushed with all of his remaining strength, but it was no use; the hound lie lifeless on him, pushing him into the soft sand. He couldn't move his body. He was, however, able to move his head and watch as Anubis battled his own demon.

His friend was standing with his feet dug into the sand behind him, still gripping the beast's jaw in his large claws. The hound was hysterical with rage and twisted its body around as much for freedom as for attack. Anubis lifted the hound high up off the ground by its jaw and it hung, feet scratching at air, trying to land a blow.

Anubis bayed toward the sky like a wolf toward the full moon, and the sand shook with fear. Alex heard a hollowed crack followed by a strangely grotesque ripping noise that filled the air.

With extreme force, Anubis separated the hound's lower jaw from its upper and tore it back to its neck. This one was dead, too. Holding it out at arm's length with one giant claw, he dropped it as if it were a piece of garbage. Anubis stood, triumphant. Stretching his arms into the air, giant claws clenched.

Once again Anubis howled in triumph. The open sky seemed to welcome his announcement. Alex heard a distant whimper. Too small and far off to be a hound, must be a jackal, Alex thought.

Still pinned under the crushing weight of the hound, Alex gave him his moment and then,

"Uh," he began, having to pause to cough out both the blood from his drying throat, and release the diminishing air in his lungs from the weight of the beast. "A little help here," he uttered, spitting out sand and blood the whole time.

Anubis quietly turned and gave a *sniff* in Alex's general direction. Alex assumed he was still in his primal beast mode and that he was just checking to see if the hound that covered him was dead. Anubis reached out and lifted the giant carcass off his small friend and removed his crook from its chest, discarding the limp body to the side as if it were a mere afterthought. He wiped his claw down the entire length of the crook to clean the enemy's blood from the shaft and returned to where he had previously camped.

"WHEN RA NEXT ARRIVES, WE GO TO MARKET."

"Right," Alex agreed softly, still trying to convince himself that dying was a good idea. The remaining hours of the night were short, but Alex did his best to take full advantage of them; that is, if sleeping with one eye open most of the night counted.

The first twinkle of daylight was peeking over the horizon, and Alex had sand stuck in more places than, well . . . places. It was a lot like when he was little, playing down at the shore and building sand castles. How ironic it was, he thought, as he rubbed the crusty sleep from his eyes, that he could recall actually building pyramids out of sand at one time. The only difference was that this was real, or at least as real as real could get.

His first shock back to this reality was the hunger that groaned in his stomach. It had been a long time since he'd eaten, and he pushed at the softness of his mid-section. He glanced over at the limp carcasses of the two hounds currently being torn at by vultures, while he noticed three jackals off in the distance trying to figure out exactly how to approach the fresh kill. It was all too possible they were afraid of his friend, who was also beginning to stir about.

The sight of last night's carnage didn't help his hunger any and made his insides turn. I suppose I could wait until we reached the market, he convinced himself.

Ra had arrived.

Market. Right now, that sounded pretty nice to Alex. Food sounded even better. Alex peered off into the distance and saw no signs of the market, of anything, and his shoulders slumped. This market that Anubis spoke of must be awfully far away. That meant more sand and a lot more sun to Alex, two things he would gladly do without right about now.

There wasn't much to breaking down the campsite, and Anubis had already gathered his belongings. Alex patted himself down and was comforted to know that both his journal and the pendant were still safe. They left for the day's journey without a word. About forty paces out from the site Alex turned to watch the jackals attack the carcasses. Fresh meat was a luxury in this wasteland, one that scavengers rarely ignored. Maybe today would be uneventful, Alex hoped.

With each passing step Alex watched the sun rise higher. He'd made every effort to walk behind Anubis and stay in his oversized shadow, hoping to squeeze out even the slightest of cooler temperatures. It wasn't until hours of trudging through the deep loose sand did they rest. Alex was tired and sweaty from the trek. He plopped down to empty his sneakers and took a moment to actually look around.

"What the . . ." Alex jumped back up, hopping on one foot, struggling to get the other sneaker back on. He couldn't believe his eyes. He looked back at Anubis with his mouth wide open.

"Did you see this?" he asked, pointing back from where they had just come.

Anubis turned and saw a familiar sight. It, however, didn't seem to faze him quite the way it did Alex. It was as if he had expected something like this to happen.

"HE KNOWS YOU ARE COMING."

Despite having just covered a vast amount of desert and enduring hours in the blistering sun, what Alex actually saw made his heart drop. He was sure he was delirious from the desert heat. But there it was. He saw it with his own two eyes. They had just traveled across nearly half the darn desert, or so it seemed, and despite his disbelief, they were still only about forty paces from where they had camped several exhaustive hours ago. They hadn't moved at all.

"SET SENSES THE LIVING. HE SENSES YOU."

Alex, both desperate and out to prove himself, was determined to beat Set's trickery, so he ran full speed, charging up and over the next dune and beyond, until he ran out of breath. Panting and bent over, hands on his knees, he looked up, and there stood Anubis in front of him exactly where he had been moments before.

"What? How did *you* get here?" Alex asked, spinning around for

another look. *"Oh nooo!* This can't be! How can this be? I don't get it," Alex whimpered. Nothing had changed. The jackals were still busy tearing and fighting over the scraps of what remained of their last battle, only forty paces from where they stood.

"SET."

"How do we fight that kind of power?" Alex begged, dropping to his knees with his head buried in his hands.

"COME. WE GO TO MARKET." Anubis raised his arm, crook in his hand, and grabbed Alex with the other. Once again the air around him jumped, and Alex felt a warm pulse pass through his body.

They disappeared.

Alex lurched forward, clutching his stomach. His head was swimming, and the sun, the entire landscape, whizzed by in front of him, slightly out of focus. The whole experience lasted only a moment. He heard a single popping noise inside his head and landed hard to the ground, out of nowhere. Instinctively, he rolled to all fours and readied himself for more projectile vomiting. Sadly, all he could muster on his empty stomach were violent dry heaves. He bucked like a Brahma bull throwing a rider for the first time. It was only after a few minutes of this rather embarrassing act did Alex realize Anubis was standing right next to him. He turned his head skyward, eyes squinting from the direct sunlight.

"Don't E-VER do that A-GAIN!" Alex yelled. Then he heard it. It was faint, off in the distance. It was people. Animals. Both. He could hear metal clanging and banging together. Everything; faint, but it was there. He looked toward the sounds. The sun made it almost impossible to see anything but the haze coming off the sand. He got up, shaking himself off.

"What did you do?" Alex barked.

"I MOVED US."

"What? Like those dogs?" he questioned somewhat nervously. He wasn't sure which he liked less, having to deal with Set's trickery or having his atoms scrambled like his morning crab cakes just to be wrenched around and dropped to the ground, heaving his guts out. He couldn't help but wonder if he was any better off. Alex knew the answer, but asking the question made him feel better.

"YES. LET'S MOVE."

"You and I are gonna have a talk when this is all over," Alex said, waving his hands in the air, and they headed off toward the sounds of the market. Several times Alex turned around just to make sure that they were putting some distance behind them.

They had much desert to cover and, despite the sounds of the market quickly filling the stale desert air, the trip wasn't any less grueling for Alex. Anubis, on the other hand, seemed indifferent, almost defiant. The sun was at its highest in the sky when they came to rest about a half-mile outside the limits of the marketplace. Anubis laid out their plan, giving Alex an idea of which items he needed for the preparation of Alex's journey to Tuat. Once again, Alex felt uneasy about his decision.

It was decided that their best chances were to have Anubis keep to the outskirts and shadows of the marketplace and have Alex enter in alone. A ten-foot tall god that looked like a dog may just attract a little attention. Then add fifty pounds of gold on him; yeah, that'll go over well. Alex laughed to himself. He listened intently, memorizing each ingredient. Only after Anubis had repeated the ingredients for the third time did Alex react.

"Dude, you don't have to tell me. I know how important it is. Do you think I *want* to die?" Alex didn't know who he was trying to convince more, Anubis or himself.

167

They were committed to their roles. Although each knew how dangerous it was for them to split up, neither mentioned it. Alex could tell that it grated on Anubis knowing that he had to wait in the shadows and hide while Alex went in exposed. Waiting wasn't one of Anubis' strengths. There was comfort in knowing that Anubis had been successful in protecting him before, but concern in that he may not be so lucky next time.

Alex trotted off toward the large sandstone pillars that capped the entrance to the hustle and bustle that played out inside. He could hear bits of music between the clattering and clanking that came from within the walls. The noises grew louder and the walls taller. He only glanced back once at where he'd left his friend, and Anubis was gone. He must have spun around three different times, his eyes searching, blanketing the vast openness of the desert. Nothing. Vanished. Fear gripped him. He was alone again, and he began to panic.

"Where'd he go?" he began. "I don't see him. What's happened now?" He tried to calm himself. No luck. It wasn't until his last turn that he saw the sulking figure dance in and out of the shadows, working its way along the left side of the wall in the distance, low to the ground. Anubis was there. He hadn't left him. He was okay.

"Get a grip, Chronos, you big baby," he poked at himself. The wall wrapped around the marketplace and rose nearly thirty feet in height. Walls this tall were usually built to either keep someone out or hold someone in, he thought, looking up at the imposing structure. With the added reassurance that Anubis wasn't too far away, he took a long deep breath as he looked up at the pillars marking the entrance and walked in.

It had been awhile since he'd seen such commotion, and he paused just inside the walls to allow for his brain to wrap around

168

everything he saw. Tan buildings lined both sides of the wide road, itself trampled hard by years of foot traffic. Tattered colored awnings jutted out from the occasional building, providing a rare opportunity away from the sun.

Then there were the people. They moved up and down the road, from vendor to vendor, picking and pawing over everything in sight. Each person was covered in some colorful array of cotton from head to toe. A fashion train wreck, he mused. Not that he dressed any better, he thought, as he looked over his own torn and tattered clothes.

So far he'd ripped his jeans. Of course, his old sneakers were losing their soles, which didn't matter since they were practically melted off from the hot sand, and he'd been dipped in dead-guy stuff. Probably still stink, he thought, as he whiffed at his armpits.

"Wheeeooowwah! That smarts!" he said, jerking his nose away quickly and coughing. A rather large woman waddled past and shot him a fairly indignant look, then shot her nose up in the air and walked off. He decided to avoid close contact with anyone from that point on.

The road was wide, and vendors lined the sides, up tight against the buildings. They were packed in and waiting to pounce on anyone showing the slightest interest in their wares. These were trained professionals skilled in the art of subtlety and sales. It was a game to them, each trying not only to make the best deal, but also to outsell the others.

There were carts and bins everywhere, full of anything and everything a person could ever want. His eyes widened. It was strangely out of place. At a glance, everything looked somehow normal, but upon closer inspection, years of pain and suffering had filled the cracks and crevices of the lives in front of him. In fact, if one was to scratch the surface of the scene before him, they would find that life itself had been eroded away, replaced. It was like Christmas, only with no cheer, too much blazing hot sun, and loads of misery.

"Oh yeah, and no stinkin' trees for hundreds of miles," he grumbled. There were large items and small ones, tall ones and fat ones. There was even a section where small animals were penned off for trading. The sound of sheep, camels and other even stranger four-legged animals filled the air. So did the odor. *"Phheww!"* On second thought, he decided it may be better to stay close to the animals, considering his own scent.

There was an area stacked with large clay pots, each about three feet high and almost as big around. A dozen men stood in a circle, looking into each of the pots, arguing and yelling. It was the same chatter, in fact the same scene, as the market back home. He couldn't understand a word they were saying, but Alex recognized what was going on. They were haggling over the goods and pricing, each trying to better the other in an already terrible deal. It was almost laughable, if it weren't for all of the suffering surrounding them.

He wondered if perhaps this market was what people referred to as an oasis. Not the typical oasis that provided much needed lifeblood from the heat of the vast desert, but rather an oasis from evil, from Set. It was a fruitless attempt at survival, at existence. His influence had made its way in through the gates, past the protective walls, and had trickled into their lives.

It was on to business. Alex made his way to the first cart on his right. Ducking in under its tarp, he feverishly searched for any of the ingredients he needed. His eyes danced as the list rolled through his mind. Oils, frankincense, cotton, something called natron, and tars.

Admittedly, Alex didn't want to know the function of a few of these. After all, it was his life they'd soon be messing with. He figured less is more in this particular case.

The first cart proved to be of no help to his mission as it was chucked full of clothing. Piles and piles of color washed across the cart in no particular organization. It reminded Alex of his own bedroom. *I'm going to have to do laundry when I get home,* his mind drifted. *That's assuming I get home.* Although fresh clean clothing right now would be a welcome change from his torn jeans and stained shirt, he didn't have time now for vanity.

He picked at the layers on the cart just like everyone else, thinking this would help him blend in more. A short elderly lady next to him looked at him and spoke. Her face was dark and wrinkled with age. Her silver hair stood out boldly against the vibrant stripes of the many layers of clothing she wore. *Man,* how do these people do it? he puzzled. It must be 140 *THOUSAND* degrees outside! Unfortunately, Alex had no idea what she said and, in a panic, all he could do was just smile and nod. He was nervous. He didn't want to draw any attention, so he moved along quickly to the next cart.

Alex correctly surmised that this wasn't going to be an easy task. He had no idea what some of the items looked like and had no way of paying for them even if he found them.

The next cart didn't prove any easier. It looked a lot like the last cart with the same wooden wheels and the same sun-faded tarp. The difference was that this one had dozens of hand-carved trinkets, mostly shiny objects and playthings for small children. He didn't understand why someone would think these items could sell out here with all of the misery surrounding them. Hope, he thought. Still, the children flocked to the cart like the teenage girls back home

171

in Ms. Trudie's shop. In fact, the similarity between these young kids and those stupid girls was almost scary to him. The attraction to all things shiny, the drooling, he mused. Yep, pretty much the same.

The next cart he came to was empty and abandoned. It looked as if nobody had occupied it for some time. It was creepy how it just stood there, empty and worn, a continual reminder of what lay ahead. The third cart had vials and casks, not unlike those that Anubis carried, full of different powders. Anubis; I wonder how he's doing? A half dozen of the locals were crushed in against the wooden sides of the cart, each trying to get their hands on the treasure inside these small bottles. Waiting his turn, Alex took the opportunity to look around and soak in the normalcy of it all. No hounds chasing, no terror waiting around the next corner. He could finally breathe easy.

"Aaiieeee!" he squeaked out a girlish yelp that sent chills up his spine and caused all sorts of looks. A roar of laughter followed, and he turned red as he looked down at his legs. Something had grabbed him; in fact, two somethings, one around each leg. Two small children, a boy and a girl, had grabbed at him from out of nowhere. Apparently hide and seek was popular here, too. He was seething from fright. Looking up at him, they giggled and ran off between the carts and down the nearest alley, jumping and dodging piles of sheets that had apparently just been dyed and laid out to dry. It may have still been his nerves settling or perhaps the familiarity of the game, but Alex was sure that he'd seen the little girl before.

"Well, I'm glad I can provide you with some entertainment," he said under his breath trying to push his heart back into his chest. Once the laughter died down, most of the crowd had dispersed. It was his turn at the cart. He ran his fingers across the tops of each vial, stopping to pick up one or two for further examination. *Hhmmm*, the colors were the same, he noticed. The last two he held gave the most promise for his needs, but just to make sure he popped the tops of both and inhaled.

One smelled like moth balls while the other had a more pleasant odor. It was the same odor he'd smelled in the cavern, masked by the stench of decay and rot. He put the stoppers back in each, wondering just how exactly he was going to buy it. The men gathered at the clay pots grew louder in their ruckus, and Alex turned his head to see what the commotion was all about. Two men had started shoving each other and shaking their fists in anger.

"That's it! If I can't pay for the items, maybe I can trade for them," he said with sudden realization. The bartering system has been around since the world started spinning on its axis, and Alex figured that trading goods was commonplace in a market such as this. He couldn't think of anything he had that others would want or need. More specifically, what did this particularly thin middle-aged man need? Alex had nothing.

Just then shouts of anger were hurled down from above. There, leaning almost her entire body out of a second story window was a stout woman casting her stubby hand into a fist and directing it downward toward this poor fellow. Alex could tell they were married right away. He'd seen henpecked before. The accosting lasted nearly three whole minutes which, Alex presumed, probably seemed like three whole lifetimes for this man who now stood pale before him. Yes! I've got it!

Alex quickly unclasped the thin silver and leather bracelet from around his wrist and held it in his hand. He stared at it for a moment. It hadn't been anything particularly special. It was just something he'd picked up at Ms. Trudie's shop one time about a year ago. He'd bought it because all the 'cool kids' at school wore ones just like it. This bracelet was one of his last attempts at vanity that he could remember. It had always been too loose on him anyway, but it just may fit around this woman's wrist.

The assault on this poor embarrassed man had caused the crowd around his cart to move on. There were looks of pity cast in his direction, something Alex believed the man was used to.

With the bracelet in one hand and the small vial of red powder in the other, Alex raised them both into the air. At first the man didn't understand as he was still busy shaking off the brunt of his wife's attack. Alex nodded once to his left hand, once to his right, and one final time upwards toward the window. The man understood immediately. A mouth full of crooked and stained teeth filled his face with a smile. He snatched the bracelet out of Alex's hand and bounded up the stairs that led from the street. Alex had his first item.

Feeling rather proud of himself, he, too, moved on down the line. It was dizzying how many carts and vendors there were. He stuck mostly to the shadows, what little there were, to keep from drawing too much attention and made quick work of the next several carts. Eyeing each as he passed, there was jewelry and even someone selling flasks of wine. No need for either, he thought.

There were few carts with food, as was expected, and these were closely guarded. The stealing of food had become commonplace for many of the people in the area, if not for themselves, then for their family members who suffered and toiled away on the ramps looming in the far distance.

The first of the food carts was stocked full of dates. Alex knew what they were only by sight. He was tempted to take some when the man wasn't looking, but was too scared of getting caught. He couldn't risk that right now. Besides, in some cultures they cut off peoples' hands for that. Alex needed his hands; he was kind of fond of them. Still, he was starving. He'd never eaten any dates before and had no idea what they tasted like. His mouth would have watered at the sight of them if it hadn't been so dry for the past several days.

Darn desert, sucks the life out of everything, he thought. He tried licking his lips, but his tongue got caught. His frustration was growing, frustration with the heat, with the pain, with the one who left the necklace on his front stoop so long ago. It was the same necklace that started all of this mess, the very necklace he still wore around his neck.

Arguments began in his head. Water would be nice. Good luck there. Water in the desert, *hah!* Heat must be getting to me. Alex had made it about one-third of the distance down the dry road when his eyes lifted.

"Oils!" His voice cracked. He needed those oils; frankincense in particular, but others, too. He'd used all of it during their escape. A worthy sacrifice, Alex thought.

This cart was set up with tiers of wooden shelves four rows high, running the length of what was almost eight feet of cart. The base of the cart was also lined with colorful items, liquids mostly, that reminded him of home again and those darn kitchen jars. He was confident that if any cart had it, it had to be this one. He started rummaging through the containers, large and small. He paused at even the slightest of similarities until he'd exhausted all but the top shelf. There were only a few vials left, and he was getting impatient.

In fact, he'd spent so much time meticulously going through each and every one that even the lady sitting next to the cart was beginning to get upset. She'd been watching him carefully with eyes like a hawk. She must have sensed something different about him. Alex could feel her cold stare icing up his neck. He'd stretch high up on his toes to reach the farthest of jars and she'd lean in, just to make sure. She was far too old to stand up for a better look. He'd pull back empty handed and she let out a, *"Humpptt."*

Alex realized he had nothing left to trade with. Even if he had, this old lady wouldn't trade anyway. She'd obviously lived a long, hard life and wasn't about to let anyone get the better of her. So she sat, leaning on her cane, staring and calculating each and every movement people made. Alex believed her entire life had been reduced to just sitting in the market watching people. By the looks of her rather full cart, she hadn't sold much. Probably because she's so scary, that's why, he thought. Must be a lonely life, he pitied. He at least had his grandmother, and she had him. If for nothing else, his grandmother had raised him right. It was always about respect between them.

But this poor old woman who reminded him so much of his grandmother, he had nothing he could give to her. He searched for something, for anything, for an answer. What would he have given his own grandmother? "Of course! That's it!" She needed attention and compassion. She needed respect. She needed someone to show her kindness. It didn't matter to Alex anymore about what he needed. It was about what this poor forgotten soul needed.

He'd noticed how difficult it had been for her to move around while she'd been busy watching him. The chair she sat in all day was hard and made of wood with no form of comfort. The hot sun couldn't be helping much, either.

Alex looked around, the woman still fixed on his every move. A piece of cloth, an old tarp perhaps, had been tossed underneath her cart. "Yes," Alex shouted, and he snatched up the roll. When he did, the old lady gasped. How odd he must seem to her, he thought. Here he was, a stranger, trying to take *her* tarp. It didn't belong to him, and they both knew it. Alex recognized the all too familiar posturing as a result of dodging blows from Jackson his entire life. He knew she was poised and ready to beat him senseless.

As she raised the wooden stick that was her cane, Alex swiped it out of her hand, poked one end into the corner of the tarp, and thrust the other end hard into the ground. He ran the remaining two corners up over the old lady's perch and fastened them to the corner posts of her cart. She was covered from the sun. Instant relief. She rocked back into her chair, puzzled at this stranger, her mouth slightly open.

Alex looked around for something else. There was more he could do. Then he remembered the dyed sheets drying in the alley where the two little rugrats had vanished. Alex disappeared out of sight for just a moment, then returned in the process of neatly folding one of those sheets into a square. The old woman looked even more puzzled than before. As he approached, she leaned back defensively as if he were going to attack. When she did, Alex tucked the folded sheet behind her back.

The woman fidgeted in her chair for a second, then leaned back into the new comfort. A slight smile formed on her dark face as she looked up at him. Her stern eyes softened. Alex smiled back at her, then leaned in and kissed her gently on her forehead. She reached out and held his hand in silence. She didn't have to say a word. He knew. Alex turned and walked away.

He took about three steps, and she called out. He didn't understand a word of what she was saying, but looked back as she was motioning to her cart, her long thin fingers pointing to the top shelf. He was slightly confused, but pulled down the one vial he needed most and placed it into her frail hands. She gave it back. He had his next item. He had the frankincense.

He walked away, tossing the bottle from one hand to the other, smiling. But it wasn't because he'd gotten what he wanted. He felt good inside about what he'd done. He helped that old lady. A simple act of kindness was all it took. She smiled. They understood each other.

Alex felt good about himself at that moment. If it weren't for all of the sadness around him, he would actually have been happy. This brief encounter with the old woman, someone's grandmother, made him long for home even more. He missed her.

But he and Anubis had a job to do first, and he knew that. He accepted it. He didn't necessarily like the idea that he had to die in the process, but if it meant freeing all of these people, Egypt, from Set's reign, then it had to be done. He was in it for the long haul.

Then he remembered Anubis. I wonder how he's doing. Where is he? Alex looked across the road toward the wall and noticed a break. A portion of the old wall had crumbled over the years, and through it he saw a rather large figure lumbering in the distance. It was out there staring back, pacing. Anubis was watching. Alex was comforted again, knowing his friend was still there. He pressed on to find the remaining ingredients.

Ten

When he saw her she was tending at a table about halfway down the market on the left. There was some shade there provided from the building behind her. It was a good place for selling stuff, he thought; highly visible. It was the same table that hundreds of other vendors tended; a cart, really, on wheels and made of wood, covered high by a colorful tarp to block out the day's passing sun.

She was a beautiful young girl, just about his age, with shoulder-length brown hair and strong features. Her skin had been darkened by years of sun, and two large brown doe eyes pierced her face. Alex noticed a deep sadness in them, even from this distance. She was thin like he was, but stood only to about his nose, which, as far as Alex was concerned, was perfect. She'd been toughened by the years of misery that he'd only seen in the past few days, but there was a softness to her that Alex picked up on even from where he stood.

This was new territory for him. He'd never spoken to a pretty girl before. In fact, he purposely avoided making any contact with them, if he could. There were times he had no choice, of course. Like in Biology, when the teacher assigned Tina Schultz, the prettiest girl in school, to be his lab partner. Let's just say, it didn't go over well. In fact, it went horribly, horribly wrong.

Most girls in his town were either stuck up or too busy hanging out with Jackson, or both, like Holley Matteson. She was pretty, too, but she knew it, and that's exactly why Alex, and most boys for that reason, never even bothered with her. He was often confused as to why girls make it so hard for guys. These same girls who knowingly flaunt their beauty and look down on most boys, most people in general, are the same idiots who ask, "I don't get it. Why doesn't anybody like me?" he spoke mockingly. "Well, being stupid is only the second reason why nobody likes you, *shheesh*," he responded to his own question.

This one was different. He could tell. He'd spotted her from a distance and he was pretty sure she'd seen him. As a typical teenage boy, uh . . . man, he strutted and strolled, taking his time and pausing at each tent, listing over each peculiar item. His mind was blank. Women will do that, he thought, smirking. That's what the Captain always said. "They'll make you gaga," he'd say.

But there was a real reason why he was here, and it was important. Despite this, strange feelings deep inside pulled at him. Boy, she sure is pretty. I wonder if . . . No! He snapped back to his task.

There are things I need to do. I'm not here to look at some dumb girl, no matter how pretty she is. I don't care how soft her hair is and how it lifts gently in the wind. Her skin *is* flawless. She has a . . . wait! And again reality was cruel.

No. Anubis. Right. He glanced at her out of the corner of his eye, beneath his locks. *Crap!* Stop it! He was getting angry at his sudden lack of control. He had a mission after all.

Is she staring at me? Did she notice me? *Oh no!* Did she see me staring at her?

Something had hit Alex in the face causing him to sputter like a water spout. A pair of birds had been killed and strung up, hanging from the cart in front of him by their feet. Alex had walked straight into them face-first, feathers and all. Spitting a mouthful out and flailing about, he looked over at the girl just as she turned away, giggling. His face reddened and grew hot from embarrassment. He was stuck, just like the jackals from this morning, not knowing exactly what to do.

In the efforts to control his movements and save himself from further embarrassment, he accidentally bumped into the cart, spilling the hot tea he'd just seen the man pour. It went all over the front of the poor man. Alex quickly ducked behind the next cart, all the while trying to quiet the man and avoid any further eye contact with the girl.

The enraged vendor behind the cart was a portly fellow about the same size and shape as Crunch, but darker skinned. He was wearing what passed for a local flavor of clothing in an oversized colorfully striped shirt and loose tan pants, only now they had a tea stain on them. A round flat hat sat upon his head. The man was furious. *Sheeesh!*

It appeared that walking into a man's dead birds was a capital offense around here. The man continued to rant, fist raised, even after Alex had disappeared around the corner. In fact, Alex was pretty sure he'd seen a wooden spoon come sailing past his head at one point.

Alex now had two goals; get the remaining items on his list *and*, of course, meet the girl. Anubis would *freak* if he knew. He shouldn't, Alex thought angrily. *I'm still focused on defeating Set. He shouldn't get upset with me. Maybe she has something on the list that we need*, he tried desperately to convince himself. *It would be foolish not to see what she's selling. It may be important. In fact, it may be the most important thing on the list.* He'd never know for sure unless he checked it out. After all, he owed it to the mission, to Anubis. Alex knew the logic was a bit twisted, but so were his feelings right about now.

He was still doing his best trying to avoid being noticed and kept to the edges of the buildings, peeking and poking in and around the carts. He was afraid that he'd embarrassed himself in front of this young beauty, so he decided to approach her cart from another direction. His hope was that she'd think it was some other idiot who had made a fool of himself. It didn't work. Her eyes caught him on his approach, and she giggled even more. "Stupid girl. It's not funny," he muttered. She . . . she *is* beautiful, though. And he was lost once again. Even more so close up, he realized.

It wasn't normal. Not like him. But he strolled right up to the front of her cart and stood. It was as if his feet were gliding, something pulling at him. His stomach felt like it was spinning, and his head felt light. Everything was dim and hazy. He was pretty sure he was having an 'out-of-body' experience. Of course, he'd never had one before, but if he had, he was pretty sure it would feel a lot like this.

This girl, this beauty, was an oasis herself in such a desolate place. Her mere existence was sending Alex into a tailspin. She was so distracting, so foreign to him, that he spent the next several moments arguing with himself. Now what, idiot? You can't turn around because you'll look stupid. Act natural. Look at the cart. See what she's selling. What *is* she selling? I still need tar and something called natron. Look down, idiot. Don't stare. She'll think you're a freak. Great, then I'll be a freak in two countries, two different times in history. Perfect.

Alex was sweating, but this time it wasn't from the hot sun beating down on his head. This time he was nervous. *Man!* Why couldn't this be like it was back in the caveman days? I could just grunt and club her over the head, drag her off to the cave, and be done with it. *Ahhh* yes, the good old days, he thought, laughing to himself. I said look down, idiot. You're drooling.

He started slowly. He turned each item over as if inspecting it for flaws. He acted every bit the expert on each item. The items in this particular cart were different somehow. They were more personal. He paused every now and then, giving a firm *hhmmm* or an occasional *ahhh*. Each time he did, he watched her hold her breath, waiting as if each item sold was going to somehow save her from this miserable existence.

Between each of those breaths she took, she would turn and tend to a young boy sitting strapped to a chair behind her; a toddler, not yet old enough to speak, but obviously plenty old enough to make a mess of himself. There was a colorful array of different foods smashed and squashed all over his face. The little guy had more food on him than in him.

At first Alex could only think of how wasteful it was to give this kid their food if all he was going to do was mash it up and wear it. But then, Alex remembered Captain Shovers always saying, "It always tastes better if you wear it first," every time he would spill something on his face or down the front of his shirt.

The difference here was that these people couldn't afford the luxury of taste. Food was much more of a necessity and given out sparingly. Alex could only conclude that this boy was greatly loved by this young girl and her family if they were willing to sacrifice something as rare as food for him.

Alex watched carefully, but when he saw her staring at him, he turned back to the business at hand. Anubis was waiting, he reminded himself, recalling that patience wasn't a strong suit with him. He was probably fuming right about now. Alex returned his efforts back to mulling through the cart, most of which he had already looked at, twice. Unfortunately, he had no use for bowls and plates or any for pots and dishware. These were cupboard items, the same stuff his grandmother pulled out for dinner each night. But he saw nothing; nothing useful anyway. Not for him.

Alex became frantic. Was that it? Was he done here? No, I can't be. He needed something. He needed a reason to stay at this particular cart longer. He knew he couldn't let this opportunity pass. She was far too pretty to let slip through his fingers.

She must have sensed Alex was done and, after forcing another spoonful of green mush into the child's mouth, only to be spit right back up again, did she turn and take a step toward him.

"Do you see anything you'd like?" She smiled at him, pulling at her hair.

"Wha?" Alex was almost knocked off his feet. This girl, this beautiful young thing who stood here in the middle of nowhere, not only had the voice of an angel, but she spoke English. He understood her. He was caught off-guard and had no idea what to do. He stood there fixated and staring into her deep brown eyes. She stared back. A fly buzzed around his face and landed on the corner of his mouth, causing him to swat away at it. He snapped back to reality. Suddenly all sorts of questions flooded Alex's head where blankness had once filled it, and he couldn't get them out fast enough.

"You speak English? How can you speak English? Where did you learn it? Who . . ." and the girl interrupted him and placed her hand on his shoulder. He turned to goo instantly. For as long as he could remember, the only time a girl, let alone a cute girl, laid a hand on him, it was to likely smack him.

"A man. He came years ago. Taught me this strange tongue. Your tongue. He was dressed like you," she explained.

"Wh-who wa-was he? What wa-was his n-name?" He stammered through each syllable like an infant learning to speak for the first time. It dawned on him that this girl, out in the middle of nowhere

184

and centuries away from where he lived, was speaking English better than he was.

"He was strange like you," she said. Alex rolled his eyes. Great, she already thinks I'm strange. She accidentally brushed his hand with hers, and Alex's mind went blank. He was a teenage boy, after all. What else would be expected? It was as if everything else around them disappeared. Nothing else existed except the two of them. "He told me to call him Gerry."

"I *like* Gerry," Alex said, smiling. The young girl laughed. It was his turn to giggle. She seemed to like it when he smiled. He flushed.

"He spoke of strange places and people. He always seemed far away in his thoughts. Papa said he wasn't right. Crazy. But I liked him." She looked through him and spoke almost as if she were in a trance. Alex was intrigued, to say the least. Now, at least, he had a reason to stay longer and talk to her.

"What's your name?" asked Alex. He was slightly shocked since this was the first time that he could remember ever speaking to a pretty girl without being forced.

"My name is Tadinanefer," she spoke softly and turned her head away.

"Tadinuniferer?" Alex stumbled. She laughed, and his face felt red and hot. Stupid. Stupid. Stupid.

"No. Tadinanefer," she corrected him politely. He was getting flustered by a pretty face. Flustered? Impossible, he rejected, his armor was as woman-proof as any man's, even the Captain's.

"Tadi-who-di-whatta? Tadi-mani-petty?" Just stop would you, you're embarrassing yourself, he thought.

"No. Ta-di-nan-e-fer," the young girl explained patiently.

"Umm," Alex scratched at his forehead. "Do you mind if I just call you Tad?" he asked embarrassingly.

"Tad is fine." She smiled sweetly, batting her long lashes and giggling. She was definitely flirting with me, I can tell. I know women. Yeah, right. But what he did know is that her voice was as soft and sweet as an angel's. His heart fluttered and skipped every time he looked at her. When their eyes caught, it was like he was flying high above, looking down on them.

"Tad-uh, umm, what does that mean? Your name," he stuttered and stammered through his words.

"Tadinanefer. It means 'She who has been given beauty.'" Her face blushed slightly.

"You got that right," Alex blurted without any thought. Now he was blushing. Idiot; why don't you ever think before you speak? His face wrinkled up in frustration.

"Is something wrong?" she asked as sweet as a mother to a child.

"Let's just say that it's been a long time since I've spoken to someone, uh well, someone like you." He smiled. He was pretty sure he was flirting, although he'd actually never attempted such a daring feat before. Battling bloodthirsty devil-hounds was even easier than this.

"My name is Alex," he said, pointing to his chest. As he did, his finger caught on his shirt and exposed the smallest bit of his pendant. She gasped and stepped backward. What just happened? he wondered. It was obvious to Alex that she was frightened. My necklace; had she seen it? Did she recognize it? Judging from her reaction, he felt it better not to ask. But it did leave an uneasy feeling in the pit of his stomach. Alex quickly covered it up and desperately tried to change the topic.

"*Heh*, uh, what are you selling?" he asked.

"Well, Alex." Tad looked into his eyes again a bit more relaxed. "I willingly sell anything from my home that will save my father

186

from the clutches of evil and return both he and my mother home safely. I sell sturdy dishware and well-stitched clothing, slightly used, but fine. Do you not need any?" There was desperation in her voice as she thrust a garment up into his face. These were literally the clothes off their backs. She *was* desperate. Based on the abundance of items in her cart, Alex guessed that sales had been slow for her lately.

"You mentioned your father? Your mother? Where are they?" he asked, but he was sure he already knew the answer. She looked at him with a mixture of disbelief and apprehension.

"My father was taken weeks ago to replenish *his* workforce. My mother was distraught with loss that she left shortly after to find him. She works on those cursed ramps, watering those that were once men. I'm all that's left behind to care for my brother." She motioned toward the young lad who now sat slumped in his chair, food dried to his cheeks, sleeping.

"*His?* You mean Set?" he asked, afraid for the first time to look directly into her eyes. When she didn't respond immediately, Alex looked up and saw that her beautiful brown eyes had filled with quiet tears. He lifted his hand and wiped them away gently with his forefinger. They were warm. She was warm. Her skin was soft.

"Yeah," Alex continued, "him I've met. We've got a dance to finish later." Alex shot a furious look back at the entrance to the marketplace.

Tad's tears had soaked into her dry skin, and Alex's comment left her with an inquisitive look on her face. How odd he must be to her, he thought. He could only imagine what she'd been through, and now this, him. He shows up out of the blue, dressed all weird and acting all stupid. She didn't ask for this, for any of it, he scolded himself. Yet, despite all of this, she was kind to him. Alex knew

187

instantly that his grandmother would like her. There can't be many left in this land whose hearts haven't been blackened by Set's far reach, he surmised.

"I have a friend. He's waiting for me to return. I, uh, I can't stay long, unfortunately. I wish I could, but I got this thing." He knew any further explanation would likely result in even more confused looks. He desperately wanted to leave a good impression. So far, so good, he thought. Of course, the fact that he was still upright and breathing through both nostrils was a good sign. He'd never made it this far with a girl before; not with a pretty one--pretty, very pretty. He was back in his trance again.

"My father has always told me that you can tell much about a person by what he buys," she said, looking up at him from under her heavy eyelids.

"And what does this stuff say about me?" Alex played along, suddenly coming to and pulling out his recently gathered items.

"You hold in your hands oils and powders, frankin . . ." She caught her breath and looked up at Alex. Her darkened face turned almost pure white. She was scared. Scared of *him*.

"What do you now seek?" she asked as if she already knew the answer.

"Ummm, *okayaaay*. I need tar and something called natron. It's white and . . ." Alex stopped. Her already large eyes had grown in size. She stepped back and virtually stopped breathing.

"I know what natron is. There's none here. You must go. Please go," she cried as she turned and hid her face.

"What? What is it? What's wrong? Did I do something, say something wrong? Man, I always screw things up when it comes to pretty girls." He hadn't realized he'd said this last part out loud.

"You hold the tools of the wicked souls. Those who take the

men and dispose of them. Those who work for *him!*" She glared at him and her soft brown eyes turned narrow and wicked. "You must leave!" She retreated even farther and placed a protective arm around her brother. He was suddenly cast back to PSA, standing in front of Ms. Flowers trying to explain away the interruption of her class yet again. She wouldn't have any excuse, nor would Tad. That much was apparent.

"Look, whatever you're thinking, it ain't it. You're wrong. Please listen. I'm doing this to *help* those people. To help those like your father, your mother. Please, I can't explain it." He had no sooner finished pleading with her when the sound of crushing stone echoed at the entrance of the market. Panic filled the walls. He could feel the rumbling beneath his feet.

One had slid and crashed sideways on the run into the right entrance pillar as if it were drunk on rage. Alex had whipped his head around already knowing what caused the thunderous crash.

He heard the hardness of chiseled stone crush with each passing step. Sand doesn't crush like that, he thought. It wasn't from *this* beast.

The other ran along the top ridge of wall to the left of the marketplace. They had locked in on Alex. The sudden explosive appearance of the hounds brought Alex back to reality in a hurry. He remembered what he was here to do. He remembered its importance. His explanation would have to wait. Tad would have to wait. He had to react. He had to save himself, to save Tad.

The beast at the entrance moved slowly and almost grinned in anticipation of what was about to happen. Great, Alex thought, he wants to play with his food. Even from a distance, this creature dwarfed everything around it. The nearest man, standing frozen in fear next to the beast, only reached its thick shoulders. The demon leaned in toward the man, uttering and growling, its drool hanging from its gums. Except for the movement of the hound, all else seemed as if it were suspended in time. Man and beast were face to face. Slowly its jaws opened, bearing all of its teeth. Its mouth was clearly larger than the poor man's entire head. Alex turned away; he couldn't bear to watch the horror. He trembled in anticipation of the unspeakable act. He heard the beast announce its intention with an earthshaking roar.

Only, the noise hadn't come from the hound at all; it came from behind the man. The man, however, passed out cold and dropped like a rock to the ground. A camel penned up in the corral behind him had let out a squelch of fear as a result of the hound's close proximity. All manner of creatures from inside the pen joined in to create a symphony of howls and grunts that echoed off the large walls of the marketplace. That same noise caught the attention of one hungry demon-beast. It moved closer to size up its next meal, pacing back and forth in front of the pen. It could have easily destroyed the wooden structure with little effort, but this was a meal worth savoring every delicious detail. Alex likened it to fine dining where even the preparation of the meal was important.

There was movement out of the corner of his eye, and Alex turned. The second massive hound, still trailing along the top of the narrow wall, wasn't as easily distracted. It had Alex's scent, and it was moving fast. The monster pulverized the stone wall with each passing step.

Two more steps and it was airborne, jumping down and landing on the roof of the nearest building. The wooden roof creaked loudly under the hound's weight. Years of sun had splintered the boards and loosened the ties. It slipped, took one step, then hesitated. Too late.

The rotted wood buckled under the stress, and the building swallowed the beast whole. There was a moment of silence followed by what Alex believed was the clamoring of the great beast trying to upright itself in such a small room. Someone inside screamed. A picture of the woman popped into his mind. No, not the woman, he realized; it was the man.

It sounded like furniture was being tossed around inside.

Alex heard yelling from inside. Not screaming, but yelling. He recognized that voice. It was the stout woman who had leaned out of the second story window earlier, the wife of his henpecked friend. She didn't sound scared, like the rest of the people scurrying about. She sounded angry. He couldn't believe it. Was she *yelling* at the *beast?* She was. She was yelling at the beast. Alex could only imagine the hound inside the tiniest of rooms sliding across the wooden floors trying to get traction, trying to get away from her. What a sight, he mused briefly.

The great monster let out a yelp of both surprise and pain.

The sounds of a great battle echoed through the window and across the marketplace. Alex's mind filled with horrible images. It must be vicious. He was afraid it was killing them. The sounds grew louder and louder. He was certain there would be no survivors. Something large suddenly slammed hard against the wall.

The structure shook as if a bomb went off inside. A crack appeared on the exterior wall and ran down to the first floor. Dust funneled out of the open window and floated away. Debris could be heard bouncing off the tops of the carts below. It was quiet. All Alex could do was stand and watch.

A blast of wind pushed at Alex as the hound came sailing through the small second story window in an explosion. Too large to fit, it took half of the wall down with it. The stout woman could be seen behind it with a large wooden table leg in her hand swinging away. A blow landed on the backside of the demon as it threw itself to safety. It had a look of fear in its eyes as it exited and flew through the air.

The landing was even less graceful. Its front leg caught on the tarp of the cart below, and the beast's momentum flung it, tail over head, smashing the cart to pieces and skidding on its side a good dozen feet into the open road. It lay there for a moment not moving. Alex desperately wished for it to be over.

Was that it? Uh, no, guess not. The hound rose slowly as if filling its lungs with air for the first time. It was definitely shaken. Alex stood, watching. The beast lifted itself from the ground, stumbled forward, and dropped again. Oh yeah, it was shaken, Alex thought happily. He was still skeptical. He'd seen these demons in action. He'd fought them before. It would take more than a tussle with an angry woman and a two-story fall to stop them.

His mind raced with options. Should he go forward and attack the stunned beast? He could run away. What about Tad and her brother? What would they do? He knew he had to stay and protect them, if he could.

The hound was standing again. This time it shook to remove the dust from its coat. It eyed Alex, gave a sniff in his direction, and headed for him at a full run. Alex turned and ran. He didn't know where, but he certainly knew why. The road that dissected the marketplace was a scene of pure chaos with people running and screaming everywhere, and now Alex was one of the masses. The hound stayed on him despite every twist and turn Alex executed trying to lose the beast in the madness of the street.

It wasn't until about his third lap around the marketplace flailing about wildly that Alex felt the full force of the batting to his shoulder from the hound. He was lifted high into the air and sent hurtling into the middle of the area that staged the clay pots. Alex landed face-down in an obliterating crash, destroying virtually every pot in the bunch. The sky was suddenly filled with the colorful powders that had filled them. He lifted his head out of a mound of yellow powder, inhaling its rotten egg smell as he did. Sulfur, he thought.

"*Auughh*. Gross."

The men who had been here earlier finding joy in their banter had quickly dispersed upon his landing and were now scattered, fleeing for their lives. As the hound circled for his second and final approach, Alex wiped the sulfur from his face and rolled over into the next pile. He felt like a turtle placed on its back trying to turn over. Rolling back and forth, he was now covered head to toe in a white powder, giving him a ghostly appearance. His hair was pure white, his clothes covered.

Billows of dust clouded the air every time he moved. But he had to move. The hound was getting closer. Finally able to free himself from the pile and push through the broken clay pots, stepping over the sulfur, Alex headed away. The hound moved faster toward its kill, leaving a path of destruction in its wake. It ricocheted its way through the food carts, tipping over and spilling the one that held all of the dates.

Terrified people, adults and children alike who once ran into hiding, were now running out into the open after the food as the dates rolled out into the road. Hungry children were scooping up handfuls and shoving them into their mouths, while the older ones were gathering bunches in their clothes. How strange it is that even in the face of danger, primal survival instincts such as the basic need for food can overcome fear, Alex thought.

It wasn't until he was about to reach her cart that Alex realized Tad and her brother had disappeared. He didn't have time to worry about that right now, not with this thing on his butt. The glimpse of a tiny foot gave away their hiding place from beneath the cart, and Alex was suddenly relieved. The tarp had been dropped in front of the shelves and hung to the ground, effectively concealing everything behind it. The chasing hound was momentarily distracted from all of the commotion in the street. Alex saw his chance. With the hound looking away, he slid under the tarp like a runner heading for home plate.

The hound turned back. Alex was gone from sight. The beast slid to a stop just in front of Tad's cart where its meal had been, looking confused. It paused for a second and started sniffing about.

Lying on his stomach next to Tad, her brother between them, Alex placed a protective arm over the two and a finger to his lips, motioning for them to be silent. They couldn't see the beast on the other side of the tarp pacing only feet in front of them, but they could hear it. Every step, every throaty breath was amplified ten-fold to their ears. It knew they were near. Alex couldn't afford the luxury of fear right now, so he turned to anger. Where the heck is Anubis when you need him? If he's out there sleeping while I'm in here battling demon-mutts, I'll have to kick his butt, too.

There, as he lay under Tad's cart, hiding with her and her brother from the hound, he saw it. Grease! Someone had used it on the axle of the cart. The grease was likely animal fat, but it was close enough, he thought. Alex carefully and quietly reached over and picked up a small wooden spoon and a vial that had fallen to the ground during the riot. He had to reach a bit, and he knew, by doing so, he risked being seen by the hound, but he had to get it. There was a bigger picture here, and he was a part of it. He needed this stuff. It wasn't tar, but it was the closest thing he could find to it. He used the spoon to scrape off all that he could without risking further exposure. The vial was filled to the brim and the stopper shoved back into its opening. It was messy and gross, but it was full. One more item remained on the list; natron. They'd just have to do it without the stuff. Anubis could improvise, he determined. He'd have to.

Tad had been watching the chaos in the street unfold in front of her as she peered through a small rip in the tarp. Alex watched her. She was no different than those who were now busy trying to feed their hunger. Seeing the others, she, too, instinctively rose to take her share for her and her brother. Alex motioned to her, grabbing her hand and pulling her back down next to him.

"No! Stay here. I'll get them for you," he instructed in a whisper. He only had one chance to do this. It had to be perfect. He searched for something . . . there, that's it. Grasping the spoon in his right hand, he gave his best pitch.

Nailed it. The spoon landed against a small clay jar three carts down. Apparently all of the time he'd spent practicing earlier this summer had paid off. He suddenly didn't feel as guilty about the shed window anymore. Again, not my fault, he clarified. Yeah, right; what shed? It exploded, didn't it?

The hound turned away hesitantly and lumbered toward the sound to investigate. It was now. He had to move while the creature was distracted. Alex pulled himself back under the hanging tarp and out into the open.

"No. Wait," Tad yelled after him, reaching out. It was no good. He couldn't turn back now. The hound stopped in its tracks, and Alex stood frozen. The great canine slowly turned its head. Its mouth was cracked like . . . like . . . *a smile?* Alex suddenly wished he

195

was invisible. A rabid white froth had formed on both sides of the beast's snout. Its eyes were glassy and fixed. It had the scent again.

Heh . . . Heh . . .

Alex was confused. Wait. What? Did that dog just laugh at me? Then an all too familiar feeling set in. It was fear. Oh crap. Gotta go. Gotta go. *"NOW!"*

Alex took off toward the fallen cart still surrounded by the crowd of people fixed on their own next meal. The demon closed the distance between them in about four strides. Alex could feel its breath on his back. It was moving fast, and any people in the way fell like bowling pins.

Alex had always been quick on his feet. It came from years of running. It wasn't like he practiced running or even exercised. He ran out of survival. Flashes of Jackson whisked through his head. What a jerk, he dismissed. No time for that now. Where the heck is Anubis? Alex braced himself for the impending attack. The hound was still in the playing mood, or perhaps it was just tenderizing the meat. It leaned into Alex hard, on the run.

Alex took the hit solidly, but was still able to control his fall. It went just as he'd hoped, and he rolled up next to the pile of dates, scooping several in his hands and shoving them into his already full pockets. The fearsome mass of teeth and muscle needed at least half of the road to slow down and turn itself around at that pace. Alex was betting on it. He took this time to grab several more dates and shove them into his own mouth. If it weren't for what felt like several broken ribs and a cracked spine, that was cool, he thought.

As for the dates, they were okay, he reckoned, but they went down like the fruit of the gods. Juice and pieces of dates covered his mouth and smeared the white powder across his face, and he looked much like Tad's younger brother. The hound circled as Alex headed back toward the cart, toward Tad.

Alex was beginning to understand these creatures. They were big. They were strong. They were hungry, but *man*, were they dumb, he concluded. Kind of like Jackson. He laughed at that thought just a little inside. It hurt his ribs. He knew he couldn't outrun it for long, so he needed to use its weakness against it. It was in a flat-out run, and they were closing in on Tad's cart fast. Then he remembered. That's it! Jackson.

He'd escaped his first encounter with the big oaf many years ago by using what the television called an 'ancient Chinese fighting style.' *Well,* that's what they said. Alex realized just how silly it all sounded now.

It was late one evening when he'd visited Captain Shovers on the deck of the Mermaid to watch old movies. Guy movies. Blood and guts. Explosions. This night they were showing old martial arts films, the kind where the guys wore long, braided ponytails. Alex remembered how funny it was to hear their voices dubbed over in English and to watch their mouths move, never quite catching up to the words.

He only had a split second to execute his next move. The words *"here we go again"* streamed through his mind, and in one fluid motion he turned on the run, took two steps backwards, and dropped to the ground. Shocked and moving too fast to change its course, the beast had no choice but to jump over him and try to clear the cart at the same time. As the hound passed mere inches above him, Alex reached up, grabbed both of the hound's ears, and pulled down, threw his feet into its hulking chest, rolled backwards, and pushed off hard into the monster's mid-section, using both its own weight and momentum against it.

It went tail-first through the back wall with the force of a cannonball. Blasting out the other side, it left a hole big enough for a car to drive through.

"WhoooWaaahhh." Alex snapped into his best martial arts pose, karate-chopping at the air. Tad was staring at him wide-eyed from underneath the cart. He crawled in under the tarp with her.

"Miss me?" he asked with a smile as he reached into his pockets and pulled out a handful of dates, giving them to Tad and her brother. He figured he'd earned the right to be a little smug given everything he'd just done. She smiled. The three of them forced the last bits of dates down their throats and waited.

They could see the dazed beast through the hole in the wall from where they hid. It was lying just outside the wall. If it weren't for its large chest heaving up and down, Alex would have thought it was dead. The demon struggled to get up, wobbly at first and unstable on its feet. It had hit the wall hard. Alex smiled at that. It shook hard, trying to rid itself of both the debris covering it and the dizziness it felt. Searching around for clues as to what had just happened, the beast locked in on the three hidden humans, took two steps, then stopped. What was it doing? Alex wondered. Why did it stop? He sat up for a better view. The beast had caught the scent of something. His eyes searched. It was sniffing the air around it. There. There was something else, something beyond. Anubis!

The beast turned slowly. Anubis stood tall and still in the bright sun, his long shadow cast across the desert sand. The hound shot out of its stance like a loaded spring. It was going after Anubis now. Anubis, however, didn't move a muscle. "Why isn't he moving?" Alex spoke low under his breath. "Move idiot, move."

"*Move!*" Alex yelled at his friend.

But Anubis didn't move. He stood firm. And when the hound lunged, Anubis simply raised his giant hands and caught it around the neck at the last possible second.

The hound choked and tried to swallow. Anubis had cut off its air supply.

He twisted its thick neck and pulled the beast apart in one singular motion, separating flesh and fur from bone, much the way a fisherman de-bones a fish.

Alex couldn't help but think how much it sounded like someone had wrenched together a roll of packing bubbles. Innards and flesh fell to the ground in a wet mass.

All that remained was the grizzly sight of the hound's head, still in Anubis' hand, its skeleton hanging from it like the tail of a kite blowing in the breeze. Anubis simply let the remains drop to his side as if they were nothing to him. He looked indifferent at the fact that he was just attacked by some freak of nature, as if it never even happened. He stood motionless and still once again.

"*Dude!* About stinking time!" Alex yelled with a mouthful of smashed dates dripping off his tongue. "Have a nice nap, did you? Could've used you a little sooner. We're dying in here, you big lummox!"

"No. Stop. Don't agitate the creature," Tad pleaded.

"Oh. It's okay. We're friends." Alex realized how strange that must have sounded as soon as he'd said it. Tad looked at him oddly.

"I *told* you, I'm here to *help*," he explained as if she understood. He knew she didn't.

The other hound had, at some point during all of the commotion, moved past its taunting and teasing of the frightened animals in the pen. It had been snacking on some poor bird, likely one of the easier preys lashed to the fence with a string. Feathers flew from its powerful jaws as it tore into the snack, pinning it to the ground with one of its sharp claws. It must have sensed the violent death of the other hound and raised its head.

A gruesome howl filled the air announcing both its pain and its intent.

Alex whipped his head around to the street. *Oh, crud!* Alex cinched his eyelids shut at the sound. Everything in the marketplace stood silent.

"Forgot about him," he mocked. Looking up from under the tarp, Alex watched as the deathly howl stirred up a storm of noise from the animals in the pen. A camel, which had just about enough of this nonsense, reared up and kicked the hound square in the snout. The unsuspected blow knocked it off its feet and through the fence. Judging by the expression on its face when it stood, it realized that this wasn't the easy dinner it had hoped for. It raised its hackle and growled back at the camel. The hound sniffed at the air and licked its lips. It had a new scent. It had Alex.

Alex was worried he'd placed both Tad and her brother in danger. *It knows we're here,* he thought. He was right. The hound moved directly toward them, and Alex saw a maniacal look wash over its face the closer it got. *That can't be good,* he thought, shaking his head; *not good at all.*

He had to lead the demon away from here, away from Tad and her brother. He had to do everything to keep them safe. With a burst of misguided energy, Alex rolled out from under the cart and charged directly at the beast head-on, catching it off-guard, but only momentarily. The hound leaned forward and shifted gears as if to say *bring it on.* It was moving fast.

They were like two drivers playing chicken, each waiting to see who would flinch first. Alex knew he wouldn't stand a chance in a head-on collision with this beast. Its skull must be inches thick. Closer and closer they closed the gap between them, neither straying off course. Only one would survive. He knew this had to be perfect; he couldn't miss. Alex was close enough to see the blood trickling out of its snout where the camel had introduced itself earlier. The hound jumped at him from its final steps. Alex's mind flashed. *Now!*

Alex slid lengthwise under the belly of the beast, once again using his finely honed baseball skills. The giant flew right over the top of him and landed, confused. It skidded to a stop several yards away, digging its claws into the hard-packed sand. Alex had already pushed himself back up and kept right on running. He didn't dare stop.

Behind them Anubis erupted through the wall without breaking stride. He came through the same hole that the other hound had created. Because of his enormous size, he didn't quite fit and sent debris everywhere, his gold armament gleaming in the sunlight as he crashed through the carts next to Tad and slid to the center of the street.

Once again a chilling thunder reverberated off the sandstone walls. It was different than before. It was an announcement.

Screams once again filled the air, and people scattered at this sight. Terror walked the streets again, uninvited. Alex didn't even turn around; he knew Anubis had come back. He knew the familiar roar. He could count on his friend. A little late, but he's here now, he thought. It was almost as if the people in the market had gotten used to the demon hounds and their destructive nature. Let's face it, Alex thought, they were only after me anyway. But this new beast, this creature that they had only heard about, his story passed on from generation to generation, it was *real!* Now that was cause for shock. No wonder they were screaming, he thought. "I'd scream, too," he said to himself. "Heck, I did scream."

Anubis stood tall in the center of the marketplace, his chest heaving, pushing out cold air from his lungs despite the hot desert sun, breath cold enough that only someone, or something, who deals with the dead could produce. People were scurrying about like scared mice. This time Anubis was the predator and the hound was the prey.

Neither beast nor boy had time to worry about Anubis at this point. One was busy chasing while the other was busy being chased. It was a deadly game depending on which you were. Alex headed straight for the broken clay pots with a plan, the same pots that had given him the ghostly hue. In fact, the mere sight of him must be as frightening to these scared people as the hound that chased him, he thought. The hound was in close pursuit. His plan had to work. He'd only have one chance. He had to stay ahead of the beast. As Alex passed the piles of clay and yellow powder, he reached into his pocket and removed the two small stones the guard had left behind. Timing was everything. The hound leapt.

Two things Alex knew about sulfur from Chemistry class. First, it stunk. Bad! Second, and . . .

"Please don't try this at home," he yelled as he passed the yellow pile, giving two quick chips of the stones.

Alex twisted and let sparks fly.

A burst of hot air lifted his hair. He heard three long and painful yelps.

". . . it burns."

The hound fell to the ground, engulfed in flames. It bellowed out the most terrible of sounds, writhing in agony. Men, old women, even small children came out from hiding and closed in on the beast, carrying anything they could to finish the job. The predator had finally become the prey. Alex didn't stick around for the final death blows; he kept running, out the entrance and into the desert, grabbing a cotton tarp left blowing in the wind from the battle; the same desert he so desperately wanted to forget. He'd done it. He'd saved Tad. Oh, and killed two mutant dogs at the same time, lest he forget. He was exhausted, but his legs didn't stop running.

It wasn't until Anubis had caught up with him did he calm himself. He knew Tad and her brother were safe, for now. They walked some distance away from the marketplace, both dressed in silence, before Alex broke down.

"The natron. I didn't get the natron. I'm sorry, so sorry." He collapsed into the sand, sobbing. Anubis simply reached into his pouch and removed a straight-bladed knife and one of his empty vials. Drying his eyes on his shirt, Alex saw the knife approaching his head and instinctively ducked out of the way. Anubis grabbed him and held him down.

"*Wait!* What're you doing? Help! *HEELLPP!*" Alex screamed. It didn't matter. There was no one. He was too tired and weak to fight back. He was defeated, and his eyes closed, waiting for the strike.

"BE STILL," came the thunderous roar. Anubis scraped as much of the white powder out of Alex's hair and from his clothes as he could, filling the vial completely.

"NATRON," was all he said.

Alex just stared up at him.

After a moment he looked back at the marketplace. He had to leave Tad for now. It was time to go. They had much to do. He'd be back. They had a long journey ahead; a difficult one, a deadly one. Alex looked up.

"Hey, wait up," he yelled to Anubis who had already started off into the desert and was tucking the cotton into his pouch as he went. He stood, weak as he was, and did his best to run up the dune after him to catch up.

They walked on silently for a while. Alex was thinking of Tad, how beautiful she was, how soft and sweet. Her eyes; *I could get lost in those eyes forever*, he recalled dreamily. He shot a glance up toward Anubis, just to make sure the big ox wasn't doing some sort of magical thingy again and reading his mind. He was fairly certain *that* would be embarrassing. Still, she was beautiful. He drifted off once again.

Anubis just walked. He was as determined as ever. His purpose was clear. Alex redirected his own focus. He knew his friend would need his help. He didn't know how, but that didn't matter. His plan was to be there when he did; only, *uh*, on time, not late like Anubis was, he scoffed. Alex, being thirteen years old, couldn't bear to keep quiet for too long.

"You're not going to tell anyone about me crying, are you?" Alex worried quietly.

"WHICH TIME?" Anubis returned.

"Shut up," Alex retorted.

"YOU ASKED," Anubis said with what was a definite smile.

Alex didn't much like it here. It was strange to him. He began summing it all up in his head. *Hot, sticky, uh, oh yeah, DAN-GER-OUS! Fluffies from hell. I mean, who the heck comes up with these things? Some dude whose parents didn't love him as a child. Parents, heh.* His thoughts led him astray.

Mmmm, boy, I miss gramma. Did she even know I was gone? It had been the weekend when all of this first started. He wasn't so sure that it was a question of time anymore. *How much time had passed?* he reflected. *A couple of days? How long had he been in the cavern with Anubis?*

Bigger questions, ones with no real answers, began to overwhelm him. Were the days even the same here as they were back home?

Had he been here longer? Was time even measured the same here? He was confident of one thing. He wasn't home. He wiped sweat from his forehead, smearing the remaining white powder, the natron, across his face.

Alex had been through so much and had no idea what the heck was going on. He still had no answers, at least none that could help. His journal, the necklace; they held the questions, *maybe* some answers, but none that he could tell. So far it was an old book and some pretty jewelry. Alex held firm in the belief that they may yet give him the answers he needed. Until then he'd just hold on to them, he conceded, as he patted the journal in its hiding place.

Alex's mind leaped ahead. There was no room for more questions in his throbbing head, but still they came, uninvited. What was Anubis' plan? How are we going to defeat Set? How do you defeat a god, was one of the more difficult and more pressing ones to tackle. I guess with another god. Good thing I happen to have one handy. *Wait, I gotta die?* What the heck. How's *that* gonna work? That's not cool. Still, then what? Does Set *really* know we're coming for him? A moment later he got his answer.

Eleven

Anubis actually heard it first as a result of his canine-like abilities, but it was soon after that Alex heard the rumbling. The rumbling gave way to howling, then he felt it. The wind was picking up. His tussled hair lifted with each gust. They pressed on over the next dune and saw something off in the distance, beyond the great pyramids. It was huge, and it was growing. A sand storm of immense size and strength rolled across the dunes, heading directly for them, and by the time it reached the pyramids, it was easily fifteen stories tall. The percussion it created ahead of itself blasted the structures and those that surrounded it like the secondary wave of a nuclear explosion.

The poor men, thousands lashed to each other, were tossed about like balloons on a string, flapping in the wind. They were entangled and beaten against the ground, against each other, still connected by the line. None could escape.

Surprisingly, even the mammoth pyramids did little to slow the horrific storm as it whisked past them and bore down on the two companions. Mesmerized, the two stood in awe at the sheer magnitude and strength of the storm. Alex's jaw dropped, his hair now whipping in the building wind.

"SET," Anubis roared.

Instinctively, they both turned and took off running back toward where they came. The sand was loose on the slope of the dune, and Alex kept losing his footing, reduced to crawling up the side on his hands and knees. Anubis was much faster and led Alex by several yards. It wasn't until he was at the top of the dune did Anubis turn, with outstretched hand,

"COME ON BOY, MOVE!" he barked with the force of a thundercloud.

There wasn't enough time for Alex to clear the dune on his own, so Anubis leapt and, in a single bound, was upon Alex, grabbing him around the waist and hoisting him up and to his back. Alex held on desperately, knowing that one slip and he'd be buried, lost forever. Anubis jumped, and in two, was leading the downward side of the dune. Too late. They couldn't escape. They were hit with a wall of sand so hard it toppled the two, and they separated. The storm pushed on Alex like a falling leaf in the wind. He twisted and bounced so many times that he'd lost his direction and almost his consciousness, not knowing whether he was coming or going. At this point in time, it didn't matter where he was; he just didn't want to be here.

Anubis could only gather enough strength to pull Alex, lifeless, toward him. He covered him, shielding him from the storm. The sand ripped at Anubis and tore down to his flesh, peeling away hair and skin. Anubis howled at the pain.

His earthshaking cry was snuffed out by the roar of the storm itself. It seemed to lag on the two, hovering and pounding, burying them inch by shredded inch. There was no shelter and the only thing to do was to wait it out. Hours of torment went by. Anubis' breathing had slowed, and Alex was getting worried. His friend, although strong and powerful, couldn't keep this up much longer. And then it happened. Anubis stopped. Everything stopped. The wind, the sand, Anubis. Alex struggled to lift the weight of his friend off him.

"*NOOO!* I can't lose you, you big dumb animal. Get up," Alex yelled as he shoved Anubis' limp body to the side and wiggled out from under. He wasn't breathing. Alex was frightened. Not like rabid-beast-dogs-chasing-you frightened, but more like I-don't-want-to-be-left-here-alone frightened. He leaned in to listen. No breath. No movement. He became frantic. "What do I do? Wait, what was it? Tip . . . open . . . seal . . . blow . . . push? Was that it, or was it push . . . tip . . . open . . . sweep . . . blow? Where's the seal come in? Crap! I wish I could remember." He was running out of time. Furious with himself, Alex decided anything would be better than having his friend die on him. He knew it was selfish, but he didn't want to be left here in this strange place alone. That means I have to put my mouth against his, his whatever that thing is, he conceded reluctantly. A mouth? A nose? A snout? Despite his dire situation, the teenage boy surfaced. *Ewwww, gross!* There's doggy drool on it. He's got *snot* on his snout! He's got *snot-snout! Awww, man.* That was the last thing he thought would ever enter his mind. Kiss a dog, he repulsed. *Blecth!* No way! No stinking way. He thought of all those he loved; his grandmother, the Captain, Ms. Trudie . . . *Tad?* Perhaps. Anubis? Yes, Anubis. And he leaned in,

"Ew . . . ew . . . ew . . . ew . . . *eewwww!*" he said as he squinted his eyes closed. He wasn't quite prepared for the deed, but was going in anyway. "Anubis better flipping appreciate this," he fussed. "His breath stinks!"

"WHAT ARE YOU DOING?" boomed Anubis in his echoed tone.

"*Yaaaaaa!* What the . . . ?" Alex screamed and pushed away. "I thought you were dead! You stopped breathing." Feeling embarrassed, he responded more sternly, "It's called mouth-to-mouth, or in your case, mouth-to-stinky-snout! I was *saving* your *life! Dude,* don't you *ever* brush?"

Alex sat back shaking off the shock that Anubis wasn't dead.

208

"What the heck happened?" he asked.

"IT IS THE SAME WAY I WILL JOURNEY WITH YOU TO TUAT."

"*Whaaa* . . . You really have to start letting me know these things, *uh*, preferably in advance," Alex shot back. Alex had no idea what Anubis was talking about, but was too mad to ask for details. Looking around, Alex sized up the damage from the storm. Far off in the distance, the desert was speckled with bodies and debris. The landscape had changed from the storm. It was obvious that Set didn't care for these people. But it was more than that, Alex thought. It was as if these people weren't even alive to Set, like they didn't even exist. They were nothing to him. Their lives meant nothing. His thoughts drifted back to Tad. She'd endured so much. He *had* to help. He was *going* to help.

Alex looked back at the marketplace far in the distance. The protective walls surrounding it were piled high with sand. It had funneled in through the entrance and spilled into the road. Fear flooded his mind. Was Tad okay? Was she safe? Did she and her brother find shelter in time? Anubis placed his heavy paw on Alex's shoulder and motioned ahead of them, toward his destiny.

It wasn't long before something else loomed in the distance. He hadn't paid much attention to it before. He'd been distracted by all of the pain, focused on the people. But it was there, just like in his history book. If I ever get back home, I am *so* reading that book, he told himself. He could easily picture the large volume propping up the end of his comfortable bed. Alex had seen several photos of it in the past. But this too was different, just like the pyramids. He recognized right away what that difference was. This one had a nose. All of those in his book, in fact in any book, the nose had been broken off, missing. But not this one. Not this Sphinx.

There it sat, untouched by years of erosion yet to come, years of wind beating down on it, sandblasting it; and before that there would be years of water lapping up against its sides, rain pouring down on it. Alex remembered reading in a magazine once that scientists had no idea exactly how old the Sphinx was. They had called it an *en-ig-ma.* He wasn't sure what the word meant, but it was the same one they used to describe it. Besides, he liked the word. En-ig-ma. An unpopular belief, the article said, was that the desert had been covered entirely by water at one time. *Anti-diluvium* they said. "Whatever," he muttered.

Was he standing here at a time before all of that? Those years of erosion they had written about hadn't happened yet. "My head hurts just thinking about all of this time-shifting junk," he complained as he tugged at his hair. But that wouldn't explain the timeline of the three, *not one*, pyramids, he thought. "*Man*, this place is screwy!"

It was a person's face carved high on the shoulders of a beast, a lion. It sat as if protecting the pyramids themselves. They moved closer, taking more caution with each step as they were within sight of the pyramids in the background. They couldn't risk being seen now. Each was tired, and it had already been a long day, although Alex somewhat resented Anubis being tired. After all, it was Alex who battled two massive hounds, not Anubis. Yeah, Anubis killed the one, but Alex sent him flying through the wall with his awesome moves. He definitely killed the other one, though, sort of. The people helped, but he torched the mighty mongrel. Anubis just hung out, probably getting a tan, he thought. Lazy.

They stopped, Alex huffing and puffing, as he leaned against the right front paw of the Sphinx. Alex looked up and wondered what he was looking at. It just seemed to stare, fixated on something. Yeah, in this place, I'm guessing more desert.

Alex sat in the shade of the statue and desperately tried to catch his breath. He tried running through the events of the day so far, but kept getting distracted when he got to the part about the girl, Tad. She consumed his thoughts. Why? She was just a girl, right? he reasoned. Except, she liked him, and that automatically put her at the top of his list as far as Alex was concerned. She obviously recognizes my extraordinary good looks, superior intelligence, and raw awesomeness, my . . . *rawesomeness*, he thought conceitedly. He made an attempt to flick his mop of hair out of his face in a 'cool' sort of way, but it ended up back where it started.

Resolute in his task, he knew they had to help Tad somehow find her parents and get her family back together again. It was larger than that, though. They had to help everyone. Alex took a deep breath and jumped up with renewed ambition.

"What about Set? We have to start making plans don . . ." He was cut off. He felt something under his feet.

The sand was giving out beneath him. Alex was suddenly jerked downward where he stood. It swirled around, pulling him down like a whirlpool. He reached out for something, anything to grab, but there was nothing there, nothing but more sand. The force was sucking him down, swallowing him whole. It was like quicksand, and Alex was sinking fast. Despite his attempts, he found it impossible to move. The sand closed in around his legs, and he was up to his waist already. Alex cried out, *"HEELLPP!"*

Anubis was quick to react and lunged at him with an outstretched paw. He laid his long body out across the sand, grasping and digging in with all of his might. His grip caught Alex by the wrist, and he held on. He wasn't about to let go. Anubis was slipping and sliding across the loose sand. He was struggling. The suction was too much even for the powerful Anubis. It pulled him down with his friend. He had no control over his fate. All he could do was hold onto Alex. It was as if the great desert herself had consumed them.

They had dropped about fifteen feet and slammed onto a solid stone slab.

"*Owww!*" Alex let out a cough to clear his half-deflated lungs. "These falls aren't getting any easier, you know," Alex quipped. "Where are we?" He coughed again. "Why am I always either underground with you or sweating like a pig in the hot sun?" Alex asked as he stood and brushed himself off. Anubis was already standing, staring at what was in front of him.

The two had landed at the top of a narrow staircase made of gleaming white marble. There was light at the bottom of the stairs. They cautiously moved in the only direction they could, down the stairs toward the light, each not making a sound.

"*Wooo-oooo. Stay awaaay from the liiight,*" Alex joked in his best spooky voice. The joke was wasted on Anubis; he wasn't even paying attention. Anubis was first to reach the bottom. He stopped and stood, filling almost the entire doorway.

"*Hey.*" Alex ran into the giant in front of him. "Dude, what's up? What's wrong?" he asked as he poked his head around Anubis' side. His eyes widened. There was only the steep marble staircase behind them, but in front of them was an entirely different sight.

It was the largest and brightest room he'd ever seen. Easily the size of a football field and rising twenty or so feet in height, the entire room was built not of sandstone like everything else in this forsaken land, but of marble; smooth, gleaming, and white. I bet Gramma would like a slab of this in her kitchen when she bakes, he thought, as he touched one of the walls. It was cold. Alex was nearly blinded by all of the white marble in the room. It seemed to glow.

212

The entire perimeter of the room was lined with simple wooden shelves, more like cubbies, standing easily to the ceiling. Each cubby held several scrolls, and bounds of stacked paper were shoved into every crevice.

Massive columns supported the great hall. These columns were different than the ornate ones he'd seen in the outer room of the chamber where he and Anubis had been held captive earlier. These weren't as ornately carved; they were smooth and capped with square tops and bases. They, too, were of marble and looked more like the ancient Greek structures he'd seen in that same darn history book. They reminded him of pictures he'd seen of the Acropolis or even Apollo's Gate.

Hundreds of simple wooden tables were placed in row after row, covering the floor. Several, at least those he could see closely, had larger scrolls laid out on them, as if for viewing.

"What *is* this place?" Alex asked from under Anubis' armpit.

They moved a few steps into the room, Alex still following. It was bright, that's for sure. Dozens of holes in the ceiling, shafts lined with marble, ran to the surface, allowing the sun's rays to illuminate the colossal underground room. Light bounced off every surface.

"IT HAS BEEN WRITTEN OF A GREAT HALL. BUILT BY THE ANCIENT ONES. HIDDEN," Anubis recounted.

"A great hall? For *what*? Why is it buried, covered under all of this sand?" Alex demanded.

"A HALL OF RECORDS."

"Records of what? You mean those flat disk things my Gramma always listens to? They're kind of cool, I guess, but I wouldn't have built an underground vault for them."

"IT IS SAID THAT THE ANCIENT ONES KEPT HISTORY

HERE." Anubis gazed around in wide wonder.

"History of *what?*" Alex asked, somewhat disinterested and remembering how difficult it had been to navigate through the Mayan Period in Ms. Flowers class with Jackson smacking him in the arm all of the time.

"EVERYTHING."

That grabbed his attention. Alex's eyes grew even larger. The magnitude of what Anubis had said was slowly sinking in. History of *everything*. His mind began to fill with visions of untold civilizations, of battles fought and won, not just here, but everywhere. Legends. Reality. Both. The answer to some of life's greatest mysteries. His heart leapt. Maybe even to . . . *aliens*, he hoped. *Yes!* That would be so awesome!

"I'd be happy for some answers," Alex said under his breath as he pushed off around Anubis, and the two separated and spread out. It was quiet down here, and Alex felt almost removed from the horrors above. Almost.

He worked his way to the right of the room, his eyes fishing for something to catch his eye. These scrolls were old. Even now they laid with years of dust on them and were made of papyrus, likely harvested from the nearby Nile River area.

The two moved on without a word, each fielding toward opposite walls of the Hall. Sharp glints of light pierced Alex's eyes as he moved closer. It seemed a bit out of place in this marble box. Curious, he hedged forward to see what was causing the reflections. Each shelf and cubby had a small nameplate of sorts inset into the edge of the wood. They weren't gold, as one would have expected in this white palace. They were some other metal, soft enough to have been carved into.

Alex stood in front of the first line of shelves and saw that each shiny plate had something etched on its face. Quickly scanning all of the plates in the immediate vicinity, his interest now heightened, he saw that each plate was different. Some had a form of writing on it, while others had only symbols. The writing was strange to him, not that he expected anything different. After all that he'd been through lately, why should this be any easier? In fact, the writing from one plate to another seemed different than the last. It was like deciphering his journal.

The answers were close, on the tip of his tongue, but still eluded him somehow. Alex got a sudden nagging feeling. It may not have been common language to him, but it was all somehow vaguely familiar. He stared for a moment, scratching the back of his head.

It came to him in a start. The journal! That's it! Alex's heart beat faster as he whipped out the leather-bound book hidden beneath his clothes. He feverishly flipped through the pages. They were there. The words, the language, even the symbols, all there! *A connection!*

"Finally!" Alex shouted.

His shout went unaware to his friend who was now twice the distance down the opposite wall as he was and focused on a rather large sheet of papyrus laid out flat on one of the tables. It was possible, Alex thought, as he looked in Anubis' direction, that his friend didn't hear him because of the size of the room. This piqued his curiosity because he was certain that a room this size should have an echo. Strangely, it didn't.

"*Hu-LLOOO,*" Alex shouted out loud in anticipation. No echo. No response from Anubis. Nothing. It was as if the walls absorbed his words. Turning back to the plate in front of him, he leaned in as if to get a better read on the inscription. The pendant sitting comfortably under his shirt suddenly became hot. There was no warning, no warm up period, just straight to hot.

215

"Ahhh!" Alex cried as he reached down his shirt and pulled it out and away from his chest. It was glowing brighter than ever. The plate in front of him depicted a series of random dots. There was no apparent order to them, no familiar structure. He had no idea what they meant, and it irritated him. He leaned in closer, forgetting the hot pendant in his hand. As he did, the plate lit up brightly. More precisely, the series of dots on the plate lit up brightly. "I've seen that pattern before," he spoke without realizing it. "I know those dots. Think, Chronos, think!" He struggled to remember. "They get brighter every time I move closer, every time the necklace gets closer. Brighter like . . . *STARS!"* he shouted.

"Leo! It's the constellation Leo! I knew I'd seen it before," he exclaimed. His mind flashed back to the deck of the Mermaid. Spent a lot of time there, he recalled fondly; late nights staring up at the stars. Captain Shovers had taught him how to navigate by using those same stars. He could even chart a course on his own by using those same stars. He'd learned the constellations well. It *was* Leo, he could see it now. What he couldn't figure out was *why* it was Leo? What significance did Leo have here, to him?

He pulled down a pile of papers from the cubby as well as an armful of papyrus scrolls and laid them out on the nearest table. A quick glance over to Anubis let him know he hadn't moved, still focused on the large sheet in front of him. This gave Alex some time to search through his own pile for clues. The first thing he came to was a drawing of a lion with the constellation superimposed over the top of the sketch. This confirmed his belief. It *was* Leo. He'd read in that same dumb history book that, like most ancient civilizations, the stars fascinated the Egyptians. In fact, he'd also read that the placement of the three pyramids actually aligned perfectly with another constellation named Orion.

Alex struggled with all of it; Leo, here and now, Egypt. "What's it all mean? Leo's a lion; I get that, but I don't remember anything about a lion carved in that dungeon," he spoke aloud. There were many scary things, but the only lion he remembered was that creepy Ammit creature that eats people's hearts, and she was only about a third lion. Heck, he recalled, the Sphinx is at least half lion. Anubis didn't mention anything about a lion. *Are* there lions in Egypt? "Humph, mostly dogs from what I can tell," he muttered to himself while glancing over at Anubis.

There were a few sheets of what looked like astrological signs, but Alex didn't pay any attention to them. The most interest he'd ever shown in astrology was flipping through the channels late at night for the Psychic Tarot-Something-Or-Other channel. A load of junk if you asked me, he thought. So he kept flipping.

Alex stretched across the table at one of the scrolls he'd pulled down and spread it out in front of him. It looked like construction diagrams, several sheets in all. The Sphinx? The reality of what lay before him slowly sank in. Construction documents on the Sphinx. "These are the plans," he shouted. "Now *this* is cool," he continued to speak aloud, knowing full well nobody was listening. As a guy's guy, Alex loved all things construction. Demolition was better, but construction was pretty cool, too. Why would these documents be here? In with all of thi . . . His thought was interrupted with sudden clarity. It was a first for him.

"*The Sphinx!* Of course! It's her!" Alex cried out. He realized he hadn't solved any of his own problems, but he was excited nonetheless. He was spitting out answers faster than he could ask the questions. "The Sphinx is Leo! Or at least she represents her. That makes sense," he decided. "But if the Sphinx is Leo, then who would someone like Orion be? He was pretty impor . . . *No way!* No stinking way! It can't be that easy," he continued.

Alex wondered if Orion could be the same person as Osiris, the king whom Anubis spoke of so fondly. Was he the same Osiris who Set had tricked, the same dude who was missing? Why not? If Set is the evil god-jerk that everyone knows he is . . . *and he is,* then the three pyramids, they're his way of showing everyone the power he holds over their beloved Osiris. This angered Alex. There was only one singular thought that entered his mind now. *"Oh, we are so going to take him down."*

The only problem with this theory was that this was supposed to be a Hall of Records. A storage facility for . . .

"Everything." Alex made his best attempt at an Anubis voice. He tried to dissect everything he knew so far. It didn't help. That means that what I'm reading is supposed to be history. Only it isn't. It's happening now. *Right now!* Alex had always considered himself to be of fair intelligence, but this stuff, this time travel mess, confused him. How is that possible? How could the Ancient Ones have written this stuff already? He was getting seriously confused. Alex remembered something Tina Schultz had said to him during Science class that one fateful day. He repeated her words out loud, "I think I got lost somewhere in the Fourth Dementia." Alex chuckled at the play on words.

Hungry for more knowledge, Alex jumped up and moved down to the second set of shelves, searching for the next big thing. He left the first pile of papers still on the table. If this were a library, he thought, he'd have gotten yelled at for that. But he needed more. As he moved in closer to the shelves, the familiar heat from his pendant began to warm his chest indicating it was glowing again. This time he was better prepared and was able to lift the pendant away from his chest before he was burned. It was hot once again.

He held it up inches from the next plate and, much the same as the last, this one also glowed brightly.

"Too strange," Alex responded, intrigued. If this is supposed to be *his* pendant, and there was a definite reaction between it and these plates, then was he connected somehow to all of this? He realized this wasn't the first time he'd considered that question, nor would it be the last. He moved away, and the plate stopped glowing. He moved forward and it glowed again. Pretty obvious, he thought. This plate was different than the last. No dots, no strange symbols to decipher. It was a picture. Three pyramids. "No brainer there. I know what those are, and if I never see one again, it'll be too soon."

He pulled down the next stack of papers and returned to the table. Alex found it odd that there was no dust on any of these papers. They were obviously quite old, but still no dust. Curious, he thought.

About midway down the stack of papers was a bound set. It looked to be about the same age as the rest of the stack but, admittedly, Alex had no real way of knowing. This interested him the most.

He looked up again at the massive figure lumbering over the table on the other side of the room. This was the first real opportunity he had to digest everything. What am I doing here? He scratched his head, wondering how he got here. Better yet, how do I get home? He gazed in awe at the figure across the room.

This thing he now considered a friend, Anubis, is a god. This last part was particularly hard to swallow. *Really? A god?* How is that even possible? He's a hairy ten foot tall creepy looking dude wearing a lot of gold. But *nooo,* as if that isn't enough, he's not just a god; he's a dog, too. A flipping man-dog. Oh, did I mention he happens to work with the dead? "Yeah, try putting that on your resume. Boy, can I pick them or what?" he finished loudly.

He pulled the bound set from the pile, sending loose papers sliding across the table and cascading down onto the floor. Alex had always accepted his untidiness. He made no excuses. His bedroom back home, covered in dirty clothes, was the perfect example of this. No matter, he thought, and he laid the bound set down in front of him. It had the same three pyramids on the front of its cover. Alex ran his fingers over it, staring. No, not the same pyramids, he discovered. Not pyramids at all, in fact.

He whirled his head around from where he sat and lifted his pendant up, toward the metal plate. It glowed. Alex hadn't noticed this before. The plate. They weren't pyramids; they were triangles, and all three were intertwined with each other just like the cover in his hand. He remembered this as one of the symbols drawn in his journal and laid the two bound editions next to each other on the table. An entire page in his journal had been dedicated to this particular symbol. It was an exact copy of the original from the ancient papers.

"Awesome," he whispered to himself. He had to go on; his curiosity wouldn't allow him to stop now. Alex opened the cover of the older manuscript, and a small slip of paper fell out and onto his lap. He picked it up and right away noticed its difference. This was machined paper, not hand-pressed from papyrus or some other ancient method. Not modern, yet definitely more recent than the rest of the stack and of the bound cover in front of him. Someone had placed it inside the cover. There was a single word written on it.

"*VALKNOT*," Alex spoke aloud. He didn't know what it meant, but he was quite sure it wasn't Egyptian. That much he could tell. There were no hieroglyphs anywhere. This was entirely different.

He began thumbing through the pages as carefully as the

excitement of a thirteen-year-old would allow. The text was angular and tall compared to English.

About a third of the way through this odd writing, his fingers landed on a hand-drawn picture of what appeared to be three men floating in the air. They were holding a round object high above their heads in the sky.

They're either flying giants or gods, he thought. He was pretty sure there were no such things as flying giants. *Uh*, I hope. I've seen some pretty weird things lately. Why not throw in a couple of flying giants, too? he thought. Probably not, though. They must be gods. "*Great*. That's *much* better, *not!* Just what I need, more gods," he said as his shoulders slumped.

Several more pages into the text, Alex came across a second drawing, a rainbow of sorts that rose up from the earth into the sky. "What's next, a stinking unicorn?" he mocked. Because he couldn't actually read the text, Alex became discouraged, closed the papers, and all that he'd seen was quickly forgotten. He turned his attention to the large set of scrolls that covered the table. Pushing the stack aside, he unfurled the first one. He immediately recognized it for what it was.

The scroll laid out the engineering documents of a great sea vessel worthy of even Captain Shovers' praise. Alex was genuinely impressed as to the level of detail provided on the drawings and figured the Captain would be, too. It was sleek and appeared to be powered by both man and wind. Dozens of oars stuck out through the gunnels of the ship. A large center mast rose up through the middle, easily two-thirds the length of the craft. A huge colorful sail was lashed to the rigging. Both bow and stern jutted up in a curved fashion with a finely carved dragon's head at the bow and the beast's tail at the stern. Alex had seen pictures of these types of ships before. They were the ships of warriors. These were the ships of . . .

"Vikings!" he exclaimed. It was almost too much for him to comprehend. His already frail sense of reality was rocked once again. "What are drawings of Viking warships doing in an ancient underground vault in Egypt?" he screamed. He pushed away the scrolls and stood, not knowing fully what to do next.

"This is insane!" Alex said and moved on to the next cubby, once again leaving his mess behind. He raced up to the next plate without thinking, and the heat from his pendant came on strong, causing him to jump.

"*Ahhh! Sheesh.* I have to stop that," he exclaimed as he pulled it away from his chest. His eyes were already searching, looking for the glow. This time it came in the form of a series of dots aligned in a circle with several lines in the center. This, too, he recognized right away. He'd seen a picture of it in the older section of his church, back and hidden away from curious eyes. On one of those drizzly Sunday mornings when church came second to his mind behind sleeping, he let off the pew and worked his way to the back rooms. It was there that he'd seen for the first time what was now glowing on the plate in front of him. It was an aerial depiction of Stonehenge.

"*What the* . . ." He stopped short. He pulled out the longest scroll in front of him and unraveled it where he stood, not bothering to even sit this time. Sure enough, a drawing of Stonehenge, only not as he'd seen it, but as it was actually built.

"*Okayaaay.* I now know two things. First, apparently everything in history is connected somehow; and second, *reeaaally* old people like to build *reeaaally* big things out of *reeaaally* heavy stuff." Alex was getting almost feverish. He ran to the next shelf, already holding his pendant high. The plate glowed. It looked like some sort of crazy stick figure of a bird with a long straight beak. A hummingbird?

"Yes. A hummingbird." Alex remembered a show he'd seen about ancient South American civilizations once. They spoke of something called sky drawings in Peru and some ancient city in Bolivia. Supposed to be the oldest known civilization, he recalled. "*Hah!* Whoever believes that hasn't spent time down here, have they?" he blurted.

This particular plate looked similar to those he'd seen on television. He was convinced they were the same. Peruvian sky drawings. It fit, didn't it? So, if *nothing* makes sense, does that mean that's the connection? he joked sarcastically.

He pulled down several sheets and spread them out on the table behind him. He was too excited to sit still, so he just leaned over, filing through the different drawings in front of him. About twenty in all, he only recognized a few from the documentary. There was the hummingbird. He got that. A monkey. He remembered seeing that, too. A pair of hand-looking thingies. Most of the rest he didn't remember.

Pushing off, he ran to the next shelf. Another plate. Another circle. It was far more complex around the outer circle than the last one, with a person kneeling in the center. Curious, he reached up and pulled down some papyrus scrolls. They dropped to the floor in a pile. As he reached to grab the closest one, his unusually large feet slipped backwards across some of the loose papers that had fallen to the floor. He fell hard. With his legs spread in opposite directions and too anxious to even move at this point, Alex opened it where he landed. Ignoring the pain, literally in his butt, he stared at the open scroll.

"My genius knows no bounds. Did I mention I was rawesome? *Did I?*" he asked out loud. He already knew that Anubis wouldn't

223

have heard him, but he asked anyway. He'd recognized immediately what it was. It was far more detailed than the metal plate, but it represented the same thing. In fact, it *was* the same thing. The scroll illustrated a large circle with what he'd counted were nineteen small block figures positioned around a circle. Inside the circle was an even larger figure, slumped over and carrying another smaller block figure in a sack. It was the Mayan Calendar.

"The Mayans," he said incredulously. Alex held in his hands proof, evidence that the two cultures were related somehow. Actually, based on what he'd seen so far, all cultures were related. Dropping one scroll and picking up the next, he held his breath. Definitely Mayan. It was a flat-topped pyramid similar to those discovered in Central America, the same type of carvings as the calendar. Mayan, he concluded.

"Nobody is ever gonna believe this. E-VER," he spoke sadly and rolled his eyes. "Not sure I do either. I need to stop talking to myself . . . like now." He pushed himself up from the floor and noticed with a glance that Anubis had finally sat down, but that he was still greatly preoccupied with whatever was in front of him. This fact was almost as interesting to Alex as the Hall of Records itself. He skirted around the table, knocking most of the remaining papers to the floor in a race to see what has kept his friend's interest for so long.

As he crossed over the vast space, he looked around, taking in everything he saw. "Man, this place is huge. I wonder how they built it?" he asked in awe. He had his answer soon enough.

He slid in along side of Anubis and leaned in for a closer look. It was a schematic of the room they were in. Anubis had been studying the plans. Actually, it not only detailed the great hall, this Hall of Records they were in, but also three separate tunnels that branched off and led to the three pyramids, as well as a series of smaller hidden chambers that ran off from it. These guys loved to build big things, didn't they? he thought, shaking his head.

He looked around the hall, then down at the large sheet again. Strangely, any notations to detail weren't in Egyptian lettering or hieroglyphs as he'd expected. This language was uniquely different than any of the others he'd seen in this hall so far. It was far removed from his own English, yet vaguely familiar, comfortable even.

Then it caught his eye; a symbol. A tiny watermark had been inked and hidden in the details. A person would miss it if he wasn't paying attention. He looked closer, pushing against Anubis now. Anubis was getting annoyed.

"HMMNPH." Anubis conveyed his displeasure. Either that or he sneezed, Alex thought. It was tough to tell.

Alex hadn't noticed it before. It was subtle, hidden almost. He looked around the hall for more clues. It was there, over the entrance, on the plate behind Anubis' head, and . . . Alex filed through the sheets on the table, slammed them back down in confirmation, then jumped up and raced back over to the piles of Mayan papers he'd just examined. It was on just about every piece of papyrus in the room, repeated everywhere he looked. More important, he knew it was written in his journal and cut deep into his pendant, or at least when light was cast through it, the symbol would reflect on the ceili . . . He lifted his head.

"The ceiling! What the heck is on the ceiling?" he asked as he slowly walked back to the center of the room, looking up. It was too large to take in standing up, so he laid himself down flat on the marble floor.

"No way. No flipping way!" was all he could come up with.

There, high on the white marble ceiling, was a picture, not painted, but carved lightly into the slab. So faint was it that only the reflected light in the room revealed the lines. It was a map. More specifically, it was a map of the world, an ancient map.

"Dude, get out of the way!" he yelled at Anubis, who had also taken an interest in the ceiling and had moved out to the center of the room, standing above him.

"I can't believe it. Nope. I don't believe it," he said as he stared, fixated on the map. "This pre-dates everything. All of our beliefs."

There in the middle of the map, etched more imposing than the surrounding continents, was a large land mass, another continent itself, lying where he knew an ocean, the Atlantic Ocean specifically, was supposed to be. He'd read stories, seen movies, and even listened to the crackpots speak of it. But it was more like the existence of aliens than a reality. The map was carved overhead as if it were looking down over all of the other ancient civilizations that existed, like it was responsible for them somehow. No, like it was the *source* of them; the source of everything. The three wavy lines, one laid atop the next, Alex knew as the universal sign of water. Well now it appears that there was a reason for that. It was the sign of . . .

"*ATLANTIS!*"

Twelve

"*Oh, my God!*" Alex cried. Anubis shot him a look out of the corner of his black, soulless eyes.

"*Umm*, sorry. My bad. I meant *Oh, my Anubis!*" Alex joked with half a smile. Anubis' expression was a clear indication that he either didn't get the joke or didn't appreciate it.

"HMMNNFFT," was the only response Anubis gave.

"Good thing I'm lying down or I'd pass out," Alex said in complete disbelief. "Did you know about this?" he asked Anubis.

"NO. I HAVE SEEN MANY LANDS WITH MY KING. NEVER THIS."

Alex stared at the strange map on the ceiling, hands crossed behind his head. His eyes ran over the boundaries, soaking in the sheer size of the mass. It was larger than any stories he'd ever heard and, according to this map, stretched from almost Florida to just off the African coast.

Anything he'd heard to date indicated it was much smaller. What he'd heard were broken pieces of purported knowledge, with some saying it was rising again in the Caribbean, while some said it was in the Canary Islands, or even back in Cuba. Well, seems like they were right. They were all right, each one, and then some. This land covered all of that space and ran northward past Ireland and southward down to about the middle of Brazil.

Each story or myth, Alex learned from Captain Shovers, was born from a bit of truth, and some push and stretch over the years to create something far from reality. He suspected that even the Captain was guilty of this, too, based on some of his own stories.

Similarly, Alex presumed, what had happened in the case of Atlantis was that numerous people had probably left off the continent, creating their own civilizations, each holding on to only a little piece of their ancestry and growing their own legend from it, the next different from the last. It would explain both the commonality of the place and the differences in the many stories. But this was just a guess, just like anyone else's. Still, Alex felt something here. It felt real. He knew it was real. It felt safe, like it did when he was home.

"WE MUST LEAVE. PREPARE," Anubis interrupted and reminded him.

"Don't you realize what this means?" Alex looked at Anubis with shock. He wanted to stay, to absorb more knowledge and information. It was the first time in a long time that something else filled his thoughts other than his home. Heck, he thought, for that matter it was the first time he could ever remember actually *wanting* to learn *more*.

"I DO. IF WE DO NOT STOP SET, THIS . . ." and he motioned around the hall, then slowly up to the ceiling, "DOES NOT EXIST."

He was right, and Alex knew it. Set was changing history, and *not* for the better. They couldn't let this happen. But there was something here, something beyond even the greatest discovery in history, or histories. Somehow, someway, it was all connected.

A growing fear, maybe even excitement, rose in Alex's stomach. He didn't want to think about it and definitely didn't want to say it out loud. It was a crazy thought, really. But all of this, the records, this Hall of Records, ancient civilizations, Mayan, Peruvian, all of it, was connected.

The water symbol, the symbol of Atlantis; it was everywhere, on all of it. His strange journal that, until now, had only given him a headache and a butt-ache, was connected. He couldn't help but wonder where the necklace came from. He felt its connection. It was his, just like the journal, or at least they were given to him. He was desperate to know from who, and more important, why him?

Alex could feel the pendant close to his beating chest. It was warm and glowing slightly. *Am I connected to these ancient civilizations, to Atlantis?* "Yeah right," he said.

He looked down at his hands, turning them over several times, half expecting to see webbing between his fingers. Nothing. He laughed to himself and shrugged. *Well, I'm a good swimmer anyway,* he thought. *Maybe that's something?*

"WHAT ARE YOU DOING?" Anubis asked impatiently.

"Nothing," Alex responded as he lifted himself off the marble, his rubber-soled sneakers squeaking across the floor. Alex looked longingly up at the map as he walked away, back toward the table.

"What's the plan?" he asked Anubis. "I mean, *besides* killing the cute, innocent child, *uh*, that would be *me?* Did I mention *defenseless?*" He smiled awkwardly at his comment. He wasn't getting anymore comfortable with the idea. In fact, he was getting less so. Not much had been explained to him so far. Things got in the way, he reasoned, like demon dogs and huge underground vaults of history and, oh yeah, let's not forget *Atlantis!* He looked back up at the ceiling from behind the table, aching to know more.

There they sat, man and beast, scouring over every detail of the schematics in front of them. Anubis showed Alex where on the scroll he thought Set was hiding. An expansive chamber deep inside the largest pyramid had been constructed with a maze of stairs and tunnels leading to it. For all purposes, it appeared the most fortified with the largest of blocks used as barricades.

"THIS IS GOOD," Anubis spoke, pointing out that particular fact.

"How's that good?" Alex quizzed, his own opinion believing it was going to make it even more difficult to take on Set.

"HE IS SCARED," Anubis explained.

"He ain't the only one. I guess what you said *sooorrta* makes sense, but how on earth do we get to him?" Alex pleaded, pointing to the structure drawn in front of them.

"LEAVE THAT TO ME," Anubis responded cryptically. Alex didn't especially like that answer, or rather, non-answer. It made him uneasy again.

"WE MUST GO," Anubis demanded and headed back toward the entrance and the marble staircase beyond. Alex gave one last longing look back up at the ceiling and sighed.

"Hey, wait for me!" he shouted after the imposing figure of a creature. Strange, how he now considered Anubis to be his friend. He trusted him. It was only a short time ago that he had feared him. Anubis was a monster in the dark, something from under his bed or hiding in his closet. Not anymore. They went on this journey together, each needing the other.

Alex caught up to him at the bottom of the stairs. He turned and looked back at the marble room, the Hall of Records. Rotating back again, he noticed the three wavy lines over the entrance and smiled. Trying to jump up and smack them with his hand much the same as football players do before leaving the tunnel and running out into their field of battle, he, too, was heading into his own battle. He missed.

It didn't dawn on Alex until they got to the top of the stairs and stood on the small landing, staring up at the small opening in the sand above. How are they going to get out? he wondered. Anubis had the answer already and, without saying a word, reached around, grabbed Alex by his collar, and lifted him high with one hand. It was effortless for him. Alex's head was shoved clear through the opening and, upon breaking through to sunlight, was spitting out sand from his mouth.

"Thanks," he yelled down sarcastically. He wiggled and managed to bring his arms up, then hoisted himself up through the hole. Okay, now I'm up, he thought, as he brushed himself off, but how the heck do I get Anubis up? I can't lift him. He must weigh four hundred stinking pounds.

"What now, genius?" Alex leaned over the opening and yelled.

"Whoa!" Alex dodged just in time to miss Anubis' crook come sailing up out of the hole. "Guess he didn't like the genius crack much," he joked.

"PLACE THAT ACROSS THE OPENING," the hollowed voice came booming from below. Alex did so carefully, more out of fear that some other flying object may come hurling toward his head. He stepped back toward the base of the Sphinx and waited. All that he'd just discovered waded around in his head.

He couldn't remember a more confusing and exciting time in his life other than when he met Tad. He sighed. One day, he vowed, one day I'll see her again. But this whole Atlantis thing? He shook his head. What the heck is that about? Outside, leaning against the massive stone structure, he stared off wondering what it could possibly have to do with this hot dry place. Alex kicked at the sand, thinking ahead toward his destiny, but wondering about his past. He didn't remember much. His memories were spotted at best, but what he did remember revolved around his grandmother. She was his whole world, past, present, and if he ever got out of here, his future. He kicked again at the sand. This time it kicked back.

Startled, his neck snapped back and forth. He didn't see a thing, but the ground grumbled and shook. A loud grinding noise filled the air. "Was this an earthquake?" he asked with a start. "In Egypt?" It certainly felt like one to him.

"*Whoooaa.*" He tried steadying himself by spreading his arms out from his sides. The ground heaved violently, and he was lifted from where he stood, flying through the air and landing several yards away, face-down in the sand. Sand and stone doused him like a rain shower. He jumped up, immediately ready for a fight, certain it was another attack from the hounds. He looked around, prepared for the next strike; only, it wasn't more demon hounds that he saw. A dark shadow cast over the area. It was big. Slowly he looked upward. What he saw made his mouth run dry. It was the mighty

"*SPHINX!*" Alex yelled, stumbling back in fear while she struggled to break herself free of the sandstone from which she was carved. It was immense. The force of her effort sent waves of stone and sand flying into the air in all directions. The noise alone was epic, and Alex found himself covering his pounding ears once again.

The Sphinx literally roared to life. Alex saw her usually placid face go evil right in front of him. He knew this could only be the work of Set. He was frantic. His friend was nowhere.

The sound of solid stone being pulled apart is a lot different than the sound of it being crushed, Alex thought. Either way, he was quite sure that neither was a good experience for him.

She pulled each foot loose one by one. "*Uh, hellooo*, Anubis?" He ran to his left to avoid her right paw, only to have to skirt the left one. Every move she made caused the air to rush, sucking him back. Only the explosive force of her paws landing on the sand would send him forward again.

Chips of stone were falling off her body and legs with each

232

crushing step. She towered over the landscape, looking down on him. One step and she could pulverize him. She moved clumsily, but moved none-the-less, and she was well over two hundred feet long and at least sixty feet tall. The ground bounced and heaved with every giant step.

She was coming after him. A five-ton stone in the shape of a paw was lowering down on him. He felt the familiar pull of air.

Alex dove to his right, narrowly missing the pummeling blow. The force of the impact sent a tidal wave of sand up six feet into the air. He could try to outrun her, but he knew it would be useless. Each of her steps covered about thirty-five feet; she'd be on him in less than two steps. All he could do was try to outsmart her . . . and stay alive.

Another monolithic paw came down hard, skimming his side, and sent him tumbling across the sand. His shirt was torn down the back. "Wow, that was close!" he quivered.

"*A-nu-bis!*" Alex screamed. "I need you now!"

With a noise so savage it caused the Sphinx to hesitate, Anubis burst through the blanketing sand where the small opening to the vault once existed, grabbing his crook as he passed through. The sand trailed off him in flight. Alex never saw anything so fierce. Anubis was ready for battle. He landed several feet away, feet planted solidly between Alex and the Sphinx, his crook in one hand behind him and his teeth bared. He was seething.

"Dude, you're always late. What's up with that?" Alex fired at him. He was clearly upset, but he couldn't help but admire his friend. It didn't seem to matter to Anubis that his latest foe was a walking skyscraper. Anubis was always prepared for battle, never scared. Running away never entered his mind.

She moved first.

And Anubis pounced, first to her foot, then scrambling up to her knee. When she lifted her foot to step, he jumped to her shoulder, and within an instant he had landed, standing on the back of her neck and riding her like a surfboard. Watching Anubis scramble up the Sphinx like that reminded Alex of Mittens and her, *umm*, unprovoked attack on him. Stupid cat, he recalled with renewed frustration and contempt.

Her movements were jerky and uncontrollable, sending Anubis sliding back and forth wildly. She didn't like someone riding her. Anubis was barely hanging on and at one point had lost his pouch having slipped off his shoulder and fallen to the sand some fifty feet below. His sharp claws were digging in. He was being bounced around like a paddle ball. Watching this, it was clear to Alex that Anubis had charged in without thinking his attack through.

Alex had never seen anything like this before. In fact, he was pretty sure that riding on the back of a Sphinx was a first for Anubis, too. Anubis had managed to stand again. It wouldn't last long and he knew it, so he lifted his crook high into the air with both hands and drove it into the back of the Sphinx's neck, and she roared.

And he roared back in defiance.

Unfortunately for Alex, the pain forced the Sphinx to buck and weave violently. She reared on her hind legs like a wild bronco, Anubis hanging on fearlessly to his crook, hesitated for a moment at her apex, then came crashing down with both feet landing on either side of Alex. The force of her landing left a crater in the sand the size of a small lake. Alex stood shaking in his sneakers.

"*Shheesh*. Can't a guy ever catch a break?" he shouted to his friend.

"FIGHT!" Anubis yelled.

"With what, you loon? In case you hadn't noticed, she's the size of a flipping freight liner! What am I going to do, tie her down and tickle her to death?" he yelled back, shaking his fist up at him.

Tie her down. The thought began to marinate in his head. *Yes!* Alex looked around. He knew he'd seen it fall to the ground. There. He raced toward Anubis' sack, which was now underneath the belly of the Sphinx. *Great*, he thought sarcastically. He had to get past her feet. He was definitely fast enough, but still, the timing needed to be perfect or he'd be a sand-patty.

He waited for the cool rush of air.

Now! Alex took off running. He made about two paces and, she landed a massive paw inches from him.

"Whoa! Shheesh!" he shouted. Alex hesitated, stepped back, then tried to time another effort.

She dropped her second paw in a crushing effort sending up a cloud of sand.

Running toward her was proving to be a far more difficult task than running away from her. It reminded him of running from Jackson all of those times. Jackson was big and clumsy like the Sphinx, and in the past Alex had been able to outrun and outsmart the bully. This should be no different except that instead of Jackson, it was three hundred zillion tons of angry, body-crushing stone. Slightly different, he thought.

"HURRY," Anubis scolded.

The Sphinx took another pummeling step.

"Hang on to your, *uh* . . . lions," Alex yelled back.

She stepped again.

"Keep her busy! I have an idea!" he shouted back up to his friend.

"HMMNFT," came the familiar response.

He was off again. He dodged and rolled around each massive paw, jumping and sliding. Almost there, he thought.

She kept moving, trying to crush him.

"*Aauugh!*" Alex landed inches from the pouch, covered in sand. "Will you stop, already?" he screamed at the Sphinx. Crawling the rest of the way, he wrapped the strap around his fingers and pulled it in close. He had to *hurry*, as Anubis put it. Alex flipped open the pouch and spread it out on the loose sand. She couldn't see him now, hidden underneath her. He only had a few moments to make this work. Alex made a quick note that all of the vials were still intact despite the fall from above. The soft sand must have absorbed the impact. He grabbed the cotton tarp from the marketplace and started shredding it into long strips. It wasn't easy. Egyptian cotton was strong. Tying each strip end to end, he tugged at the knots to draw them tight.

Another paw landed too close. Alex sensed her frustration. He was annoying her. He was good at that, annoying people. *Usually* people, he thought.

"How you doing up there?" he yelled, unable to see Anubis.

"I SAID HURRY," Anubis urged.

"Yeah, yeah, keep your skirt on, you baby!" Alex teased. Anubis swung, hanging from his crook, trying anything to keep the Sphinx's attention on him rather than Alex. Alex's task was difficult enough, and the giant paws crashing down around him didn't make it any easier.

She leaned. The air rushed.

"I'm doing all the *hard* work!" Alex shouted back. Anubis bounced and slid part way down the Sphinx, digging his long claws into her back to stop. Steadying himself, he leapt back to the safe grip of his crook.

"THEN DO IT FASTER!" Anubis roared down from above.

Alex was done. All knots were checked. He scooped up the rather large pile of cotton in both hands, then struggled to stand up with it. It was heavy and long. I hope this works, he thought.

"Catch!" Alex instructed Anubis.

Alex threw the end of the cotton up to Anubis with the accuracy and force of a professional baseball pitcher. Anubis only had to reach out for it to land squarely in his hand, the other still holding on to his crook for balance. "Nailed it! Man, I have to try out for the team this year."

Alex took the other end of the long roll and ran as fast as he could. Well, as fast as any awkward teenager could in loose sand with large stone blocks smashing down around him, but he managed. Around the first leg, loosely or it won't work, he told himself. Back around to the second leg he went. Careful. Watch it! Keep going. Again and again he circled. Keep it loose, Chronos. One more time around and, "There! Done!" he said with an air of satisfaction.

"Now!" he shouted up to the sky as loud as he could, then ran for cover. That's all Anubis needed to hear. He wrapped his end only once around his crook and jumped, pulling the end of the cotton line down with him as he fell to the ground. He landed in a cloud of sand. It was now or never. Anubis gave the end of the line an enormous jerk, and it went taunt, each strand tightening around her front legs, closing them together and pulling them up toward her chest. It worked perfectly. Her inertia sent her tumbling forward down on to her front knees. She gave one last bellow as she fell.

The Sphinx landed in an earth-shattering crash, sending another tidal wave of sand ten feet high across the desert in all directions. The resulting force cracked her face, shearing off her nose. It slid,

237

crashing to the ground, missing Alex by inches. Her feet had crumbled beneath her, and she was poised as she was before. She sat stiff and silent, as if nothing had ever happened. The only sign of the battle was her now imperfect face.

"HMMNFT." Anubis climbed back on to her shoulders, wrapped both his giant claws around his crook, and gave one good yank.

"Hmmnft." Alex agreed. He began taking up the remaining cotton line, knowing they would need it for the next critical step in their journey. He didn't want any mistakes.

They moved on, toward the unknown. The pyramids loomed in the distance and the hour was late. The cover of nightfall would soon be on them. This was good, Alex thought. Now dying, that's *not* good. They had all of the items necessary for Anubis to perform his duties. "Nothing but courage stopping you," is what Ms. Trudie would always say.

"Yeah, well, Ms. Trudie hasn't had to fight devil dogs, now has she? Except maybe the kind you eat," he added. "She hasn't had to battle giant stone creatures either," he continued. "The worst she's had to deal with were the tourists on sale days." Bad enough for sure, he would agree, but still, not like this. Nothing like this.

Without words, they headed south of the pyramids, avoiding exposure among the encampments. It was dusk when they came to the trench dug deep and long into the sand, the same trench that housed the slaves, beaten and bloody. The death moans were still there, haunting the stale air. Alex still had terrifying visions of the scenes he'd witnessed here upon first arriving. Unfortunately, they both knew this was going to provide the best cover for their dangerous task. They needed concealment.

As they made their way toward the edge of the trench, Anubis retrieved his old and tattered cloak he'd worn in the dark cavern. They were close to Set now, and it was imperative that they drew no attention to themselves, and let's face it, a ten foot tall dog-faced god was a bit of an attention getter, Alex thought.

Searching for the nearest stone stairs, they descended to the depths of nightmares. Anubis hunched over as he walked, trying to give the illusion of a much smaller being. Once at the bottom, they stuck to the shadows, keeping out of any light that existed for the sole purposes of exposure.

The night was getting cold, and the death around them made it even colder. They made their way to the farthest reaches of the trench, ducking and hiding at every movement or noise. At last they found a small room carved into the wall of the trench, hidden from sight. Only the door left them exposed. Anubis gave a quick *sniff* to the air inside and said, "CLEAR."

Alex darted in first, followed by Anubis, who had pulled some wooden crates across the open doorway as he entered. This was the best they were going to get. It was quiet and out of the way.

The room was small and bare, as if nobody had stayed there for some time. They each gave one quick look around, then sat facing each other in the center of the room. The remnants of where a small fire had been tended by the previous occupants were between them. Alex pulled out his two stones, gave them two quick chips, and the fire was lit. Anubis rolled out his pouch to his side, displaying each component necessary to complete his task.

Alex sat quietly, remembering all of the trouble he had to go through just to get this stuff. He thought of Tad once again. He was going to miss her; her large brown eyes, her soft gentle skin, and her pretty smile.

Anubis laid out the familiar vials, small and large, focused on the mission. He pulled the frankincense out from its strap. The oils followed, then the natron.

"It was all I could find. I was a bit busy, you know, kicking demons all over the place," he said in quiet defense. "It'll work, won't it?"

"IT WILL WORK," Anubis replied. Alex wasn't so sure. Earlier it had been up to Alex to mix the correct ingredients for their escape. This time it was up to Anubis. Alex was fine with that. He figured that it was likely his friend had done this six or seven thousand times, so why not? The large flask was removed from the pouch, and ingredients were carefully measured and added in specific proportionate sequence.

Anubis took out the vial of grease that Alex had gathered from the axle of Tad's cart. Removing the lid, he placed it at the edge of the fire. The air in the cold damp room was a mixture of death, oils, and frankincense, not a pleasant odor. It made Alex's stomach turn. The room began swimming.

The natron was necessary, according to Anubis, to extract the moisture from his body or something like that. Alex wasn't sure; he wasn't listening. His head had started spinning since they sat down. His nerves were on end and his eyes had closed. Thoughts of dying consumed him, and he was uneasy. His body rocked back and forth uncontrollably. The question of what was happening barely formed in his thoughts. Alex cracked his eyes open for a split second before he passed out. The last thing he saw was Anubis sitting in front of the fire, chanting something. His eyes had glossed over.

When he next awoke, Alex was walking beside Anubis in a field of wheat. The horizon ahead was darkening. The two walked for several yards before Alex spoke.

"Am I . . ." he started.

"STAY CLOSE. IT IS NOT WHAT IT SEEMS," Anubis instructed. Alex could hear whispering all around him. The wheat was moving. No, he realized, *something* in the wheat was moving. He couldn't make it out. Everything was a slight haze to him, just out of focus, but he did as Anubis said. He stayed close. His head didn't hurt like he thought it would, but it was definitely foggy. They made it over the next hill and down to the shore of a small, dark lake. The water was eerily calm.

"Water? Where'd the water come from? I thought we were in the desert?" Alex asked, somewhat scared by its mere existence. He knew it wasn't right, out of place.

"SILENCE," Anubis demanded. It was plain to see this new place didn't smooth his edges any. The sky was blackening. An old wooden boat was beached on the shore. They shoved off and climbed in. Anubis stood at the bow staring out over the dark water. His weight alone pushed the boat several inches into the water, and it skirted just above the waterline, moving slowly.

Strangely, neither was rowing. The boat moved on its own, as if being pulled toward something. Alex sat to the back and searched out across the lake, wondering what the other side held.

The sky had turned completely black, and only the glow from his pendant gave off any light. He reached down and held it out in front of his chest so he could see. Fog was rolling in, and it became thick, too thick to see. Alex could deal with all of that. He'd been through worse, but the quiet was what made him nervous. This place, the lake, was devoid of any noise, as if they were in a vacuum. Even the water made no noise as it lapped against the sides of the small boat.

As he sat contemplating the finality of his immediate future, a soft, muffled sound broke the silence.

Did something just hit the boat? Alex wondered. *Nah*, he thought, as he looked around. There's nothing out here. Anubis hadn't moved; couldn't have.

Alex's mind drifted back into thoughts of his fate. He was confident that this whole idea of dying was a bad idea. He desperately wanted to change his mind. *I could swim for it*, he thought. *Nah!* Besides, how was this gorilla going to do anything without me? His thoughts were broken once more.

There it was again, only louder. His heart raced. Alex actually felt it this time. There was something in the water underneath the boat. He rose slightly from where he sat and looked up at his friend. Nothing. Anubis gave no reaction, still focused on the mystery of the distant shore. It was like he hadn't felt a thing. *I definitely felt that. How could he* not *have?*

"Hey," Alex whispered, "did you feel that?" No response.

"*Hey!*" he prodded a bit louder.

The third one came quicker and harder. The boat rocked in the water. He was certain now. A definite hit! What the heck was that? He stared over the edge, peering into the emptiness, only this time it wasn't empty. He caught the tail end of something ghostly white, something big, swimming fast in the depths below. In an instant it was gone and the water was still again. He shot a look up at Anubis for some hint that he, too, had seen it. "Really? Nothing? Are you kidding?" Anubis hadn't faltered. He was still unaware.

"Tell me you didn't feel *that?*" Alex spoke even louder. There was no sign of acknowledgement from Anubis. In fact, he gave no response at all. Alex was incredulous. *I can't believe he didn't feel that.*

The fourth time wasn't as subtle. Something slammed into the wooden vessel from below.

The boat heaved, and the wooden slats of the hull cracked open. Water was coming in at his feet. He'd been knocked off his seat, but quickly recovered and steadied himself, looking anxiously once again over the side and into the watery unknown. He saw something large sink away from the surface, then he lost it. It had disappeared far below them, cloaked by the dark waters. A chill raced up Alex's spine.

He looked up again at Anubis. It hadn't even fazed the brute. Something wasn't quite right with his friend. Did he even know what was going on? Seriously, Alex thought, how could he *not* know? For a moment Alex began doubting himself. Was I dreaming? Am I dreaming? He looked back down into the water and had his answer.

"What the . . ." Alex stopped as if something had reached down his throat and pulled the words from his body, leaving him gasping for more. It was rising fast, coming closer. Long, sharp fangs came into focus first. Narrow slits followed to the back of its large head, revealing its eyes. It was a snake, a sea snake, unlike anything he could have ever imagined. Its form wasn't solid and whole; it was transparent. Its long body and split tail whipped behind it, propelling it upward toward the boat, mouth open and ready.

"*Oh nooo!*" Alex yelled. There was no time for reaction. Alex closed his eyes. There was only the noise.

The beast had severed the hull, sending thousands of shattered pieces flying through the air in all directions. Alex was in the water swimming frantically. It was freezing. His lungs were filling with the deep poison each time he took a breath. He was under, sinking. His thoughts drifted to his grandmother, to Tad, to . . .

Suddenly he was coughing. Air was pushing its way past the water. His body reacted violently, rejecting the vile intrusion that had entered his lungs. The dark liquid erupted from his mouth.

His lungs were clear again.

"Uhhgghh. What just happened?" he asked Anubis who was now standing over him, looking puzzled.

Alex was lying on a pebbled beach, soaked to the bone. They had reached the other side.

"YOU SCREAMED. YOU WERE IN THE WATER. I PULLED YOU OUT," Anubis explained in his usually loud and broken fashion.

"I *don't* scream!" Alex corrected him. "Are we here?" he asked, simply to change the subject before Anubis could respond.

"WE ARE HERE," Anubis proclaimed, revealing a large gate behind him as he moved aside. The fog lifted slightly, still concealing what Alex presumed was the real danger. Alex didn't get a warm fuzzy feeling from the large gates, but then, he wasn't expecting one. They were ominous, but he felt as if they beckoned him to enter. It was a feeling he wished he didn't have.

He was standing before them, gazing up at their immense size. Something was odd. He looked down. How could this be? He was dry. They had only just walked a few feet from the shore where he lay soaked to the bone. Anubis just stared down at him. Yeah, that helps, he thought, as he rolled his eyes.

"How'd I get . . ." He was interrupted by the grating of stone across the earth. The gates didn't swing open; they slid apart, allowing those who enter full passage. I'd hate to get caught between them when they were closing, Alex considered as he passed through.

What little fog that had lifted to reveal the gates had returned, heavier than ever, and Alex thought it wise to stick close to Anubis as they made their way in.

Thirteen

It wasn't long before their bodies became engulfed in the dense fog, and Alex trailed off behind Anubis. He lost sight of his friend in the thickness of it all. He tried calling out, but the heavier the fog was, the louder the wind became. It was no use. The wind was a deathly sound, like the wails and moans of the men who had passed through here before, begging for mercy and forgiveness.

The fog was at its thickest, and his head was quickly filling with doubt. He couldn't see more than a few inches ahead. Anubis, his only form of protection, was gone. This wasn't a place he wanted to be. "What did I let that big jerk talk me into?" he questioned nervously. The moans became louder and louder. It felt like he was going insane. He covered his ears and closed his eyes tightly to try to shut out the evil forces lurking around him. When he opened them again the fog had lifted. He found himself in the middle of a room lying on a cold stone slab. He couldn't move. There were no ropes, no bindings that he could see, but he was immobilized.

"Where am I? How the heck did I get here?" he asked aloud. His own voice sounded muffled to him. Anubis was beside him kneeling next to a large scale. Alex's mind flashed to the carvings from so long ago. This must be it, he considered. He was able to just lift his head slightly to survey the rest of his surroundings.

It was a dark room, but merely in the sense that there was no artificial light. It was like being outdoors underneath the night sky, only without the stars. Except for the cold slab that he was on, the only things in the room were Anubis and the scale. Alex noticed that his overly large friend wasn't wearing the old cloak that had hid him away in the shadows earlier. He must have removed it at some point. Instead, he was once again displaying his full dress gold.

Although he couldn't see them, Alex had an unsettling feeling that there were others, too, lurking just out of sight. He could feel their presence, almost hear them. Anubis was busy chanting something, intent on the function of the scale and the task at hand. That's a good thing, Alex thought. I need him to bring his A-game.

Out of the corner of his eye, he saw her; a most beautiful woman, only she wasn't a woman at all. Alex's eye caught on something. No. What? "Wings?" his muted voice broke, not realizing it. There were *wings* on her back. His mind was racing once again.

It felt as if none of what he saw was real, like he was dreaming. He must be dreaming. She couldn't be human. But then if she was here with them, with Anubis, she *could* be a goddess, he decided.

She wore a large feather in her headdress and had those wings on her back. He knew. *That's it! That's who it is!* Based on Anubis' description, she must be Ma'at! Alex watched her closely. She was glorious in even her simplest of movements, seemingly kind and just in everything she did. Although he couldn't see her feet from where he was, she appeared to glide when she moved. The air around her swirled in admiration of her existence.

Although beauty such as hers would normally be calming to most people, Alex was growing more and more panicked. He was certain there was something else in the room. *What's that?* More movement. To my right. I heard something. Alex twisted his head right to left and back again, searching for the source of the sound. It was a strange sound, a throaty growl muffled by the thick air. Whatever it was, it had four legs. Alex could hear the patter of paws on the ground next to him. His mind jumped to the hounds.

246

It was another attack; it had to be. Alex tried desperately to move, but couldn't. Something was holding him down, growing tighter with every movement. Anubis. He must see them. Alex couldn't understand why his friend didn't react. He was usually first to a fight. *We need to attack before they do.*

"Anubis, look out!" Alex yelled. He sounded like a barking seal. It was no wonder Anubis didn't respond. The growls he heard became deeper. His eyes desperately searched; he needed to know. *I can't see.*

Struggling to move the only part of his body that he could, Alex stretched his neck to the side and saw the most hideous creature drift into focus. His breath went cold. Frost was settling on the stone slab. It was a sight so unbelievable, he couldn't look away. *Sheesh!* That would give my nightmares, well, uh . . . nightmares. She was there. The four-legged, butt-ugly freak show from the carvings was here. *YIKES!* Alex reached back for her name. *I think Anubis called her Amment? Amnet? No, Ammit. Yeah, that's it!* Ammit *was* real, or at least as real as everything else he'd seen lately.

She was darker, more ominous than the carving. Her teeth seemed sharper than he recalled, too, but then,

"Of course they were," he chided. She was close enough that he could count each tooth, even smell her vile breath. She was a gruesome being with froth surrounding her mouth and a long hissing tongue spitting out between her powerful vice-like jaws. Alex had a bad feeling about this. She approached the scale and took her place. Ammit looked eager, he noticed, like a dog waiting for a bone. Alex moaned at this. He found her being here bad enough, but her being hungry was just plain wrong. He knew why she was here, but knowing didn't help matters much. He struggled more. *I didn't mean it. I didn't mean to scare the cat! I promise I won't do it again.*

247

There was movement just beyond. It was Anubis. Alex watched helplessly as he placed something on the scale. Something was driving him to look. It was a lot like poking a bee's nest with a stick; *I know what's going to happen, but I do it anyway.* His stomach turned a bit, and it made him feel flush. He knew deep down what it was, but desperately wanted to deny it. He remembered Anubis' story all too well. He'd tossed it over in his mind dozens of times since. *If only he'd move. I need to know.*

He got his wish. Anubis moved.

"*Wha . . .*" Alex cried out. It was still beating; each pulse sent ripples up the thin chains to the top of the scale and seemed to amplify in the quiet room.

It was a heart, *his* heart, on the scale, opposite a . . . a feather. He glanced over toward Ma'at. She wasn't wearing it anymore. He instinctively reached for his chest. Looking down, all he saw was his pendant glowing brightly and sitting in a hole where his heart was supposed to be. It felt warm. *Am I dreaming? I flipping better be!* Only he and Ammit seemed truly interested in the outcome. She was salivating in hungered anticipation. After all, she was the Devourer of Souls. Her eyes met his, and she licked her lips in confidence. Perhaps she sensed something that he couldn't.

The scale creaked under the weight of his heart. *This is it,* he thought. It wasn't until this moment that he questioned whether he had gone too far. A haze fell upon the room and blanketed everything he could see. No longer was he restrained. His lifeless body was whisked away by a sudden wind. He looked down at his freed hands; they were changing. His solid form was turning to vapor, disappearing into the haze, only his mind remained. "Oh no, I've failed," he spoke softly. A single tear ran down his cold cheek.

"*I'VE FAAAIILLED!*" he yelled.

His body lifted up and slammed to the ground. Air was forced from his lungs, and he coughed violently.

His eyes opened slowly while his lungs gasped for air. He was back in the small stone room hidden in the far reaches of the trench. The familiar stench of death was around him. It was quiet except for the occasional moan hidden in the distance, from those who had barely survived, beaten and fallen. He was wrapped tightly from head to toe in the cotton and lying next to the fire. Anubis hadn't moved, still sitting across from him, legs crossed.

"Did I pass?" Alex asked quietly.

"YOU DID," responded Anubis with his eyes shut. He looked like he was meditating.

"So, am I a mummy or can I get out of this?" Alex asked. "How did I even . . . you know, I don't even want to ask," he decided.

Anubis opened his eyes. The vials that had been laid out were empty. He carefully capped each one and placed them back into his pouch. He moved around the fire toward Alex. It had been a long time since Alex had seen him move on all fours.

Anubis reared up one of his large paws and bared the razor sharp claws in the flickering light of the fire. He brought them down quickly and precisely, gliding just over Alex's body. Within a feverish instant, he was done. Alex was free.

The cotton wrap lay shredded across the damp floor.

"That's it? I'm dead?" Alex asked, patting himself down to see if there was anything out of place. His heart was right where it should be, his necklace dangling to his side, still glowing.

"I don't feel any different," he continued.

"WE HAVE MUCH TO DO," Anubis pushed.

"Can't we just take a rest?" Alex asked and started to lie back down, closing his eyes for a long nap. "I mean, it *is* still dark outside," he continued as he blindly pointed to the doorway to prove his point. As he did, the sun broke over the horizon, fell down the stairs of the deep trench, and peeked into that same doorway.

"Crap."

Alex doused the fire, and Anubis was once again under his tattered cloak. They were close now and couldn't risk any mistakes. Alex, under the misperception that being dead gave him new-found powers, decided it would be smart to kick the wall and test that theory.

"Owwwooo!" he howled. "What good is being dead if you still feel the blasted pain?" he argued while hopping on one leg and holding his damaged foot in his hands.

"ARE YOU FINISHED?" Anubis said, shooting him an icy stare.

"Done," he responded, deflated, as he limped out the door following Anubis. The sunlight hadn't yet fully penetrated the corners of the trench, and most of the occupants were still asleep, or had died, Alex fretted. Anubis moved the boxes and crates cautiously, listening to the quiet around them. When he felt that everything was as it should be, the two edged out, once again sticking to the shadows.

There were the occasional moans and discomforted cries that echoed off the stone walls, but always just out of sight. This added to Alex's current state of anxiety. He knew that the sun was rising rapidly, and that brought with it sights that he so desperately wanted to avoid. Gruesome, sickening visions were stuck in his mind forever. He didn't need a refresher course. He remembered vividly what this place looked like during the day and was anxious to be somewhere else, anywhere else, and fast.

Except for his strange clothes, Alex could blend in if he needed, but Anubis, there just isn't any hiding a ten-foot tall cloaked figure, human or otherwise. They were both keenly aware of the difficult task ahead, but now they had the advantage. According to Anubis, Set wouldn't be able to detect them. The element of surprise was on their side. They were going to need it.

It was risky as they made their way through the debris and bodies strewn across the trench, past the wounded and sick, under the rising sun. It had to be done. They had to get out. The trench was nearly flooded with light.

The rather odd pair moved quickly, concealing themselves as best they could. It was fortunate that most were too busy tending to themselves to worry about these two strangers lurking about. They made for the nearest stair leading up to the surface, back to the hot sand, and into battle.

Reaching the top, there was no turning back. At least down there, Alex reflected, they could hide, but not now, not again. They were done hiding, done running, and if Alex never saw another giant demon dog again, he'd be happy.

Alex quickly sized up their position. The two were still a ways from their destination, but close enough where they could hear the crack of the whips. He and Anubis were now standing just off from the pyramids and the ramps that surrounded them. It wasn't possible to charge up the ramps and attack from the front. It was too obvious and too dangerous. They'd be seen instantly, causing panic and alarm among the slaves. Set would no doubt be warned in advance. As he remembered it, the drawings from the Hall of Records, those same drawings that occupied Anubis' attention for so long, had indicated a tunnel running from the Hall up to the largest of the pyramids. That's where Anubis guessed Set would be.

"Think, Chronos, think," he mumbled, lost in thought. It was obvious that the same people who built the Hall built those tunnels. So if the design was the same, then . . .

"There has to be shafts, airshafts for breathing," he exclaimed. "We need to find a shaft."

"HMMNFT." Anubis agreed. It was some distance from the Hall of Records located underneath the Sphinx, and the pyramids. "*Ooh*, yeah. Sorry about the nose," Alex said through his teeth at the Sphinx. "*Not!*" The tunnels were built pretty much in a straight line, which means they would have to pass . . . just about under . . .

"There." Alex pointed to the area where the animals had been tied up at the base of the ramps. "That's where we need to be." It appeared hopeless. There was just a bit too much open space between where they stood and the animals in the distance for Alex's comfort. We need a diversion, he thought. His eyes sparkled in excitement. He had an idea.

Alex spun around to Anubis, grabbed his pouch, and started rifling through it blindly. He found it. Pulling out a piece of the wadded up cotton they had used from, *well, uh*, his death, he curled it into a tight ball at one end, leaving about a four foot length dangling behind. He reached back into the pouch and pulled out a vial. Nope. He pulled out another. Not it either. He blindly palmed the next one. He'd found it.

Removing the lid to the vial that held the oils, Alex poured out its remaining contents, soaking the ball of cotton completely. Alex then reached into his own pocket and once again removed the two small stones. They had come in handy in the past. Now all he needed was a target.

As if on cue, he glanced up and saw a tired old man shuffling through the sand leading three scrawny camels and a donkey, each carrying a sack of something or other. He had his mark, took three quick chips of the stones, and he spun the ball of flaming cotton around three times, holding the tail end firmly and let it sail through the air.

The unsuspecting caravan moved on quietly for about ten long seconds. The air suddenly filled with chaotic barks and squelches. The donkey bucked and jumped trying to get rid of the smoldering pack on its back. The cracking of the whips went silent.

All eyes were on the old man who, try as he could, had no luck controlling the four scared beasts. The poor man was swung back and forth while each creature tugged and pulled on the next. *Let go,* Alex's mind screamed in regret. He *really* should let go.

The animals took off running in different directions. The man was slammed to the ground and lifted back up again. His efforts made no difference at all. Then the flames came. The donkey's pack was on fire. Needless to say, this didn't help matters for the old man, who was continuing to be thrashed.

"*Oooh,* that'll leave a mark," Alex said out loud. Then he heard that familiar voice in his head again.

Run.

He hadn't seen Anubis speak, but then, he never saw Anubis speak, even when he bellowed loudly. Alex eyed his friend as he passed. It *was* Anubis. He was sure of it. It sounded just like the dog that saved him back home, the same one that separated him from Jackson's fist. That was so long ago now, a distant memory. Not a pleasant one, mind you, but a memory still. Boy, did he have some memories now. He wondered if anybody back home would ever believe him. In truth, it didn't matter. He just wanted to see his grandmother. Under cover of the commotion, he swiftly followed Anubis back up toward the base of the ramps swinging wide of the old man, his camels, and the fiery donkey.

Anubis was far more graceful than Alex who, at some point on the run, decided that a head-first homerun slide made better sense than something more covert. The problem was, as Alex discovered, this maneuver made it far more difficult to avoid the lesser pleasantries of an animal pen. He slid across the muck and finally stopped at the base of a rather foul smelling and ratty looking camel with matted hair. Alex's own head stuck sideways into a pile of camel dung. It was packed into his ear.

"*Uuggghh!*" he said as he wiped at his face and dug out his ear. The flies were already at home. I guess it could have been worse, the camel could've . . .

"*Aww, man!* He *spit* on me," Alex complained.

"SILENCE," Anubis boomed. This in itself wasn't silent and caused a slight ruckus among the animals still tied to the posts. Fortunately, they were well hidden from sight and nobody paid any attention to it as the old man had finally broken free and was now chasing the beast, yelling what was obviously the Egyptian equivalent of profanities.

Well, Alex conceded, might as well look around while I'm down here. He pushed the muck back and forth, careful not to stir the animals any more than he had to. The last thing they needed right now was to get caught. *Agghh, gross!* Alex had heard that camels were stubborn when they wanted to be, but when the ratty looking one finally moved out of his way Alex heard a dull, almost hollow, noise.

It was soft and muffled from being covered in a week's worth of muck, but it was definitely not sand. She must have stepped on something. He crawled up under the camel and cleared an area of about three by three from atop the wooden lid. He'd found one of the shafts they were looking for. Alex struggled with the lid, tugging and pulling at it with no luck. He looked up at Anubis, who was merely watching.

"Are you enjoying this?" Alex scolded. Anubis leaned over and popped it off with a simple flick of his wrist.

"Again, I loosened it," Alex claimed as he did his best impression of a flexing bodybuilder.

"You don't want to mess with these guns," he said, kissing each of his biceps.

"CLEARLY," Anubis scoffed and jumped down the narrow shaft.

"Not cool, dude. Not cool," Alex responded as he followed down the shaft behind his friend.

"OOOOFF. Ow. Sorry."

Alex had landed some distance below and directly on top of Anubis. The tunnel was dark, and it took some time for Alex's eyes to adjust. Anubis didn't have that problem.

Alex noticed right away that the tunnel sloped downward below the base of the pyramid. He was right. It was one of the tunnels leading from the Hall of Records. It was a small passage, built for humans' use, not an oversized behemoth like Anubis, so he dropped to his canine position and continued on all fours. Alex followed him, trusting his friend's instincts. Those instincts hadn't failed him yet, and now wasn't the time to doubt them.

They were shut off from everything. It was deathly quiet. No noise from above could reach them down here, and the air was stale from lack of use. Alex's heart was beating faster with each step. It felt like his lungs were collapsing. He tried not to think about what was at the end of this tunnel. He knew deep down that whatever secrets this pyramid held, whatever evil forces waited ahead, it was going to be nothing like he'd ever experienced before. The demon hounds, the Sphinx, were likely all child's play compared to what was ahead.

A set of stairs descended before them, heading down deeper into the unknown. The smooth slab walls of the tunnel had turned to large sandstone blocks, probably as a result of the pyramid construction going on above. They moved downward into the depths of the pyramid. Another shorter tunnel carried them from the bottom of the stairs and ended at a slab. Light flickered off the wall at the end of the tunnel. Muffled noises came from beyond. Someone or something was on the other side. Neither spoke. They were close. Alex's heart, his pure heart that had passed the greatest of tests, beat loudly and uncontrollably. As long as it wasn't on some scale somewhere and was still in his chest, he was happy.

Anubis growled lowly from deep within his chest. Alex could see his friend's reflection dancing up on the walls of the tunnel. His hackle was up.

"*Sshhhh,* quiet," Alex whispered. "We don't want him to know we're here." Anubis' teeth were showing. His canine warrior instincts were taking over, and it was hard for him to control them.

They crept up to the slab, realizing it was the only obstacle that stood between them and battle. The slab was positioned about a foot in front of the opening to the tunnel and allowed for those who knew its secret to just squeeze by if necessary. Alex slipped in and peered around the edge, making use of his thin body.

There were two opposing columns about Alex's height in the middle of a grand room. Each held a shallow pan full of firelight that trickled throughout the room at the top. A large empty throne sat at the opposite end of the room from the slab that now provided them with their only protection. It was made of stone and looked uncomfortable, Alex concluded. The back of the throne had been intricately carved into the large head of a jackal, a headdress at the top. We're definitely in the right place. He scanned the room.

Oh crap! Alex mouthed quietly with his lips.

More hounds; two more to be exact. They were lying at the base of the throne, one on each side. One was busy licking its paw while the other appeared to be sleeping. Well, this sucks, he regretted. I was kinda hoping we'd be done with those mutants. His thought was broken by something familiar. "Where is that sound coming from?" he asked, annoyed. It's the same noise they'd heard from the tunnel. It sounded like chanting to him.

He turned to his left to see four men on their hands and knees. Their heads were tucked in low to their chests. It was them. They were the ones chanting. The light from the pans poured over their backs, and Alex could see their gilded skin, suddenly verifying what he'd already suspected. It was the same four bald dudes from before, he concluded. These were the same men who carried the golden cage; Set's golden cage! Alex felt a wash of desperation. His head whipped back and forth, searching. "What's that noise?" he whispered to Anubis. Indeed, there was a noise. "What is . . ." He turned around to see Anubis seething loudly from his mouth, and foam had begun to push through his sharp teeth. Anubis sensed something. Danger? Set?

This place wasn't nearly the size of the Hall of Records nor was it as ornate as the outer chamber of their former prison, but it held something just as important as both. It held their destiny.

The room was rather stark and bare. Alex thought it looked unfinished or temporary somehow. That made sense since the pyramid above was still being constructed. All those people; he could feel their pain down here. According to the drawings he'd seen, a maze of stone had been placed above, making it near impossible to navigate to its location. It was built as a secret, to hide something. The tunnel they had just travelled had been built by someone else, another people, and perhaps an entirely different race. It was from another time, something earlier than the pyramids.

The space in front of him was longer than it was wide and had the familiar support columns that the other places had. The inside was sparse and, unlike the outer chamber from before, had no carvings on the walls. To the left, next to the men on the ground, was the gilded cage in which Set was carried. Four golden staffs leaned against the wall. Although light from the pans played against the columns and reflected off the cage, the room was somewhat gray. The air felt heavy. It reminded Alex of a tomb.

Alex's eyes darted around, searching the corners for every detail, looking for the one they came for. He saw nothing else, but he somehow knew he was here. Anubis knew it, too. Doubt entered Alex's thoughts. Had they been discovered? Had Set known all along?

Out of the corner of his eye Alex saw something shimmer. There was another movement from inside this stark room where there had been none before. Turning, it came into focus. "Whoa!" he exclaimed as he stepped back behind the slab. Set appeared to have walked out of thin air. Well, actually he glided, Alex noticed. "Why do these people insist on gliding? Don't they have feet? It's kinda freaky," he scolded quietly.

Turning to Anubis, who was crouched behind him and ready to spring, Alex began to quietly devise a plan.

Fourteen

"I think if we move left, hidden by . . ." He was cut off. Anubis had launched himself clear through the air directly at Set, announcing himself the only way he knew how. The walls shook from his thunderous cry.

He'd waited long enough. He was attacking. It was a battle to the end, and they both knew it. For Alex and Anubis, there was no failure; they had to win. They had to for themselves, for those who suffered, for all of Egypt.

"So much for the element of surprise," Alex yelled after him. Set let out a high-pitched screech in response.

Alex buckled to his knees, covering his ears. It was the same noise he'd heard days before at the base of the pyramid upon Set's arrival, only this time it echoed off the stone walls of the interior chamber. The hounds rose ready for a fight, barking wildly at the intrusion. The chanting stopped. Set caught Anubis in flight, spun, and threw him hard, back against the large thick slab that concealed the tunnel, causing it to crumble and reveal Alex's hiding place.

Anubis groaned softly, shook his head, and slowly lifted himself back upright, spreading his fists wide and pushing out his massive chest he responded the only way he knew. It was a terrifying roar that seemed to echo endlessly.

Alex hadn't moved since they had peered around the slab that once hid them from danger. The shock of his friend being tossed around effortlessly was wearing off when he saw the four men charging at them. The hounds were still barking in the distance. It was at that point that Alex knew his role in all of this. He would fight man and beast; Anubis would battle Set. Alex rushed at the group of oncoming men, giving his own version of a battle cry.

"*CRRAAAPPPP!*" he shouted as he snatched one of the thick golden staffs leaning against the wall as he ran by. He rounded on the first one and caught him in the fatty part of his stomach, causing him to lurch forward and spin over the staff. Alex had knocked the wind out of him.

The other three men, whom Alex only now realized, were actually rather large in size, circled him. Alex was able to keep them at bay only for a few seconds, by swinging the staff on end wildly in a circle. This gave him time to think.

Anubis returned from where he'd landed with a vengeance. There was blood in his eyes, and Alex, as busy as he was, could see it. He ran at Set from across the room and at the last possible second jumped to his right, rebounding off the last support column eight feet up from the floor. Spinning in the air, Anubis landed both of his hind feet on Set's shoulders, knocking him to the ground. Set was recovering and scurrying about on his back when Anubis pounced yet again and sunk his feet into Set's chest. It was looking good until Set reached up and grabbed one of Anubis' legs and twisted hard.

Anubis collapsed under his own weight, the broken leg unable to support him. He was in agonizing pain, but was able to slide himself behind the nearest column. Alex could do nothing. He felt helpless, but he had his own problems. The men were closing in on him. Breathing heavily, Anubis gritted his teeth, grabbed above and below the break, and snapped it into place.

Alex knew the pain was unbearable, but he also knew that Anubis wasn't about to let a measly compound fracture slow him down. Anubis stood slowly, still leaning against the column and keeping his weight mostly on the other leg. Now it was Set's turn to attack.

The deadly foe took a swiping blow clean through the same column Anubis was leaning against and into the back of Alex's friend, knocking him against the closest stone wall. Alex could only watch as his friend was being batted around like a toy. Anubis had lost his concentration, but for only a moment. He won't do that again, Alex thought. He was right.

Alex was busy with his own fight, but every now and again could see that Set and Anubis were locked in combat, each clawing and biting. It was more like watching two wild animals fighting than two humans or even two gods, bestial in nature.

Set was strong and many times looked as if he was winning. Alex was worried. Had Anubis met his match? Set was much stronger than Alex had expected. Did Anubis underestimate Set's power? This was Anubis' fight. He was fighting for his king, Osiris. He was fighting for Isis, his queen. Anubis needed to win, to defeat Set. Alex understood that.

So much was riding on Set's defeat, and here, locking horns with what was probably the world's most evil being, none but he and Anubis were aware of the battle taking place below the ancient pyramids. None would know why they were free. If they defeated Set, future generations would likely never know either. Historians always get things wrong, or at least that's what Alex was quickly learning.

One of the men decided he had enough of this boy and stepped in a bit too close. The sound reminded Alex of cracking crab legs at dinner.

Alex clocked him in the head and didn't even know it. He couldn't keep up the swing much longer. His arms were getting tired. He had to move quickly while the one man was down. Alex leapt over him and ran, carrying the staff with him.

He saw Anubis and Set in each other's clutches swatting and tearing at each other. Set had the upper hand and was forcing Anubis to the ground. His leg didn't have enough strength to push back, and it was buckling. Alex had to help his friend.

The men were behind him; now was his chance. Anubis had told him that Set couldn't sense the dead. Well, I didn't make that trip to Tuat for nothing, he thought. Let's see if it's true. Cautiously, carefully, he made his way to Set undetected. It's true! His heart raced. He doesn't know I'm behind him. Alex could feel the adrenaline pumping through his body. He lifted the heavy staff over his head and brought it down hard against Set's back. The staff shattered.

Set merely turned, unaffected by the blow, and swatted Alex like a fly with the back of his long thin hand, still squeezing Anubis around the neck with the other and pinning him to the ground. Alex was thrown across the room and against the far wall, crushing the solid stone behind him.

"Uunnggghh!" It hurt badly, but he didn't die. "Of course! I can't die. Cool!" he said with a painful smile.

Anubis saw his chance. While Set was distracted with Alex, Anubis grabbed Set's hand from around his throat, arched up off the floor, and pushed Set back over his head with his feet, rolling to a stand. His friend was up again and safe for the moment. Hah! Safe, that's a joke, Alex thought. Alex heard the rush of the men's feet behind him too late. One had grabbed him and pulled his arms behind him tight. Alex struggled, but it was no use. The man had him.

"*Dude!* Your breath *stinks!* Haven't you heard that gingivitis is the *second* leading cause of death in the world?" Alex said. It was the first thing that came to his mind. He figured if he couldn't get free, he'd at least have some fun teasing the man. Unfortunately for Alex, the man understood nothing he'd said and just looked puzzled. He did, however, close his mouth. For that, Alex was grateful.

A second man, whip in hand, reeled back and sent about three cracks against Alex's face and jaw. The first one split the air and landed.

"Aaaaggghh," he cried out defiantly, and the man was angry. The second one tore flesh from bone.

"AAAGGGGG," he cried out in pain, and the man smiled. The third one sailed through the air with deadly accuracy.

"Uunnggghh." Alex's head hung limp, but it wasn't joy that filled the man; it was horror.

Anubis had returned to the aid of his friend, slashing his sharp claws across the back of the man holding Alex.

"*AAARRRRR!*" He let go of Alex and dropped to his knees, clutching at the open flesh peeling down his back and writhing in extreme pain. Alex turned to see what had just happened, his own face split and bleeding in three distinct places.

"Meet my friend Anubis. He, however, is the *first* leading cause of death in the world," Alex taunted at the man.

Alex wasn't paying attention when the man with the whip let another one sail at his head. Anubis caught the end just as it cracked at Alex's ear and gave it a hard yank, pulling the man up to him. He lifted the man, dangling from the whip wrapped around his wrist, to his face and growled. The man screamed, and Anubis simply discarded him, sending him against the gilded cage, breaking two of its supports. He wasn't Anubis' fight. Having escaped what was sure death, the man got up and ran across the room and out the entrance, screaming the entire time. Guess we don't have to worry about him anymore. Alex laughed to himself.

"And don't forget to change your shorts when you get home!" Alex yelled after him, shaking his fist. Anubis turned his attention back to Set, who was now breaking the hounds free from their bindings to the floor. They were salivating.

"Oh great!" Alex shouted at Anubis and pointed toward the hounds. "See what you can do about that, too, while you're at it, would you? I can't do everything, you lazy slug!"

The first hound was past Anubis and on Alex in seconds. He didn't have time to think. The rabid beast lurched at Alex. Alex leaned to his right just in time, grabbing the remains of the broken chain still around the demon's neck as he went by. *Brilliant*, flashed through his mind. The hound pulled and tugged at the chains, trying to rid himself of his unwanted passenger. Alex pulled himself, dragging along behind the beast. He slid his hands under the collar that held the chain and hoisted himself up onto the hound's back. Okay, now this is officially the most stupid thing I've ever done, he thought.

"*Wooaaaa . . . aaahhh . . . aahhhhh . . .*" he shouted in rhythm with the bouncing of the hound. The beast was crazed and desperate. It slammed itself against the columns, the men, the walls; anything to rid itself of this weight. "Oh no!" Alex cried. It was heading for the cage. This was going to hurt, and he knew it. The beast couldn't control itself. It bucked once, twice, and on the third and final time, Alex pushed off while the hound jumped madly into the already broken cage.

When Alex looked up again, the beast had crashed through the gilded cage, impaling itself on a sheared post through its side. It struggled, letting out a small whimper, then it stopped. It was dead.

It wasn't over. Alex stood only to find another man swinging at him with his golden fist. The blood on his face was beginning to dry. Alex moved his head in time to absorb the blow with his shoulder. I would have thought being dead would ease the pain. It didn't, and he grabbed at his shoulder. Jackson had hit him there once. It felt the same. Alex looked around the room for his friend. He wasn't going to get any help this time.

Anubis was rushing at his enemy with the force of a tsunami, building steam. Set lifted his hand toward the heavy stone throne at his side and waved it toward the rushing Anubis, sending it slamming against Alex's friend. A normal man, a mortal, would've been crushed. Not Anubis, not a god. He simply leaned into it with his shoulder and met it, exploding across his back and sending large chunks everywhere, including missing Alex's head by inches.

"*Hey!* Do you mind? I'm working over here." Alex landed a punch squarely against the face of one of the men, sending him back against the wall. The impact of soft bone against hard stone knocked the man out cold, and he slumped to the floor. It reminded Alex of the last time he faced Jackson. A smile came over his face. Boy, that one felt good. So does this one actually. I should totally be a boxer, or a professional baseball player. He grinned smugly. Maybe both, he thought, as he dodged a flying post. "I can't believe that missed."

In an instant, Alex felt something slam against him, and the air was forced from his lungs. The second hound had built up a head of steam and caught Alex on his side, sending him tumbling across the floor and landing limp at the base of one of the columns. Anubis was near enough that he rounded on the demon and bit him on his back, clean through his spine, snapping it in the middle. He cried out in a feverish rage.

265

Flesh was still hanging from his sharp teeth. Spitting it out, he raced to his friend's side, forgetting the surrounding danger in the room once again. It was just long enough for one of the men to charge Anubis. What a mistake. Anubis stood and hip-checked the man into one of the shorter columns that carried a fire pan on its top. The resulting impact caused the heavy stone column to teeter and fall, pinning him to the ground, dousing his face and chest with flames. He screamed in horrific pain. Anubis laid his crook next to the man and reached down, placing his large hand on his forehead. A look of comfort washed over the man's face. Anubis twisted his head with a quick snapping motion, and he was dead.

Alex was groggy and still shaken from the hit. His ribs were hurting and he had severely twisted his ankle. Seeming to sense that Alex was okay, Anubis climbed the adjacent wall, sinking his sharp claws into the stone as he went. When he reached a sufficient height, he pushed off into the air and dove at Set.

Set was waiting this time. He raised his hand and stopped Anubis, suspending him in the air mere feet from his target. Anubis was dangling there, several feet off the ground, like a puppet, and Set was his master. Set slowly turned his hand over, and Anubis' body spun helpless over to his back. Arched in suspension, Anubis howled in pain as Set clutched his open hand together into a fist. He was crushing him without even putting a finger on him. Set had what looked like a crooked smile upon his depraved face.

Alex had to do something. He was moving slowly, but was still able to drag his beaten body over to the man whose body lay charred from the fire. Alex looked away from the sickening sight. Holding his ribcage tightly, he picked up the forgotten crook and slid on his side, trying to avoid any pressure on his bad ankle. He pulled himself up behind Set, once again undetected, and hooked

266

the wicked creature around his neck with the crook, pulling him back hard with all of his weight.

The maneuver caused Set to break his concentration on Anubis, and Alex's friend dropped to the floor. He wasn't moving. Set responded by snatching the crook from his hands and slashing at both he and Anubis violently with it.

Set screamed wildly with rage.

The crook was strong, making for solid, backbreaking blows, each more painful than the last. Alex couldn't die, but he was being beaten to within an inch of his life. He couldn't move and, when he tried, the force of the crook on his bleeding back would send him back to the ground. Both Alex and Anubis were near defeat. He looked at the carnage all around him, then at Anubis, his eyes lifting.

"It's hopeless. We can't win," Alex forced out of his cracked ribs, reaching out to his friend. It was a desperate attempt. He was desperate. Set was moving in for the final deathblow. It was going to end soon. Alex closed his own eyes in acceptance. He could do no more. He was ready to die.

"WE MUST!" Anubis boomed. He took a difficult breath and beckoned, "MY EGYPT. MY BROTHERS. I MUST CALL UPON YOU. COME TO ME."

Alex looked one last piteous time at Anubis. The deep black of his eyes had gone cloudy white.

"*Nooooooo!*" Alex cried. His own voice echoed off the walls and vibrated the ground. Vibrated the ground? Wait, it can't be. But it was. He felt the ground vibrating, trembling, beneath his hands. The walls of the pyramid began to shake. With all that he'd been through, he couldn't help but wonder if this was how it was going to end. Anubis didn't move. Alex felt alone, and tears came to his eyes once again. What was he going to do? He couldn't take on Set, not

267

if Anubis couldn't. "You big dope. Why did you have to fight him? Why?" he cried as tears began to streak down his bloodied cheeks.

The rumbling became louder and louder. Fear swept over Alex. Something was coming. Outside on the ramps, men were fleeing; animals broke free from their ties. In the distance the sun cast a massive shadow across the land.

A vast army extending the entire horizon, a thousand rows deep, covered the dunes in a feverish storm. They were coming fast. They rolled down the hill, moving as one. Their screams and battle cries came from years of torture and abuse. It was the dead. They rose from the mass grave where Alex and Anubis had laid captive so long ago, from under every grain of sand, from every corner of Egypt across time. Alex had his proof. The dead did move, and they were coming.

Set, too, had felt the trembling and had stopped his assault on Alex. He stood there listening, wondering, a look of knowing on his face.

Anubis hadn't died. Now that he was free from Set's imprisonment, his own living tomb, he could summon the dead. He can *lead*, Alex thought. Now was the time. Now it was Set's turn to feel fear, to feel pain, to suffer. He stood there, sensing what was to come. There was nothing else he could do. Alex watched as the dead descended upon Set like a swarm of locusts, hundreds, thousands, carrying him at Anubis' bidding down below, to be judged--to Tuat. The walls of the pyramid were coming apart. Whole columns were splitting, cracking to their base. The hordes folded in on themselves, sucking Set down with them. In a moment they were gone. The room was as it was before, quiet. Anubis had disappeared, and Alex was alone.

The dust was settling around Alex as he sat in bewilderment.

Wondering what had just happened, he realized his friend, too, was also gone. Where's Anubis? Set's gone. Where's Anubis? The floor where everyone was, the army of the walking dead, was solid. He shook his head. How'd they do that? Where is everybody?

"Uh, *hu-lloooo*," Alex spoke, breaking the silence. Nothing.

He slowly got up, using the crook to help. His ankle was still throbbing from the pain, his back was bruised and achy, and his ribs were most likely broken, but he was alive. Tears were drying on his face. He hoped his friend was still alive.

Alex hobbled to the door on the far side of the room, the same door the man had run screaming through, and he looked back around one last time. The battle was fierce, but had they won? If they had, then at what cost? It was easily an hour before Alex saw the break of day at the end of the narrow hall. He'd forced himself through difficult passes and up steep hallways, but he was here. Finally, he was here.

He could hear shouting and cheering. The once half-dead men who toiled away under the cracking of a whip were now free from their bindings and cheering, thousands of them. None knew what had happened, only that it had happened.

The sun blinded him as he crossed the threshold and moved out onto the ramp. As he raised his hand to shield his eyes, his weak ankle turned, and he lost his balance falling backwards.

Someone, or something, had caught him before he hit the ground. Alex looked up, the sun still shining in his eyes. A shadow moved across, and more tears flooded his eyes. He'd almost given up. It was Anubis!

"Where did you go?" Alex asked, wiping his eyes. Anubis lifted his friend back up onto his feet. He didn't wait for Anubis to answer. He threw his arms around him and squeezed hard.

269

"What happened to Set?" Alex blurted out, still hugging his friend.

"SET?" Anubis asked.

"Yes, Set, you moron. What happened to him?" Alex asked imploringly, pushing away and looking up at Anubis with anticipation. Anubis didn't answer right away. Instead, he looked like he was thinking about his response, perhaps savoring it.

"HE FAILED." Anubis smiled.

"*Failed?* What do you . . . *ahhh*, he *failed!*" Alex thought for a moment. "*Ooooh*, Ammit?"

"AMMIT."

"*Yikes!*" Alex shivered. "I don't know what it is about that creature, but she gives me the chills."

"HMMNFT."

The two walked down the long, worn ramp together, supporting each other as they went. As Alex struggled, his leg dragging behind, he took a long look around. He saw change. Where there once stood three pyramids, now there was only one. Any other day, any other person, and this would have been shocking. But to Alex, after all he'd been through, he just chuckled.

"They don't put stuff like that in the history books, now do they," he said. But it was more than that, more than just a change in the landscape. He saw hope where there had been none.

Surprisingly, Alex realized, not a single person was paying any attention to the pyramid or the ten-foot tall god dressed in gold battle armament walking among them.

The scene here was totally different than before. The people were lively and smiling, patting each other on the backs. Family and friends were rushing to the once slaves, embracing them. How he missed his own family, his grandmother, Captain Shovers, Ms.

Trudie, Crunch, even Mittens. Okay, not Mittens, but definitely everyone else, he corrected himself. They were his family. And now, so was Anubis. Yeah, how am I going to explain this one to Gramma? *Uh*, Gramma, this is Anubis. He's staying for dinner, is that okay? He allowed himself to let out a small laugh.

I'm so going to sleep for like eight days straight, he thought. A jolt was sent up his leg to his shoulders each time he took a step. He began mulling over the events in his mind as they made their way through the crowd and down the ramp. Okay, first a big explosion rips apart my shed, followed by a long hard walk in the desert. Lots of heat. More heat. Some sun, and oh yeah, more heat. Mix in some sand, plenty of sand. Let's not forget the dang demon mutts. I'll never look at the neighbor's dog the same way again. And the Sphinx! Actually, I'd rather just forget about her. No way would anybody believe me anyhow.

Now Atlantis! *That* was cool! Just think . . . Alex's mind drifted far away and dreamed of strange lands and stranger people. Snapping back to the present, he looked around at the moving landscape, then up at Anubis. Guess I'd better be careful of what I wish for. He smiled. He couldn't have wished for anything better.

He picked her out in the middle of all of the confusion. For a second he thought he was delirious or perhaps had been hit too many times in the head. She was running, pushing through, up the ramp. His senses tingled. It was her! It was Tad! His face beamed brightly and, although it hurt, a smile split his face from ear to ear. This was exactly what he needed. He forced himself to stand straighter, ignoring the pain. She ran right up to him and kissed him on the cheek. He blushed. She blushed. In fact, there was a slim chance that even Anubis blushed. She was no longer scared of Anubis.

271

"What was that for? Not that I mind." Alex's face hurt; not from the slices where the whip had split his skin, but from smiling so hard. He'd do it all again for just one more kiss from her. A tall thin man appeared from the middle of the crowd. He was a simple man, still frail and weak. He placed his hand on Tad's shoulder.

"My daughter tells me she believes it's you who's responsible for our freedom," Tad's father said as he approached, holding out his other hand to thank Alex. "I think I agree," he said, staring up at Anubis anxiously.

"But how do you . . ." Alex looked at Tad. She was smiling.

"Gerry," was all she said, continuing to smile up at him.

"Remind me later to discuss this Gerry fellow with you. Something tells me that he has more to do with all of this than I had first thought," he replied, waving his hand around.

"Come. Let me help," Tad's father insisted, grabbing Alex's arm.

Seeing that Alex was hesitant, Tad explained, "My father was a healer before he was taken from us. Let him help." She batted her large brown eyes at him, and he melted instantly.

Alex smiled weakly.

Her father went to work on his ankle and his ribs, wrapping both tightly with the help of Anubis' remaining cotton roll. The pain was intense, but he wasn't about to show his emotions in front of her.

"Well, now what?" Alex asked sadly, searching for an expression on his friend's face. He already knew the answer.

"OUR JOURNEYS HAVE ONLY CROSSED. THEY ARE NOT COMPLETE. I MUST SEARCH FOR MY KING. MY OSIRIS. EGYPT DEMANDS IT."

This was his home. Although he didn't want to admit it, Alex knew they would have to leave each other. He knew it was time to go. It was strange that his best friend wasn't a person from home,

272

not a human at all, but a god; and an odd looking one at that. They had become close. Alex had heard of things like that; well, not the god thing, but that sometimes the strongest of bonds are forged out of combat, sharing harrowing experiences.

He didn't want to leave his friend, but still, Alex was excited to go home. He thought about it. Alex had always known what he needed to do to get there. He'd never tried before because, as much as he longed for the comfort of his home and the love of his grandmother, he still needed to be here, helping Anubis. People often speak of destiny. Alex wasn't sure if this was his destiny, but he was confident that it was part of it, a part of something much bigger. Going home was never an option until this was done, until they finished the deed.

"Wait, the deed; of course, Alex, you idiot! *Duh!*" he spoke in sudden realization. Alex pulled out his journal and read the small inscription carved into the thick worn leather spine. He'd briefly forgotten the journal during the battle. "Deed. Let's see. There it is," he mumbled to himself. Alex knew exactly what had to be done. But where? His eyes sought feverishly for the perfect spot. He couldn't do it out in the open for all to see. He'd cause mass hysteria.

They moved as a group, all of them pushing through the scattering once-slaves to the base of the ramp. A handful of tents for the guards were a short distance away, and Alex led the way. Anubis was still cautious, forever the warrior, sniffing back and forth for any danger. Making their way into the heart of the encampment, they found a small tent. Most of the accompanying equipment was still there. The recent inhabitants must have left in a hurry, Alex thought.

Before he ducked in, he leaned over to Tad and whispered something in her ear. Her face lit up like a lamp. She smiled. Alex

273

said his goodbyes to her and her family, then he and Anubis ducked inside. It was difficult to leave her behind. He was resolved in the fact that he would see her again one day. That thought made him warm inside. Before Alex could open his mouth, Anubis spoke.

"YOU MUST GO," he bellowed loud enough that the flap of the tent fluttered.

Alex felt a little put out. Was he more saddened by this than Anubis?

"But what about us, our friendship? We're friends, aren't we?" he said, concerned.

"FRIENDS. YES. WE WILL BE TOGETHER AGAIN," Anubis responded.

"But how? How do you know?" Alex questioned.

"BECAUSE IT HAS ALREADY HAPPENED," Anubis explained.

"Yeah, *that's* a load of hooey," Alex spat back.

"DUDE, TRUST ME."

"Hey, you got it right!" Alex said gleefully. The conversation was over as quickly as it had started.

It was Set all along, Alex thought. The clues, the riddle, the deed, all led to the same place in time, the same place he currently occupied. It was always about Set; he knew that now. But *now* it was over. He glanced up at Anubis. A look of understanding was shared.

Now I can go home, he thought. Boy, that sounds good. Anubis placed his large paw on Alex's shoulder, causing him to buckle slightly under the weight. The behemoth gripped his shirt and pulled him right back up. Anubis quietly turned and walked out of the tent, dropping to the ground on all fours to make it through the opening.

Alex held out his journal, rubbing the palm of his hand across the flat cover as if it were a long lost friend. He was anxious to finally get home. Looking down at it, he was discouraged that he hadn't figured out all of its clues. The necklace was still a mystery as well. He knew there was a connection with all of it. *Once I get home, there'll be plenty of time,* he thought.

Alex was ready. He knew what he needed to do. It worked getting here, but now all he could do was hope that it would work again. He desperately wanted to be home. It felt like eons since the shed had exploded in front of his eyes, although, admittedly, he wasn't looking forward to the feeling he had the last time it had happened. That, he could do without. He lifted his hand to his face. *Maybe they won't be there when he gets back.* The gash in his leg from when Jackson was chasing him had disappeared; maybe these would, too. He didn't want any scars on his face. After all, he was just a boy.

Alex turned over the journal. His shirt was glowing brightly from his necklace as if it knew something was about to happen. *Another connection,* he thought. Stroking the spine of the journal with his thumb, Alex spoke those words out loud once again, *"Through time and space I will travel to mend the deed unraveled."*

He had to reach into his shirt and pull out the pendant; it was burning his chest hairs; well, what was one day going to be chest hairs. He could tell it was getting strangely dark outside. He thought he heard thunder rumbling in the distance. *Great,* he thought sarcastically. *Now we get rain.* The setting sun was forcing rays past the dark clouds directly through the slits of the tent. The necklace began to spin like a top, sending pictures and symbols everywhere against the canvas.

He didn't hesitate. He didn't even think about it. He just did it. Alex thrust the pendant into its resting place on the cover. The tent flopped and fluttered in the growing wind. Some invisible force took hold of his body, twisting and bending it. The sand beneath his feet shifted. The visions that suddenly filled the small tent and trickled into his head weren't any clearer or any more familiar than last time; still, unfamiliar people and places. One day, he thought, they'll all make sense. He couldn't be concerned with all of that right now. He was busy being thrashed about.

His body shook. Intense sound flooded the tent, a noise so great his ears were starting to shut down on him. Here we go again, he thought. The sand floor rose from the ground, pushing him with it. He was helpless, but tried to pull his body inward this time. It was no use. His twisted ankle and broken ribs were working against him. A familiar blue light erupted outward from the small tent. It shot out to the horizon as far as the eye could see, piercing the now dark and tormented sky.

With each pulse of light, the tent flap shuttered open, revealing his friends looking on, smiling and waving goodbye. The scene took him back to that day. They could see him! That means my grandmother, she . . . she saw me. *She knew!*

Uh-oh. Here it comes. His stomach twisted into a ball once again. That familiar vomiting feeling entered his throat. The tent was whipping violently in the wind, pulling at its stakes. A final gust and it was sent off through the air, high above him, hovering in nothingness. Everything was silent. He was floating in an infinite space surrounded by unfamiliar stars warping in and out of reality. He liked this part; it was calm, and all of his pain was gone.

"Home," he said.

The dark void that wrapped him, all that he could see, was suddenly ripped apart with a single explosion of noise and flash. In a spark, he was gone.

THE END